The Remington's recoil rocked his shoulder, and the bullet hit home—the man spun half around and fell onto his hands and knees. But Bill knew there was no time to pat himself on the back. Gunfire was coming fast and furious. Bullets were hitting the ground all around him and one plucked at his left shirtsleeve.

If he took time to aim now, he'd be a target they couldn't miss. He fired anyway, hastily, knowing he was burning ammunition, but hoping to stop them.

It didn't work. They were still coming. Teeth clenched, Bill fired again. *Get one more! Make the sons of bitches pay! Let the world know that Wild Bill Watson went down shooting!*

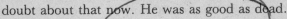

Because their bullets were going to find him. No doubt about that now. He was as good as dead.

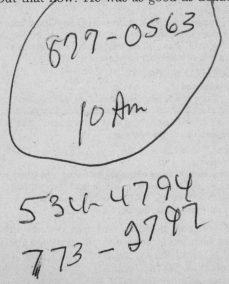

DOYLE TRENT

FIRE AND GUNSMOKE

ZEBRA BOOKS
KENSINGTON PUBLISHING CORP.

ZEBRA BOOKS are published by

Kensington Publishing Corp.
475 Park Avenue South
New York, NY 10016

Zebra and the Z logo are trademarks of Kensington Publishing Corp.

First Printing: June, 1993

Printed in the United States of America

Chapter One

They halted before they started down a long gentle slope to the cabin a quarter mile away. Their eyes squinted across the yucca and cane cactus, and studied the cabin, the corral, the brush along the creek.

"Think he sees us?"

"I'd bet on it."

The two men shifted in their saddles. Their horses, a bay and a sorrel, stamped their feet to shake flies off their legs.

"What makes you think he sees us, Sheriff?"

"There's a horse in the corral down there. If he wasn't there he'd be horseback somewhere, and he'd turn out all his other horses."

"Think he'll fight?"

"He's got that kind of reputation. They call him Wild Bill."

"Way I heard it, he loped right through a bunch of Comanches over in Texas once. The Indians had him and some others trapped and somebody had to go for help. Bill Watson had the fastest horse, and he rode

5

right through the redskins with the reins in his teeth and a Colt six-shooter in each hand.''

The younger man, with a deputy's badge pinned to a sweat-stained shirt, grunted. "Well, there's two of us and we got some repeatin' rifles.''

"I don't want any shooting if we can help it.'' Sheriff Bowman was middle-aged, with a sun-wrinkled lean face and thick dark eyebrows. He squinted from under a dirty gray Stetson. "We ain't here to run him off. Not yet. Just serve him with a court order.''

"Can he read?''

"I think he can. If he can't, I'll have to read it to him.''

"If he's down there, he's in that shack, watchin' us.''

"Yeah, he's watching us.''

"We can split up, come at him from two directions.''

"No. We don't want to look threatening.''

"Think it's safe to just ride down there?''

"He's wild, but he ain't crazy. And I made sure everybody knows where we're going, in case we don't get back.''

"So if we don't get back, them other deputies'll know where to look?''

"That's it.''

Though the two men wore law officers' badges, they were a different breed. Bowman could be mistaken for a southwestern cattleman, in his flat-brim hat, faded blue cotton shirt, and duck pants stuffed into the tops of high-heeled riding boots. His six-gun rode high on his hip in a worn leather holster. The young deputy wore a derby hat with dark curly hair showing under it. His baggy wool pants were held up by red suspenders, and his boots were the flat-heeled kind. He carried a nickel-plated, double-action .38 in a low-hanging holster. Both men had lever-action rifles in boots under their right knees.

"I don't know about you, Sheriff, but I aim to get back, and if that mick down there puts up a fight I'll carry him to town across his own horse." As he talked, he put his hand on the butt of the .38.

Sheriff Bowman turned in his saddle and studied the younger man a moment, then said, "Tell you what, Jameson, maybe you'd better wait here. Maybe I can head off trouble if I go down there by myself."

"Nope. I got orders from Mr. Howser hisself to go with you to serve these papers. In case there's some shootin'."

"You're my deputy, but you get your orders from Hunter Howser, is that it?"

"Huh," the young man snorted, "you think I'd work for the wages this county pays?"

Sheriff Bowman squinted at the far horizon, thinking without comment. "All right," he said finally, "but keep that gun in its cradle and keep your hand away from it."

"If he threatens me, I'll plug 'im."

Shaking his head sadly, the sheriff touched spurs to his bay horse and rode off the hill, heading for the cabin on Otero Creek. He kept his free hand on top of the saddle horn, away from the walnut-handled hogleg pistol. Jameson rode alongside. They rode slowly, with caution.

Wild Bill Watson watched through the dirty glass in the only window of his one-room, dirt-floor cabin. He jacked the lever on his Remington rifle partially down to be sure there was a cartridge in the chamber. He recognized Sheriff Bowman, but not the deputy. The deputy was new in Colfax County.

They weren't bringing good news. Lawmen never brought good news. Lately, the law dogs were nothing more than tools for the goddamn lawyers and judges. He had nothing personal against Sheriff Bowman, but he didn't like what he represented.

Bill Watson was thirty-four, just under six feet, slender, in fact a little underweight. He had the lean, flat-sided hips of a man who had spent much of his life on horseback, and the dark leather face of a man who had spent all his life outdoors. He didn't intend to grow a beard or mustache, but he shaved only once a week.

Holding the rifle ready but not pointed at anyone, he stepped outside the door. He stayed close to the door, ready to duck back inside if need be.

He yelled, "Whoa, right there. Don't come no closer."

The two reined up again. "Bill Watson?" the sheriff yelled.

"One and the same."

"I've got a court order for you."

"The hell you beller."

"Yep."

"What's it say?"

Sheriff Bowman yelled, "It's what the lawyers call a show-cause order. It means you have to go to court and argue about who owns this piece of land here."

"I don't know nothin' about no courts."

"I'll read it to you if you want."

"I can read it."

8

"Fine. But I have to hand it to you myself so I can say I did."

"Is that all you want?"

"That's all today."

While they were yelling back and forth, Deputy Jameson allowed his horse to move to his left, trying to get some distance between him and the sheriff. Bill Watson snapped the rifle up to his shoulder, but didn't squint down the barrel.

"Tell that deputy of yours to get back over there. Tell 'im right now."

"Jameson," the sheriff said in a conversational tone, "come back here. Turn that horse back. I told you I don't want any trouble."

"That goddamn mick's got a rifle in his mits. He can pick us both off before we can get any closer."

"He ain't gonna shoot unless you look dangerous. Now get over here. And keep your hand off that pistol."

Growling, the deputy in the derby hat turned his horse back alongside the sheriff's mount. "There's gonna be some fightin' sooner or later, and we might as well get started."

"Stay right here and keep your gun hand in plain sight. I'm going over there." To Watson, he yelled, "I'm coming up. We don't want any trouble. We're not here to force you off your land. All right?"

Bill lowered the rifle, but held it waist high. The hammer was back and his finger was on the trigger guard. "Come ahead. Just you."

Still growling, the deputy said, "We're the goddamn law. How come you're lettin' him tell you what to do?"

The sheriff ignored him and rode his horse forward

9

at a slow walk. When he was within talking distance, he said, "I've got a court paper here. The law says I have to hand it to you and read it to you if you can't read yourself."

"I said I can read."

Sheriff Bowman had to half turn in his saddle to open a saddlebag behind the cantle. He pulled out a sheaf of papers, separated one, and held it out. Bill Watson took it with his left hand.

"See you got some more."

"Yeah," the sheriff sighed. "I got more papers to serve." He leaned forward in his saddle and crossed his arms on top of the saddle horn. "I don't reckon any of you folks have hired a lawyer."

"Don't know no lawyers."

The sheriff swept his right hand in a half circle, taking in the land around him. "All this, who owns it and who doesn't, is being argued in the courts. The grant people have got lawyers crawling all over each other. I sat in on some of the court proceedings, and nobody was arguing for the anti-grant side."

"I don't know nothin' about no lawyers and courts."

"Well," the sheriff said, straightening in his saddle, "It has to be lawyers and courts instead of guns. There's been too many folks killed already."

"We'll see."

"It's a hell of a mess. The U.S. government should have straightened it all out before it got started." He sighed again. "But I'm an officer of the law and I have to do what the law says. Sometimes I wish I didn't."

"You asked for it."

"Yeah, I reckon I did. Well, you've been served. That's all I came here for today." Sheriff Bowman turned his horse around. Looking over his shoulder, he tried to joke. "Don't do nothing I wouldn't do on a bicycle."

At his deputy's side again, Bowman said, "Let's go, and don't look back."

"We're gonna have to kill 'im sooner or later. He ain't gonna go to court."

"All I can do is hope."

The sheriff touched spurs to his horse and struck a trot, heading northwest. Deputy Jameson got his mount alongside, bouncing uncomfortably in the saddle. "Don't you wild-West micks ever ride at a canter? This trottin' is too hard on the ass."

"I'm not a mick, and this gait will get us farther than a canter, as you call it."

"Who are we servin' next?"

"Arnold Peterson is his name. He lives over near where the Vermejo and the Otero come together."

"Is he another western-bad-man desperado?"

With a sideways grin, Sheriff Bowman said, "If you think Wild Bill Watson is dangerous, wait till you meet Pegleg Pete."

Chapter Two

It was late May, and the signs of spring were everywhere. Green grass was crowding out the old dead grass. The yucca, which was so thick the horses were stepping around it, was slowly giving birth to stalks of pods. Little gray pocket gophers were out of hibernation now and running through the grass ahead of them, stopping at their holes in the ground and sitting up on their hind ends to see what was coming before disappearing. The country was mostly rolling hills, but with high, flat-topped mesas sticking up in all directions. Arroyos, some deep, but most shallow, cut across the land, making wagon travel difficult, but causing no problems for saddle horses. To the west the Taos Mountains rose into a purple haze.

"Sure glad to see spring," Sheriff Bowman mused as they rode out of a shallow arroyo. "Thought it was never gonna quit snowing."

"Snow don't bother me none," the deputy said. "Sometimes it makes the 'lectric rail cars spin their wheels around the Loop."

"Whoever wrote that poem about the snow, the

beautiful snow, wasn't a cattleman. It does make the grass grow, however. Snowmelt soaks in better than rain.''

"I'll take the streets of Chi.''

With a glance at his deputy, Sheriff Bowman said, "How do you know when it's spring in Chicago? If it wasn't for warmer weather you wouldn't know the difference. Those city buildings never change. Out here everything changes. You can watch it change, and you can breathe the difference. You don't know how to appreciate spring till you've lived through a winter in northern New Mexico Territory. It can get damned cold around here and the snow can get damned deep.''

"When that happens I'm gettin' outta here.''

The sheriff said no more, but he couldn't help thinking, *Good riddance.*

Pegleg Peterson's cabin, corrals, and sheds were on the Vermejo River, four miles northwest of the spot Bill Watson had picked out on Otero Creek. It was a good spot for a ranch, well-watered, with broad draws and valleys to shelter livestock in the winter. Tall cottonwoods and shorter elms and willow trees grew along the Vermejo. Willow bushes, alder, and elms along Otero Creek provided a break from the northern winds.

Again, the lawmen stopped to study the buildings before approaching them.

"Don't see anything alive,'' Bowman mused. "Hope we didn't ride all the way over here for nothing.''

"Can't we just stick the paper in the doorjamb or somethin'?''

"Nope. The law says I've got to serve him personally.''

14

"Well, how in hell can you do that if he ain't home?"

"We'll have to wait till he gets home."

"We still got another paper to serve, ain't we?"

"Yep. The Cruz family, brother and sister, over in the high hills."

"We gotta do that today?"

"We don't just have to today, but I'd like to. I'm spending so much time serving these damn court papers, the rustlers and road agents think there's no law in Colfax County. And the damn rustlers from Texas are getting meaner all the time."

"Well, I'm sure glad we don't have to do it all today. My ass already feels like raw meat."

With more sarcasm than he intended, the sheriff said, "I'm sure sorry about your ass."

"Whatta we gonna do, set here and wait? I could use a drink out of that brook."

"All right, let's go up to the cabin, but keep your hand away from that pistol." Bowman urged his horse on in a slow walk, his right hand on top of the saddle horn.

"He could be watchin' us from inside like that other mick did."

"No, don't think so. There's no horses in the corrals, and that tells me he's gone horseback somewhere. He runs about a hundred and fifty head of cattle here and he can't keep track of 'em sitting in the house."

"I don't see no cattle."

"He doesn't keep 'em at home. Folks consider this territory free range, and they graze their stock over a lot of country."

"This ain't free range."

15

"Nobody's proved that to them yet."

"Well." Jameson rested his hand on the butt of the nickel-plated .38. "We'll have to prove it to 'em."

"Keep your hand away from that goddamn pistol, hear? I don't give a good goddamn who all is paying you, I'm the sheriff and you do what I say. Hear?"

"Shit."

"You think you're tough? You think you're handy with a gun? Huh! These folks have lived by the gun ever since they were big enough to pick one up. Old Pegleg, now, he's lived with the Indians and he's fought the Indians, he's lived with the Mexicans and he's fought the Mexicans. The Civil War was potato soup to him. He can shoot the nose off your face at three hundred yards."

"I ain't scared."

Bowman didn't comment on that, but he couldn't help thinking, *You ain't got sense enough to be scared.*

The cabin was built of a combination of logs, rough lumber, rocks, and tarpaper. It consisted of two rooms. A rock chimney stuck out of one end, and a wooden water barrel sat on a bench beside the one door. Bowman hallooed the house again, then dismounted. He opened the lid on the water barrel, picked up a dipper made from a gourd, and dipped it half-full of water.

"Here," he said to the deputy. "Wet your pipes."

Deputy Jameson pushed back the derby hat, allowing thick dark curly hair to fall over his forehead, and took the dipper from the sheriff's hand. He drank with a series of gulps, said, "Aaah," and handed the dipper back. "I gotta admit, the water around here tastes good."

"It's snowmelt out of the creek. The best drinking

16

water there is." Then with a small grin, he added, "Unless there's something dead upstream."

"Huh?"

"Best advice," the sheriff said as he refilled the dipper, "is never drink out of a creek unless you know what's upstream. Could be a dead animal full of maggots, could be cowshit, could be some cows standing up there in the brush somewhere pissing in the water." He grinned again as the deputy swallowed a lump in his throat.

"The stinkin' Chicago River is better than this."

"But"—Bowman grinned—"it sure does taste good." He drank from the gourd dipper.

Deputy Jameson stretched his legs one at a time, then sat carefully on the bench beside the water barrel. "Damn knees get cramped in that damned saddle."

"You ought to let your stirrups down a hole."

"If I did that, I'd bounce on my ass even more."

Shrugging, Bowman said, "Well, it's a sore ass or cramped knees, take your pick."

They waited, the deputy sitting on the bench, the sheriff cross-legged on the ground. The sun was slowly sliding down toward the back side of the Taos Mountains. Jameson said, "I could eat a tenement-house rat. Wonder if there's anything to eat inside."

"Bound to be."

"Why don't we go in an help ourselfs?"

"No. When you're sheriffing, you're gonna miss a meal now and then."

"I thought these wild-West micks was stuffed full of hospitality."

"If I was starving I'd eat whatever I could find in there, and old Peterson wouldn't complain a-tall. But

17

we're not starving. It won't hurt you to miss your dinner today.''

''Missin' meals is somethin' I don't intend to get used to.''

''You can go back to town if you want. It only takes one man to serve a court order.''

''I was told to go with you.''

''Yeah.'' A frown crossed the lawman's seamed face. ''Old Howser hollers 'Frog,' and you and your partners jump.''

''As long as he's payin' us, we'll jump when he says to.''

''Yeah,'' Bowman grunted, ''I used to work my ass off trying to keep the peace and chasing rustlers and tracking robbers. Then the damned easterners and Englishmen and Dutchmen went and bought half of New Mexico Territory, and I'm s'posed to run off the folks who've settled here.''

''Them Englishmen and Dutchmen seen you need some help.''

''Yeah,'' the sheriff grumbled, leaning back on his elbows, straightening his legs. ''Yeah, sure.''

They fell silent, the deputy thinking about how hungry he was, the sheriff wishing he hadn't run for reelection and was raising beef or running a store, or just about anything but what he was doing. Goddamn the U.S. Congress. Could have claimed the land for the U.S. government. Goddamn lawyers and judges. Could have kept their noses out of it. Hell, if old Maxwell had known how much trouble he was causing, he would have given the land away. He sure didn't intend for this to happen. Too bad he had to go off and die.

Damn it all, anyway.

With his stomach gurgling, the sheriff leaned back on his elbows and thought bitter thoughts. He could resign. Let old Howser and his hired bullies do their own dirty work. The grant company was just using him and the law.

Deputy Jameson was dozing on the bench, his head down and his chin almost touching his chest. The horses stood with the reins down, switching their tails and stomping their feet. Then the sorrel horse's head came up. Its ears twitched. Sheriff Bowman got slowly to his feet, careful to keep his hand away from the hogleg pistol. He wasn't at all surprised when a hard voice came from somewhere.

"Don't move a hair. If you wanna keep on breathin', don't move a inch."

Chapter Three

Without turning his head, the sheriff asked, "Is that you, Peterson?"

"Yeah, and who are you?"

"I'm Sheriff Bowman. I'm not here to give you any trouble."

The deputy had jerked upright, eyes darting in all directions. Bowman whispered to him, "Do like he says and sit still. Reach for that gun and you'll be dead in a second."

"What are you here for?"

"I've got a court paper to serve you. It doesn't say you have to get off your land. Not yet, anyhow."

"What does it say?"

"It says you have to go to court and argue for your property."

"I ain't gonna argue with them damned lawyers for what's mine."

"Listen, Peterson, can I turn around so we can face each other?"

After a pause, the voice said, "All right, turn around

21

slow. And tell that other feller to take that pistol out of its holster and put it on the ground."

The deputy said, "I ain't gonna do it."

"Do it, goddamn it, or I'll be packing you back to town dead."

"Aw, shit." Jameson took the butt in two fingers and, with a grimace, carefully put the .38 on the ground.

"Now stand away from it."

"Aw, shit."

"Do like he says."

Jameson took two sideways steps, eyes moving in the direction the voice was coming from.

"All right, Sheriff. Turn around."

A short, husky man, wrinkled, with a gray beard and walking on a wooden leg, came from around a corner of the cabin. He wore a ragged black broad-brimmed hat, and he held a Winchester lever-action carbine ready to aim and fire.

Stopping ten feet in front of the sheriff, where he could cover both men with the carbine, he said, "Now speak your piece."

"The paper is in my hip pocket. I'll read it to you if you want." He reached for the folded paper and unfolded it.

"I can read."

"The law says I've got to hand it to you. Here."

"Put it on the ground."

"It might blow away."

"Let 'er blow. I got a paper in the house that says ever'thing anybody needs to read."

"Listen, Peterson, I'm trying to be a friend. You can't ignore a court order."

"You ain't no friend. Nobody wearin' a badge has ever said anything I wanta hear."

"Take it, will you, and read it. You've said you've got a deed to your land. All you have to do is go to court and show that deed."

"I done that. They had to admit it's got Lucien Maxwell's signature on it, but they said it's only good for two sections. Mr. Maxwell and me, we laid out twenty sections."

"If it's properly marked and spelled out on the deed, then that ought to be the end of the argument."

"Them smart-mouth lawyers can talk around anything. Only thing they can't outargue is this." He raised the barrel of the carbine.

"That's not the way to settle it, Peterson. If we're ever gonna have law and order, we have to settle disputes in court."

"I don't like courts. I don't like them god-almighty judges that set up there and look down their noses at us like we was lice. I don't like them lawyer fellers that git rich 'thout doin' a day's work."

"They work. They just don't work with their hands."

"They work at gettin' their hands in other folks' pockets, that's what they do."

"Now, that ain't always so. If we're gonna have law, somebody has to learn the law and be able to thrash it out in court. Here, take the paper, will you?"

Reluctantly, the short man reached out a hand covered with skin that looked like old dried leather. He took the paper and put it in his hip pocket.

"Read it, will you? And do what it says."

"I'll read it when I get good and ready, and maybe I'll do what it says and maybe I won't."

"I hope you obey the court. We don't want any trouble."

The short man shifted his weight onto the peg leg. His small squinty eyes glanced at the deputy. "What about him? I heered about him and his bunch takin' over Springer and Raton. I heered they was hired by the company."

"If I can help it, they won't cause any trouble either." Bowman looked down at his boots a moment. "I was elected sheriff, but sometimes I'm overruled by the county board and the courts."

"I heered the gov'nor gave 'em the right to shoot folks off their land."

"He authorized a militia, but he didn't tell them to shoot anybody. And he has since rescinded his order."

"He done what?"

"He took away what authority he gave them. They have no authority now."

"Then, if they're not militiamen no more, what're they hangin' around for? Ever'body knows they don't belong in this territory."

The answer to that question had Sheriff Bowman worried, but he didn't want to say so. Instead, he said, "We'll go now. I'll take my deputy's gun and give it back to him when we get out of sight." Without waiting for permission, he walked over to the bench, picked up the .38, and stuck it inside his belt. "Let's go," he said to the deputy.

Pegleg Peterson watched them, putting his weight on his good leg now, while they mounted their horses and rode away toward Springer, the county seat. "Goddamn law," he muttered to himself. "All it does is give some gut-robbin' sons of bitches a license to steal. God-damn law."

Two miles southeast of Peterson's cabin, the sheriff squinted at the Taos Mountain, and allowed, "Be dark before we can get to the Cruz place. I wasn't figuring on having to wait so long for Peterson. Here, put this in its cradle and keep it there." He handed the deputy his gun.

"We goin' back to town now?"

"Yeah. I'll ride over to the Cruz place tomorrow and serve them with the court order. I'll go by myself. I'll stay in Cimarron tomorrow night."

"Mr. Howser said I'm s'posed to go with you."

"I said I'm going by myself and I'm going by myself, savvy?"

"Mr. Howser ain't gonna like it."

Wild Bill Watson believed the worst danger he faced came from the ex-militiamen, but there were other dangers. There were the cattle thieves. Being from Texas himself, he knew how they operated. They crossed the border in gangs and rode west until they found a ranch or farm with a small herd of cattle. Then they helped themselves, exchanging gunfire if they were challenged. The ranchers and farmers had no hired guns, and were so badly outnumbered that all they could do was try to get away and ride like hell for Springer and the sheriff. Chances were, the sheriff was out of town, and his deputy, if there was one, would refuse to leave town. He was there to keep the peace,

25

he'd say, and would have to wait for orders from the sheriff.

By the time the sheriff was told about it, the thieves would be halfway back to Texas, driving the stolen cattle ahead of them. They'd always manage to cross the Texas border before the law officers could catch up. And if Texas lawmen questioned them, they'd say they were driving back cattle that had been stolen from them.

Wild Bill had come by his handful of longhorn cattle honestly. At the time, he was riding west, leading a packhorse, heading for Elizabethtown on the side of the Taos Mountains. Gold and silver were there, just waiting for him to pick it up, he'd been told. Men were getting rich. He could get rich, too.

But soon after he'd crossed over into the New Mexico Territory he began to have doubts. Too many folks were going the other way. The creeks had been panned out, and the land worth digging on had already been claimed. However, there was a million acres of good grazing and farming land over west if a feller wanted to go into that business. It was U.S. government land, not yet surveyed, but soon would be. When it was, the folks who were there first could claim first homestead rights. Just pick out a good piece of land and settle on it.

So Bill had ridden on. Hell, he had nowhere else to go. He had a year's pay in his pockets, winnings from an all-night poker game, and two good horses. But no plans for the future. Not until he caught up with the sodbusters.

He saw them far ahead on the plains, too far at first sight to tell how many there were. When he got closer he counted twenty-three cows and four bulls, all bony longhorns, spotted, brindle, and roan. The brand was so old the hair had grown over it, and he couldn't make it out. There were two men—rather, a man and a boy about fifteen—and a woman. The woman was driving a covered wagon pulled by two big horses. A two-wheeled cart was hitched to the back of the wagon, carrying a walking plow and two gunnysacks of grain. The man and boy were keeping the cattle moving at a slow walk. When they saw Bill coming up, they stopped and sat still in their saddles.

"Howdy," Bill said, smiling, careful to do nothing that could be interpreted as a threat. They could see for miles behind him, and they knew he was alone.

"Howdy." The man had a hollow-cheeked face and buck teeth. He wore bib overalls and scuffed brogan shoes.

"The cows are fat," Bill said by way of conversation. He pulled a small sack of tobacco out of a shirt pocket. "Good grass around here." He offered the tobacco and a sheaf of papers to the man.

"Thanks." The man rolled a cigarette and handed the sack and papers back. "Cows and horses're doin' fine. Better'n we are."

Holding the reins between two fingers, Bill rolled a smoke, struck a wooden match on the fork of his saddle, and lit it. "Havin' hard times, are you?"

"Yep. Out of grub and out of money. Ain't seen no game in four days. Might have to butcher one of our own cows to keep from starvin'."

The boy said nothing, only stared. A sun-bleached cowlick hung from under a shapeless brown hat.

"How far to the next town?"

"Don't know. Ain't never been in these parts before."

Bill drew deeply on the cigarette, blew out the smoke. "Well, I've got some sowbelly and spuds and beans and coffee on the packhorse. We can eat for a day or two."

"You willin' to share with us?"

"Yep." Squinting at the sun, Bill said, "Takes a while to boil beans and stuff. We better set up camp somewheres and get started cookin'. Any water around here?"

"Feller said there's a crick 'bout a mile west. We was headin' for there."

"I'll go on ahead and get some water boilin'. See you there."

Next day, Wild Bill Watson bought their cattle.

Now he was fighting to keep them.

Chapter Four

There were five of them, and they saw him coming. No use asking what they were doing. They were driving eighteen of his cows and their calves east. The cattle had been grazing along Otero Creek a mile northwest of his cabin. The cows were half-wild and well-fed on the spring grass. All the riders had to do was keep them going in the right direction.

Almost half his herd and half his spring calf crop was being stolen while he watched. Like hell.

Bill got down, lifted the Remington out of its boot, knelt on one knee, squinted down the barrel, and fired at the closest rider.

The range was too great for accurate shooting, but at least the rustlers knew they were in for a shooting match. Two fired back, but their bullets fell short.

Bill's horse, a long-legged dun, was used to gunfire, and it jumped sideways a little, but didn't stampede. Leaving the horse, Bill walked closer to the riders, knelt again, and fired again. Still too far. Three more shots came from the rustlers. One kicked up dirt twenty feet ahead of Bill.

What Wild Bill hoped to do was scare them into just getting themselves away from there. They knew they'd been seen. Unless they had murder on their minds as well as cattle stealing, they'd just ride away.

But they didn't just ride away.

Instead they rode in a big half-circle. Two rode at a gallop to his right and three rode to his left. They were still too far away to shoot, but they'd soon have him in a crossfire, and they'd get closer. Sure enough, while he watched, they dismounted and started walking his way, rifles ready. He could lie flat on the ground and make a small target of himself, but so could they.

Bill fired at the three on his left. They hit the ground. The two on Bill's right opened fire. Bill hit the ground, flat. Then the other three stood and came closer. When Bill raised up on knee, the two on his right opened fire again. He could hear the bullets thudding into the ground. They had him in a trap and the trap was about to be sprung.

He realized then that he'd done something foolish. When they'd moved to either side of him and gotten afoot, he should have climbed on the dun and ridden for safety. He would have lost some of his cattle, but he would have saved his life.

No, by god. He'd be damned if he'd run. And it was fifteen or more miles to Springer and the sheriff's office. And the sheriff was probably somewhere serving court papers, anyway. Maybe if he could drop a couple of these gunslammers, the others would run.

Trying to ignore the gunfire coming his way, Bill got up on one knee, took aim at a man on his right, and squeezed the trigger. The Remington's recoil slammed his right shoulder. But his bullet hit home.

The man spun half around and fell onto his hands and knees.

There was no time to pat himself on the back, Bill knew. Gunfire was coming fast and furious. The bullets were hitting the ground all around him. One plucked at his left shirtsleeve. If he took time to aim now, he'd be a target they couldn't miss. They'd get him. He fired anyway, hastily, knowing he was wasting ammunition, but hoping to stop them. It didn't work. They were still coming.

Teeth clenched, Bill fired back. Get one more. At least one more. Make the sons of bitches pay. Let the world know that Wild Bill Watson went down shooting.

The bullets were going to find him. No doubt about that now. He was dead.

Maybe. Maybe not.

A crazy screeching yell came from the north. A gun boomed. Not a .44–40, but a big gun. Sounded like a Big Fifty. Gunfire ceased for a moment, then resumed as furious as ever. But it wasn't coming his way.

Carefully, Bill got to both knees. The wild yell came again. It sounded like a Comanche on the attack. The big gun boomed again. Men yelled. Three men ran for their horses. Another lay on his back in the grass. Lay still.

Bill recognized the shooter then, recognized his ragged hat, recognized the way he limped as he gathered the reins of his horse and climbed into the saddle. Bill ran to his horse, mounted, and spurred out after the three running rustlers. Riding hard, he tried to get one of the men in his gunsights, but the dun horse was jumping yucca, dodging cholla cactus. Bill reined up long enough to take aim. The horse snorted and ducked sideways at the sound of a gun going off on his back, but was easy to control.

Another rustler was down.

Bill waited then for the shooter from the north to catch up. When he did, neither man spoke for a moment, just sat their saddles and grinned at each other. The shooter was short and thick, with a gray beard he'd trimmed with sheep shears. When he pushed his hat back on a nearly bald head, he said, "Whatta you think, Bill, think we orter get after them other two?"

"Wal, dunno, Pete." Bill reached for the makings and started rolling a smoke. "They're halfway back to Texas by now. What brought you over this way?"

"I wanted to talk to you about them court orders the sheriff is handin' out, and I brought this here buff'ler gun hopin' to shoot a buckskin for dinner." Pegleg Peterson nodded toward one of the downed rustlers. "Three of 'em ain't goin' back to Texas."

"One of 'em is still breathin', I think. What should we do with him?"

"I ain't no doctor, but I doubt he'll live long enough to ride a horse to Raton or Springer."

"Raton is a little closer, but like you said, he won't live long enough."

"Maybe we orter hang 'im. Put 'im out of his misery."

"Let's go see what he looks like."

Peterson had fashioned a leather cup in his right stirrup for his wooden leg, and he rode a horse as easily as a man with two good legs. Together they approached the wounded man. Bill had put his rifle back in its boot under his right knee. Peterson was carrying

32

his long-barreled Sharps rifle across the saddle. The rustler was flat on his back, staring at the sky. "Looks dead," Bill allowed.

"We don't have to worry about 'im, then."

But suddenly the man sat up, a six-gun in his hand. A gun popped. Popped again. The man flopped down onto his back, kicked twice, and lay still.

Glancing from Bill to the prone man and back to Bill, Pegleg said, "You didn't have that shootin' iron in your hand when we rode up here. How . . . ?"

"Takes practice," Bill said matter-of-factly. "Sometimes it pays off."

"Well, I'll be go to hell. Sure paid off this time. He had us cold."

"He fooled me."

"Now we for sure don't have to worry about what to do with 'im."

"I reckon I oughta go fetch that sheriff or one of his deputies."

"I reckon. Speakin' of which, did he pay you a visit yesterday?"

"Yeah, him and one a them mean-looking jaspers from somewheres back east. He had a court paper."

"I seen 'im before. He's one of them militiamen brought here by Jim Masterson. Sheriff tol' me the gov'nor took their authority away from 'em, but some of 'em stuck around anyways."

"That one wore a deputy's badge."

"They're meaner'n rattlesnakes, and they'll strike just as fast. Uh, what did your court paper say?"

Bill reached for the makings again, and offered them to Peterson. "Naw," Peterson said, "I usta smoke,

33

but I run outta tobaccer once for a long time, and got out of the habit.''

"The paper said I have to go to court in Springer and prove I own the land I'm usin'. I can't prove it 'cuz I don't own it. I just squatted on it.''

"So did a lot of folks. Hell, they had two million acres to squat on. Anyways, I got a legal title to twenty sections. Mr. Maxwell hisself signed it.''

For the moment, the dead rustlers were forgotten. The two neighbors had more important things to talk about. They sat their horses and talked.

"Reckon you'll go to court, then.''

"I went once, and it didn't do no good. They agreed it was Maxwell's signature, but they said I owned only a couple a sections.''

"What're you gonna do?''

With a sigh, Peterson said, "I'll go back to court. Show 'em my deed again and listen to them lawyers try to prove it's no account. What about you?''

"I ain't got a deed. Reckon I'll just wait for 'em to run me off. I ain't gonna make it easy for 'em, but sooner or later I'll have to gather my stock and go back to Texas. I can sell 'em in Texas or I can just drive 'em to the railroad and ship 'em somewheres. If they don't kill me first.''

"Hell of a note. The land company's got two million acres they ain't usin', and they can't stand to see a feller get some good out of it.''

"I heard they're claimin' land that goes plumb up into Colorado.''

"It does. Mr. Maxwell tol' me hisself. His land starts just this side of Taos and goes north all the way to the other side of them Raton Mountains.''

Finishing his smoke, Bill pinched it out, held it in his hand for a moment to be sure it was out, dropped it. "I'll go to Raton and hunt up the laws. It's closer. Won't get there till after dark, though. These dead men are gonna be stiffer'n boards by the time I can get back with some men to bury 'em."

"I'll catch their horses and offsaddle 'em. Watch out for them militiamen. If they see a squatter in town, they'll sure as hell give you troubles."

Grinning a wry grin, Wild Bill said, "Trouble is my other nickname."

Chapter Five

The town of Raton was divided. Every man, woman, and child was either grant or anti-grant, even those who weren't affected one way or the other.

Ella Fitzwater wasn't affected, but she had a strong opinion, and anyone who disagreed wasn't welcome in her Willow Springs Liquor and Games. She named her establishment after the original name of the town, which she liked better than Raton, which was what the Mexicans called the gray, long-eared squirrels that scampered through the trees in the nearby mountains.

Ella was no classic beauty, but she was a handsome woman in her early thirties, with long dishwater-blond curls hanging to her shoulders, a slim waist, and enough flare to her hips and bosom to make any man want to reach out and grab a feel.

They didn't dare. A Hawken black powder rifle was on display over a mirror behind the mahogany bar, and with it she could hit a dime at a hundred yards. At two hundred yards she could hit a silver dollar or, better yet, a twenty-dollar gold piece. She had a collection of bent gold eagles she had won in bets. Any man who grabbed a feel found himself challenged to a shooting match. Men who knew Ella or knew of her didn't try to grab a feel.

Accurate shooting was a skill she had acquired growing up on a poor cotton farm in South Texas where small-game kills meant the difference between eating or going hungry. And it took so long to reload the muzzle-loading percussion gun that one shot had to do it.

But being sole proprietor of a drinking and gambling establishment, she couldn't afford to be standoffish. So when she saw Bill Watson step through the open door, she shouted across a crowded room:

"Wild Bill, you rangy old son of a pup. C'mere and let me buy you one."

Bill Watson spotted her and aimed his boots in her direction, an oak-handled six-gun hanging on his right hip. " 'Lo, Ella. How's the girl? Keepin' ever'body happy?"

"Happier'n a skunk suckin' eggs. Ain't seen you in a couple months. What brings you to town?"

"Got to find a deputy and some men with shovels and go out and bury three cow thieves."

"Well, now." Ella's hazel eyes widened. "Do tell. Step up to the bar here and give me all the details. I'll keep buying as long as you keep talking."

The bartender, a skinny young man with sparse hair plastered to his head, reached for a whiskey bottle. "None of that," Ella said. "Pour some of that good Kentucky bourbon. This here's a friend of mine." She stood beside Bill and put a hand on his left shoulder.

Whiskey was poured. Bill downed a shot glass full, put an exaggerated grimace on his face, said,

38

"Gawwwd. Now I know why they call you Ella Fire-water."

Playfully, she tapped him on the jaw with bare knuckles. "You think that's potent? Joel, pour him some of that sour mash."

The skinny bartender reached under the bar for another bottle, filled the shot glass again. "Go ahead," Ella teased. "Throw that down your gullet."

Bill held the glass out at arm's length, pretended to study it, brought it up under his nose, sniffed it. "Wal." He studied it further, turning the glass in his fingers. "Tell you, Ella, if it kills me I'll never speak to you again."

With a chuckle, Ella said, "It won't kill you, but I can't guarantee you'll ever again speak."

In one fast gulp, Bill swallowed the whiskey. Using every once of determination he had, he managed to keep his face straight, though he couldn't keep from blinking back tears. When he tried to talk, only a thin screech came out. Ella stood back and smiled. "Want another?"

"Now, that . . ." He had to clear his throat. "That there is a man's drink."

"Fill it again, Joel."

Another drink was poured. Bill held it up at eye level, licked his lips, and took a sip. "Good likker like this," he allowed, "is s'posed to be savored." He smacked his lips. "Yessir, you ain't s'posed to chug it down like it was beer."

"All right, all right. Now. Tell me about some dead cow thieves."

"A-hum. Wal, now, if I had a glass of cold beer to cool things down, my squawk box'd work better."

"Draw one," Ella ordered. Within a minute, a mug of beer was placed in front of Bill. He took a swallow, smacked his lips. "It undoes the damage that whiskey done."

"Now then. Talk."

Bill told her all about it. "It was my lucky day. Old Pegleg was comin' over to talk about the court orders Sheriff Bowman is handin' out, an' he was looking for some wild meat at the same time, an' he was packin' his old buffalo gun, an' that old smoke pole'll knock a bull elk over at five hundred yards, an'—"

"Wait a minute," Ella interrupted. "Back up a step. What's this about Sheriff Bowman delivering court orders?"

So Bill told all about that, too.

"Why, that . . . it doesn't surprise me. I hear they've been holding court down at Springer, and the grant company's got a whole crew of lawyers bending some judge's ear."

"The paper I got don't say I have to git, but it says I have to go to court and satisfy the judge that I've got a right to be there."

"The next court order will tell you to git."

"Prob'ly will. Wal." Bill drank the rest of his beer. "Reckon I'd better hunt up the laws and tell 'em what happened."

"I'll go with you."

"Why would you do that?"

"I don't know." Ella smiled a weak smile. "I just can't keep my nose out of other people's business, I guess."

* * *

The town of Raton was only a watering hole until the Atchison, Topeka and Santa Fe finished laying rails over the Raton Mountains and built its repair shops there. That made it a fast-growing railroad town. It was also in the middle of good grazing lands, and there were as many cattlemen and cowboys on the plankwalks as railroaders.

It was in Raton that Bill first began to realize he might have to give up the land he'd settled on. Until then he'd never heard of the Maxwell land grant or the Maxwell Land Company. He'd stepped into Ella Fitzwater's place for a beer, and was soon in a conversation with other drinkers standing at the bar. When they heard he'd driven some cattle onto the grant and was building a cabin, they told him all about it.

And when Ella heard about him, she stepped up, introduced herself, and offered her advice: "Don't quit the country yet. Them grant people ain't nothing more than vampires and land pirates, and most folks in these parts ain't giving them an inch."

Bill didn't know what to say to that. He went ahead with his cabin, but didn't invest much money in it. Hell, he didn't have much money. If he had to git he wouldn't lose much. But he was told about folks who had built fine homes on the grant, and ranches and farms. And about the Mexicans who'd grown orchards and even built churches. He became friends with Pegleg Peterson, his nearest neighbor. He rode up into the high valleys and saw the Mexican farms with neat green fields of squash, corn, beans, and grain, irrigated with water from the Vermejo, or the Cimarron or the Otero. The Mexicans were friendly people, deeply religious. Their houses, built of adobe and rock, were well-built and well cared for. They'd been here for two centuries.

The first time Bill saw Eileen Cruz, he fell in love.

Eileen Cruz was every man's dream, with expressive brown eyes, a smooth light-brown complexion, a straight nose, full mouth, and a fine woman-figure that no amount of clothes could disguise.

Ella Fitzwater was a good-looking woman, but Eileen Cruz was a beauty.

Now as he walked on the dark street with Ella at his side, he figured she was his second choice. Then he grinned a wry grin in the dark. His fantasies were turning into delusions. What choice? Who would have him?

"I see a light in the sheriff's office," Ella said, "but it doesn't mean somebody's there. They keep a lamp lit all night."

"If there's no deputy there, where is he?"

"Home, probably. We've got a town marshal that stays up most of the night, but his jurisdiction ends at the town limits."

"Oh. Wal . . ." Bill's boots thumped on the planks. "I was figurin' on stayin' in town tonight anyway. I already put my horse in a pen at the livery barn."

"Nobody's going down there to hunt for dead men in the dark."

Sure enough, the door to the deputy's office was locked. When Bill rattled the door, a voice from inside yelled, "Hey, unlock that goddamn door. Unlock this here goddamn cage an' lemme outta here."

"That," Ella chuckled, "is Henry Volmos. Every time he comes to town he gets tanked up and gets arrested for shooting that old cap-and-ball pistol he carries."

42

"Is a man named Duncan still the deputy here?"

"Yeah, and he's a grant man. He's gonna try to give you a bad time."

"Think he'll get mad if I go to his house?"

"He'll get mad no matter what you do. That's why I'm going with you. He won't give me any trouble."

"Why, because you're a woman?"

"Because I won't take any guff from him. And I've got a lot of friends."

Deputy Duncan was about to go to bed, and he grumbled at having to stand in the front door of his board-and-batten whitewashed house and listen to a tale about rustlers and dead men. After Bill had finished talking, he held a lantern up to Ella's face.

"Is that you, Ella Firewater?"

"The name's Fitzwater."

"I like Firewater better. What're you doin' here?"

"I'm here as a witness."

The deputy was a plump young man with a handlebar mustache. He stood in the open door in his sock feet, pants, and undershirt, scowling. "A witness to what?"

"To Bill's report. To prove that Bill complied with the law and reported the shooting to an officer of the law."

"He's a grant squatter. He just said so."

"Nobody's proved yet he doesn't have a right there, and what's that got to do with cattle thieves and a killing?"

"Well, there ain't no use ridin' down there in the dark. Them dead men ain't goin' nowheres." Deputy Duncan's forehead wrinkled as he thought about it.

"You, Watson, you be in front of my office at first light in the mornin'. Hear?"

"I'll be there."

"And you, Ella Firewater, you mind your own business."

"This is my business. Bill's a friend of mine."

A sneer came over the deputy's face. "I'll bet. Every man is a friend of yours."

"Not every man. You ain't."

Chapter Six

It was a gopher that had given Ella her stake—one of the little ground squirrels that resembled half-grown prairie dogs. Ella and her husband, Joe, had been infected with gold fever, and they settled in a one-room tarpaper shack on a creek five miles west of Elizabethtown. Joe panned and picked until he was so weary he could barely eat his supper of Indian bread, fried rabbit, and beans. He found nothing. Not even a promise of gold or silver or anything else. Ella suggested once that they give up and go to some town and get jobs and earn a decent living. Joe wouldn't hear of it.

"Ever'damnbody else is findin' color, and I'll find somethin'. Just stick with me."

She stuck with him, using her Hawken rifle to shoot squirrels and rabbits to eat. She was used to poverty, and knew how to make a meal out of anything available. Twice, she saved them from starvation by slyly encouraging men to challenge her to a shooting match. Only twice. After that there were no challenges.

Then Joe walked away. He'd been in a deep depression for weeks. He refused to talk much, and ate so little that she was afraid he'd lose what strength he had left. She tried to coax him to eat more until he yelled at her to quit nagging. One morning he rolled up a blanket, stuck his old Army Colt inside his belt, picked up a loaf of bread, paused in the door, and said simply, "Goodbye, Ellie."

At first she wanted to run after him, beg him to come back, promise him anything. But she had nothing to promise. She had nothing. For a time she hoped he would change his mind and come back. She would be a better wife—somehow. She would win more money with her shooting skill, or sell the Hawken if she had to, to eat better. She would make love to him when he was too tired to make love to her. She would do anything.

With a borrowed washtub and a scrub board, she took in washing. That kept her from starving. Her eyes were always on the road where she'd last seen Joe. He didn't come back.

Ella cried at times. She would die rather than let anyone see her cry, but at times when she was alone she let the tears fall.

Then one morning everything changed.

Joe had dug a narrow ditch to carry water from the creek to the shack, and Ella went out at daylight to fill a water bucket. The ditch was dry. Walking up the ditch toward the creek, she soon discovered why. A pocket gopher had dug its burrow so near the ditch that all the water was pouring down the gopher hole.

"Goshdammit," Ella muttered as she hurried back to the shack for a shovel, "I'll show you how to dig, you little booger."

What she dug up were flakes of gold, and nuggets

46

as big as her thumbnail. "Huh?" She couldn't believe it. By the time she'd finished digging, she had a teacup nearly full of gold. And there had to be more where that had come from.

Quickly, without breakfast, she walked the five miles to the land office and filed a claim. Not until she was sure the claim was properly recorded did she let it be known that she had found gold.

Elizabethtown was dying on its feet. The mines were petering out. People, like Joe, were giving up and leaving. Then Ella's find brought new hope, new excitement. The town was alive again.

Ella was no miner, and she sold her claim for two thousand dollars. She counted the money over and over. U.S. greenbacks. There wasn't that much money in the world. With the money and her gold sewed inside her petticoat, she took a stage to Raton. There, instead of working in a hotel, she bought it.

The Shuteye Hotel and Cafe catered to the laboring men, but that was fine with Ella. Laboring men were the only kind she knew. When the Santa Fe Saloon was up for sale, she sold the hotel and bought the saloon. She renamed it and made some improvements, such as etched-glass lamps hanging from the ceiling, a hand-carved mahogany bar, a long mirror behind the bar, and new tables and chairs, and she turned the saloon into a popular drinking and gambling place.

Men. Bless them. Damn them. They couldn't believe a woman saloon owner slept alone. Propositions were as plentiful as horseflies. Some men were humble, hopeful. Some believed they were God's gift to women, and they would be doing her a favor by going to bed with her. None got anywhere with Ella—until she met

47

the rancher from over near Mount Capulin. Him, she allowed into her bed—until he realized his ranch was not on land claimed by the land-grant company. When he joined the grant crowd, Ella kicked him out.

She came from a poor working family, and she sympathized with poor working people.

For over a year she had been sleeping alone. She had no intention of sleeping alone the rest of her life, but she was discriminating. She wanted a man, but not just any man.

Wild Bill Watson might do. She wasn't sure. Something about him appealed to her. Maybe it was the recklessness in his pale blue eyes, and his sense of humor. Maybe it was because of the story she'd heard about him shooting his way through a gang of scalp-hunting, bloodthirsty Comanches. Or the way he defied the grant people. Or because he was from South Texas.

Wild Bill was a possible. But she wasn't sure.

"Where are you bunking tonight?" she asked as they walked back to her place in the dark.

He wished he'd taken a bath before he came to town, and washed his clothes. But her question gave him hope anyway. "Wal, uh, ain't decided yet."

She quickly dashed his hope. "The Shuteye Hotel is still a good place, even though I don't own it anymore."

"Wal, uh, I was thinkin' maybe . . . ." He tried to put an arm around her waist.

"Forget it, Bill."

The three dead cattle rustlers were stiff with rigor mortis, and couldn't be tied onto a crossbuck saddle.

48

Wild Bill had tried to tell Deputy Duncan they'd need a wagon, but the deputy refused to listen to anything a squatter had to say.

"We'll have to bury 'em here," Duncan said. "I don't reckon you've got a shovel?"

"Yeah, I've got a shovel," Bill said.

"Go get it."

The deputy and two volunteers had helped Bill pick up the bodies and lay them side by side. Blood had gathered in their joints and coagulated so the joints were stiff. Whatever position they were in when they died, they were still in.

"Give 'em another warm day, and they'll bend," Bill said, squinting at the sun. "Might take a couple more days."

Moisture around the dead men's eyes had dried, leaving the eyes wide open, but sunken and hollow.

"They're gonna start stinkin' in another day," a volunteer said. He was a cowboy from one of the ranches southeast of Raton.

"That's for sure," said another, "an' the satchel birds're gonna git at 'em."

"What's the matter," Deputy Duncan sneered, "got a weak stomach?"

"I can handle 'em if I have to," the cowboy said, "but it ain't somethin' I do for fun and games."

"I'll go get a shovel," Bill said.

The deputy had gone through the dead men's pockets, finding a few coins and some U.S. greenbacks, which he stuffed into his own pockets. "Not a damn thing to identify 'em," he grumbled. He unbuckled their gunbelts and stacked their guns and holsters in a small pile. Pegleg Peterson had already stacked their

49

saddles near where one of the men had fallen. Their horses were running free somewhere, out of sight.

It was two miles to Bill's shack, but he rode there at a slow gallop, grabbed a long-handled roundpoint shovel, and carried it back across his saddle. By then it was afternoon, and none of the men had had anything to eat since early morning.

"Whatta you say, Duncan," the cowboy asked, "shall we dig three graves or one big one?"

"A big one. You, Watson, you can start diggin'."

The cowboy said, "You start it, Bill, an' I'll spell you."

For a moment, Bill thought he'd tell the lawman to do his own work. He wasn't the man's hired help. But, to get the job over with, he started digging.

The grave was deep, and because the arms and legs on two of the bodies were spread, it had to be wide. They stacked the bodies three high, put their own saddle blankets over their faces, then filled in the hole. Deputy Duncan managed to tie their saddles on the packhorses.

"There's gonna be a coroner's inquest," he said. "You're gonna have to be there, Watson. You and Peterson."

"When?"

"Make it day after tomorrow. Right after noon. I've already wired the sheriff, and I'll wire the coroner. Be there. You and Peterson. Don't make me come and get you."

Bill said no more, but just got on his dun horse and rode away.

* * *

50

It was up to him to tell Pegleg about the coroner's inquest, and early next morning he saddled a fresh horse and rode northwest. There was little chance that he would find Pegleg at home, but he hoped to at least leave him a note.

Surprise. As soon as he rode across Otero Creek, he saw the short man working on a corral. He knew he'd been seen, and he hoped he'd been recognized. He was.

"Git down, Bill. Coffee's still warm. If it ain't, I'll heat it up."

Bill put his bay horse in a corral, loosened the cinches, and pulled the bridle off. The horse would probably lie down and roll on the saddle, but it would do no damage. Inside, Bill was surprised at how clean and neat Pegleg's house was. Everything was in its place, and there were no dirty dishes in sight.

With his wooden leg thumping on the wooden floor, Peterson put a piece of dead cottonwood limb in the two-hole stove, and while the coffee heated, they sat at a homemade table and talked.

"Is that Duncan feller still the deputy at Raton?"

"Yeah, and he ain't any friend of the anti-grant folks. He calls us grant squatters."

"Gave you a bad time, huh?"

"Naw, but he might of, if it hadn't been for Ella Fitzwater. You know her, don't you?"

"Sure, I know Ella." Pegleg's beard divided into a grin. "She's sure got no use for the grant side."

While they sipped coffee, Bill told about burying the bodies, and about the coroner's inquest. "I reckon I'll show up. I'll tell my story over again. The deputy wants you there, too."

Leaning back in his chair, Peterson allowed. "Was a time when you just buried the dead thieves and forgot about 'em. Now we got to have law and order, and when a man gets kilt somebody has to do some explainin'."

"I reckon there oughta be some official words said."

"Next, they'll be tellin' us we can't keep guns to protect ourselfs."

"Huh," Bill snorted. "They try that and the Civil War'll be fought all over again."

Pegleg grinned, but he was only half joking. "The day's comin', Bill. The day's comin'."

Chapter Seven

The inquest in the deputy sheriff's office was short. The coroner was a fat man who had to leave the top button on his striped wool pants undone to relieve the pressure on his big belly. He asked few questions. Sheriff Bowman had arrived on the train from Springer with the coroner. Wild Bill Watson, Pegleg Peterson, and Ella Fitzwater were there. A smattering of townspeople stood inside, leaned against the walls, and listened, out of curiosity. Then another man entered, a tall man wearing a bushy mustache, a homburg hat, a shirt with a high collar, a necktie, and a dark broadcloth suit with the pant legs stuffed into the tops of cattlemen's riding boots. He looked like a man who couldn't decide whether he wanted to dress like a cattleman or a city businessman.

Bill and Pegleg didn't recognize him, but Ella whispered, "That's Hunter Howser. Look out for him."

For the third time, Bill told the story. Pegleg backed him. Deputy Duncan told where the bodies were found. He said guns were found near the bodies, and all had been fired since they'd been reloaded. But, he said, he saw no cattle or horses.

The gunfire had stampeded the cattle, Bill allowed, and Pegleg said the dead men's horses were more than happy to run free after he'd pulled the saddles off.

Sheriff Bowman asked his deputy if he'd written down a description of the dead men. "Why, no," Deputy Duncan answered. "I wish you did," the sheriff said, "in case somebody comes around asking about 'em." The deputy said he'd remember what they looked like.

Then there was a long pause as the two lawmen and the coroner tried to think of more questions. That was when the tall man spoke:

"This whole tale sounds very suspicious to me."

"Why do you say that, Mr. Howser?" the sheriff asked.

"We have three men shot dead. We have two men who say they were trying to steal some cattle. We have no cattle and no horses. How do we know the deceased weren't merely moving their own cattle across country, and how do we know these two squatters didn't murder them for their cattle and horses?"

When no one answered, he directed his next question at Deputy Duncan: "Did you look for livestock?"

"Why, no. We had to bury the dead, and we didn't have time before dark to do much of anything else."

"Sheriff," the tall man said, "I insist that you do some further investigating. This matter cannot be closed until you do."

The sheriff's shoulders slumped. He looked at his deputy, then at the coroner. He spoke with resignation, "All right. You've got a point. It will take all day

54

and then some, and the judge is gonna have to get somebody else to serve his papers."

"You have plenty of deputies to do that."

"No, Mr. Howser." The sheriff had squared his shoulders. "Most of these deputies were picked by the county board, and they're getting their orders from . . . One of them, Jameson, said he gets his orders from you. I don't like the way they do things."

"Then, you do your job."

"I'll do the best I can." Then to Bill, the sheriff asked, "What brand are your cattle wearing?"

"A Cross J. An underslope in the right ear."

"And you, Peterson?"

"A Rafter P. A swallow fork in the left ear."

"All right. My deputy and I'll ride as much of the country around there as we reasonably can. If we see any cattle wearing brands or earmarks other than them, we'll try to find out where they came from."

"Don't forget the horses."

"We'll look for horses, too."

Whispering, Ella said to Bill, "Told you he's a troublemaker."

Another long pause, then the coroner said, "Well, all I can do right now is rule that the cause of death of three unidentified men is gunshot wounds, and they died at the hands of one William Watson and one Arnold Peterson. Without the bodies, that's all I can say at this time. If you want to exhume the bodies, Sheriff, I can perform autopsies. It's up to you and the prosecuting attorney."

"We'll see."

Everyone except the officials and Hunter Howser trooped over to Ella's saloon for a drink after the inquest. Already leaning on the bar was Henry Volmos, badly hung over and drinking to get well. A shaggy, mongrel dog stayed by his side.

"Hey, Hank," Ella said, "you can't sober up that way."

Volmos appeared to be in his early sixties, grizzled, weatherbeaten, with a three-day growth of gray whiskers. He had lace-up, high-top shoes on his feet and a ragged straw hat on his head. In between were baggy denim pants held up with leather suspenders. A big-caliber hogleg pistol was in a holster on his left hip. "Ain't tryin' to sober up. Ain't no law ag'in' drinkin'."

"What about your sheep?" Ella asked. "And your dog. He wouldn't let us feed him, and we had to put him in a pen over by the livery barn. You get locked up again, and he might starve."

"I shorely do thank you for that, Eller. This here dog ain't no animal, he's my partner." Volmos burped and wiped his mouth with the back of his right hand. "Them sheep is bein' watched by a Messican kid and two dogs. Them Messicans is damn good sheepherders."

"Just the same," Ella said, "you ought to sober up and go home, or back to your camp, or wherever."

Swaying, unsteady on his feet, the older man said, "Purty soon I won't have no place to graze my sheep. Them grant men said I gotta move."

"Don't move yet. This thing ain't over."

"Well, I'm gonna have one more shot of whiskey. Then I'll go."

"All right, but I'm telling you as a friend, go home."

Volmos was forgotten as Pegleg, Bill, and Ella stood at the bar, each with one foot on a brass rail. The two men drank beer. Ella drank water. "I've seen what liquor can do to folks," she said. "Sometimes I feel guilty about selling the stuff. Someday I'm gonna find some other business to get into." They had another round, talked about the grant versus the anti-grant people, and Wild Bill said, "I don't get this Hunter Howser. What's he up to?"

"He's a mystery," Ella said. "He came here from somewhere back east, and he wasn't here a week till he had a bunch of those ex-militiamen around him. Somebody said he's one of the conglomerate that bought the grant, but somebody else said he ain't. One thing we do know is the county board hired some of his toughs as deputies."

"I don't like 'im," Bill said.

"The grant people like him," Ella said, "but I'd trust him as far as I'd trust a rattlesnake."

Pegleg drained his beer mug and ordered a refill for himself and Bill. That was when they heard gunshots coming from the street.

Everyone in the saloon hurried to the door to see what was happening, expecting to see a gunfight. They were disappointed. What they saw was Henry Volmos firing his old Colt Dragoon at the sheriff's sign hanging over the plankwalk. Volmos was staggering drunk, waving the gun in his left hand, pointing it at everything in sight. His dog was beside him. The street was empty of people, but faces were plastered to windows from inside the buildings.

"Oh, for the love of . . ." Ella gathered her skirts and ran to the shooter, stood in front of him. "Hank, put that gun away, will you?"

"Nossir, by god. That damn deputy is one a them grant people, and I'm a-darin' 'im to come outta there and face me like a man."

"Hank, I don't think he's in there. Put the gun away and come with me, will you?"

"Nossir, by god. I'm tellin' all a them grant sons of bucks to come shootin', 'cuz old Hank Volmos is ready for war." He burped, and his breath made Ella cringe. The Dragoon was raised for another shot.

But Ella got between the gun and the sheriff's sign. "You wouldn't shoot a friend, would you, Hank?"

"I wouldn't shoot you for anything, Eller, but I wisht you'd—"*burp*—"get outta my way."

A few of the townspeople had cautiously stepped outside now, but were staying close to the doors so they could jump back inside.

"S'pose I said I wasn't gonna get out of your way, what would you do?"

A blank look spread over the old man's face. "What'd I do? Danged if I know. I"—*burp*—"ain't never had no friend get in front of my gun before." *Burp*.

"Tell you what. Put that gun away and come back in my place, and I'll get something to eat for your and your dog. If you ain't hungry, your dog is."

"My dog is hongry?" The old man reached down and scratched the dog behind the ears. A bushy tail thumped the ground. "You hongry, podner? No dog of mine is gonna go hongry."

"He won't take feed from anybody else, you know. Come on inside and I'll get your something to feed him."

"Aww. But I got two more loads in this here pees-tola that I ain't busted yet."

In a soft voice, as if she were talking to a child, Ella said, "Let the hammer down easy, Hank, and put it in its holster. That's the way. Now, come back inside." Ella took him by the arm—his gun arm—and led him inside the Willow Springs saloon. Onlookers stepped back to make way. The dog followed. She got him seated at a table, ordered him to stay awake a few more minutes, then hurried across the alley to her house and kitchen. When she returned with a half pound of beef rump in her hands, the old man was slumped in the chair, slipping into unconsciousness.

"Hank, wake up. Wake up a minute. You've got to feed your dog."

"Huh? Oh"—*burp*—"yeah." With shaking hands he took the meat and put it on the floor. The dog gulped it down in a few seconds. Ella put a tin pan of water on the floor. The dog ignored it until the old man shoved it toward him, then he lapped it up.

Finally, Henry Volmos crossed his arms on top of the table and put his face between his arms. The dog lay at his feet, licking its chops.

"Well," said Wild Bill Watkins, "now that the shootin's over, it's time for me to start for home."

"Me too," said Pegleg Peterson. "Gonna be dark before we get there."

The two men retrieved their horses from a livery pen and rode out of town, angling southwest where there was no road, not even wagon tracks. Peterson was riding a blue roan with a long back and long neck, and he had two pads, a hair pad and a doubled saddle blanket, under the saddle. Bill had been curious about the two pads, and now he nodded at the saddle and asked, "How come all the stuff?"

"Oh, this old pony's got such high withers it takes two pads to keep the saddle off his wither bone. I cut a slit in the front of this hair pad so it fits around the top of his withers, and it works purty good."

"I had a horse like that. The saddle was always eatin' hair off of 'im."

It was dark by the time they crossed the old Santa Fe Trail, which was abandoned now that the Sante Fe railroad ran from Colorado all the way to El Paso. About a mile from Pegleg's place, they split up, Bill angling southeast from there. A quarter-moon put out enough light that he knew where he was and which way to go. If he didn't know, the horse did. He allowed the horse to walk, enjoying the night breeze and the stars spread clear across the sky, so close he could almost grab one. He started singing softly to himself: "Oh, that ol' yaller moon . . ."

Ella Fitzwater entered his thoughts, and again he mentally compared her with Eileen Cruz. Ella was some woman. Eileen was a lady, a beautiful lady. He wanted to see her again, if only from a distance. Just look at her, admire her.

"Aww," he grumbled aloud. "Forget it. It's hopeless. Forget it." He couldn't forget it.

Not until—for the second time that day—he heard gunshots.

"Oh-oh," he said, reining up sharply. Four shots came from the northwest. Another. "That ain't no drunk shootin' at a street sign," he muttered. Wild Bill spun the horse around on its hind feet. "That's some-body tryin' to kill somebody.

"That's somebody tryin' to kill Pete."

Chapter Eight

The one-legged man put his horse in a corral, tossed him some hay, went into his house, and lit a coal-oil lamp. He sat on a kitchen chair, leaned over, and unstraped his wooden leg. He straightened suddenly and grunted with surprise when a gunshot came from outside. A bullet shattered the glass in the kitchen window and slammed into the wall over his head.

Hopping on one foot, he blew out the lamp, grabbed his Winchester carbine off the wall, and looked through the bottom corner of the broken window. It was so dark outside, he could see nothing to shoot at. A muzzle flash caused him to duck under the window. Another bullet broke more glass. Then a volley of shots poured through the window, punching holes in the wall across the room.

Pegleg Peterson had built his house with walls thick enough to keep out the winter cold, and to stop bullets. As long as he stayed under the window he was safe. There was another window in the other room, but the quarter-moon put out enough light that he could barely see the outline of it. Anyone who tried to climb through would be an easy target.

No one tried. It was a standoff. The shooters could send lead flying through the window all night. They could shoot splintery holes in the plank door. But Pegleg was sitting on the floor under the window, just waiting for someone to show himself. There was only one thing he feared.

And sure enough, it was happening.

Another volley came through the window, and two more holes were punched through the door, but what worried Pegleg was the sound of men's voices just outside the window. The men were staying low, under the window, and cursing.

"Goddamn wood won't burn."

"Need some littler sticks."

"Keep watchin' that winder. Don't let that old sumbitch show his face. I'll whittle some splinters off this here tree branch."

"I'm watchin'."

It was quiet for a minute. Pegleg wanted to look out. He had to. He started to stand on his one foot. Two shots from outside buzzed like angry bees past his head. No way could he poke his carbine out the window and point it down at the men under the window. Putting the rifle down, he unholstered his .45 Peacemaker. Cautiously, knowing he could lose his right arm, he poked the gun through the window, aimed down, and squeezed off two rapid shots.

"God damn. The old sumbitch almost got me. Hey, over there, pour it to 'im. Keep him away from that winder."

Shot after shot came through the window and pounded the far wall. The window in the bedroom was shattered with a rifle butt. Pegleg watched, waited for a man to appear. Only an arm appeared, an arm with a pistol in its hand. The pistol popped, but the shooter kept his head outside and was only shooting in Pegleg's general direction. Pegleg fired back. The arm disappeared.

"Cain't you get a fire goin'? Don't you know how to start a fire?"

"I ain't no goddamn wild-West bozo. Why in hell didn't we bring some coal oil?"

Pegleg started to poke his Peacemaker through the window again, but a volley of gunfire drove him down. Five seconds later, he tried again and managed to get off one shot before splinters from the windowsill peppered his face.

"I got 'er goin'," a man said outside the window. "Let's vacate the premises before that one-legged old fart gets lucky."

When the shooting stopped for the moment, Pegleg could hear a small fire crackling, and then he could see a faint glow under the window. Hopping on one foot, he grabbed a bucket two-thirds full of water from off the stove. He knew the flame would illuminate his head when he looked outside, but he had to do something. Quickly, he took a look, then started to pour water from the bucket onto the flames.

Two rifle shots tore holes in the bucket and knocked it from his hands. Most of the water spilled onto the floor.

"Well, that does it," Pegleg said to himself, standing on one foot beside the window. "If I try to run outside, I'll be cut in two with rifle bullets. If I stay inside, I'll be roasted alive." He snorted. "Huh. I couldn't run outside if I wanted to. All I can do is hop on one foot."

Crawling on his hands and knees, he made his way to the kitchen chair. There, he sat on the floor and strapped on his wooden leg. Then he stood and walked, peg leg thumping, to the window. The fire was climbing up the wall. If he as much as looked out now, his face would be a target hard to miss. He remembered leaving another water bucket outside on a bench beside the water barrel. If he could just get out there . . . no, that would be suicide.

"Well, hell, Pete, you didn't expect to live forever," he said to himself. "But by damn I ain't gonna just sit in here and burn to death."

Desperate, he picked up the carbine, stuck it through the window, and fired two shots. The return fire forced him back.

Then another shot came from somewhere. It sounded different, like a six-gun instead of a rifle. The bullet didn't hit the house or come through the window. The pistol popped again. Then the rifles opened up again, but now they were aimed at somebody else.

"Bill?" Pegleg said aloud, though he knew no one could hear him. "Is that you, Bill?"

Wild Bill Watson couldn't see who was shooting, but he could see the muzzle flashes in the dark. Dismounting, he walked toward the house, ready to drop to the ground if bullets came his way. He saw the flames eating at the house, right under the window.

"Goddamn," he muttered. "They're tryin' to burn 'im out."

A hundred feet from the house he dropped to one knee, waited for a muzzle flash, then fired at it. He wished he had his Remington rifle. It was more accurate at a distance. But the Smith & Wesson six-gun could throw a lot of lead. He fired again at another muzzle flash.

A man yelled, "Shit, he's got some help. Over there. Shoot the shit out of 'im."

Bill flattened himself on the ground while bullets sang deadly songs around him. He returned the fire, heard a man yell in pain. He rolled over and over when rifle bullets searched the ground where his shot had come from. If they kept searching, they would find him.

He wondered if Pegleg had been hit. Was he dead, or, worse yet, lying wounded in there where he'd be burned alive? Goddamn.

On one knee, he squeezed off another round, then flattened and rolled. Bullets searched for him.

Then rifle fire came from the window. A man yelled, "Shit, there's too many of 'em."

Under his breath, Bill said, "Pete, you old son of a gun. Give 'em hell."

"God damn, let's vacate this place."

Fumbling in the dark, Bill reloaded his six-gun, fired three shots in the direction of the yelling, and flattened himself.

Hoofbeats. They were leaving. Another shot came from the window, but it was a shot in the dark.

The fire was climbing higher.

Standing, Bill holstered the Smith & Wesson, and

ran toward the house, yelling, "Pete, it's me, Bill Watson. Don't shoot, Pete, it's me."

He got to the house at the same time Peterson opened the door and hobbled out. Without a word, Bill grabbed the bucket from the bench, dipped it into the water barrel, and threw water on the flames. Again and again. Now the water level in the barrel was dangerously low.

Pegleg had grabbed a shovel from somewhere and was trying to smother the flames with dirt.

Dipping the bucket into the barrel again, Bill got only a quarter-bucketful. There wasn't much more. He tipped the barrel, picked it up, and emptied it into the bucket. He threw what water he had onto the fire. That was it. Grimacing, he took off his shirt and used it to beat at the flames. Pegleg kept throwing dirt.

"Goddamn," Bill muttered. "Goddamn, goddamn."

"We're makin' headway," Peterson yelled. "We're gonna whup it, Bill."

Sure enough. The wood was wet now, and the flames were sizzling. Sizzling and dying.

The two men kept battling the fire until finally only a few hot ashes were left. Bill straightened his back with a groan, breathing hard. Peterson leaned on his shovel handle.

"It looks," Bill gasped, "like you still got a house."

"Don't . . . look like it done . . . much damage."

"It'll smell . . . like wood smoke for . . . a while."

"I c'n stand the smell . . . as long as the wall is still strong."

They were silent until their breathing returned to normal. Now that the flames had died, the two men

68

could see only vague shapes of each other in the dark. Wild Bill rolled a cigarette, lit it, then threw it down. "I've had enough smoke for tonight. Any idea who they was, Pete?"

"I couldn't see any of 'em, but I got an idee."

"Them militiamen?"

"None other."

"They wanted to kill you to get your land, huh?"

"Yup. And they wouldn't of had to kill me, just burn up my deed so's I couldn't prove I own any land."

"I been expectin' 'em over at my place. I ain't got a deed, though. All I got is a six-gun and a rifle."

"That's enough to make 'em wanta kill you."

"Or scare me off."

"Either way, they want us all off."

"Makes a feller scared to sit in his shack at night with a lamp burnin'."

"If you do, you're a target they can't miss. If they hadn't of had burnin' on their minds, they could of just shot me."

"Looks like they took to ridin' at night so nobody can recognize 'em. That deed you've got, Pete, do you keep it here in the house?"

"Yeah, but after tonight I think I'll find someplace else to keep it."

"Maybe, next time you go to court you can leave your deed with a lawyer. If there's one that's on our side."

"Hell of a note, ain't it? A feller can't rest in his own house."

"Use to be the Indians a feller had to be scairt of. Now it's the goddamn militia. The so-called militia."

69

"Well," Peterson said after a pause, "they won't be back tonight. I'm gonna hit the blankets. You can bunk here tonight if you want to."

"Naw. I've got a horse over there somewheres. I'd better find 'im and get on home." Wild Bill chuckled without mirth. "They might of already burned me out."

Rubbing his bare arms, he chuckled again. "I hope they at least left me a shirt."

Chapter Nine

Arnold Peterson had been just about everywhere between Missouri and California. Raised in Indiana, he left home at age fifteen and went west looking for adventure. He trapped beaver in the Dakotas, panned for gold in Colorado, tried vegetable farming in Utah. He bought and sold horses, cattle, and wagons. And everywhere he went he fought Indians, claim jumpers, card sharps, and road agents. When the Civil War broke out, he went back to his home state and allowed himself to be conscripted. He was inducted into the Union Army as a private and he stayed a private. Not because he wasn't a good fighting man—he'd had plenty of experience—but because he'd been living the wild free life so long he was out of the habit of taking orders. When other soldiers complained of too little food or bad food, sleeping on the cold wet ground, long marches, and the dangers of battle, Private Peterson just grinned. It was nothing new to him.

And when the war ended and ex-soldiers talked of going west where land was free for the taking, where veterans got favored treatment in their quest for land,

Peterson knew exactly where he was going. He'd trapped and hunted in the Cimarron Valley, the Moreno Valley, and on the plains. It was a mighty country where rivers rushed down the mountains, springs poured out of the hillsides, and grass of all kinds—wild wheat, grama, timothy, buffalo, brome, and june grass—was plentiful. He'd lived with the Mexicans, the Muache Utes, and the Jicarilla Apaches. He agreed with them that all of north-central New Mexico Territory belonged to them. It did not belong to a man named Maxwell, who'd inherited half from his father-in-law named Miranda and who'd bought the other half from a man named Beaubien.

The Indians had been there since time began, and the Mexicans had been there since the first Spanish colonizers. Never mind that Governor Armijo gave it to Miranda and Beaubien. When the United States kicked Mexico out, the land belonged to the United States. It was the spoils of war. Everyone knew that.

And when the U.S. Congress ruled, even before the Civil War, that the land did not belong to the United States, no one took it seriously. The old grant covered too much territory. Some said one and a half million acres. Others said it was two million acres.

Let them argue about it and fight about it. There was more country than anyone could keep track of, and Arnold Peterson went back there to resume the wild free life.

He married an Indian woman and lived with the Utes. When the Utes and Apaches clashed, he fought for his wife's people.

That was how he lost his right leg.

The arrow was buried clear to the bone about halfway between the knee and ankle. Arnold Peterson pulled it out himself, and walked, bleeding badly, back to the Ute camp. Yellow Rose, his squaw, made a poultice of moss from the Cimarron River to draw out the poison. The medicine man danced and threw ashes to the wind god. The elders chanted and drummed on their tom-toms. It didn't work. Gangrene set in. The leg had to go.

With a long-bladed skinning knife, sharpened on sandstone until it would whack a hair in two, Peterson began to cut the leg off himself. He cut until he struck bone. He could cut no farther. An ax acquired in a trade with the Mexicans finished the job. Peterson fainted. By the time he awakened, the stump had been cauterized with a red hot iron and bandaged loosely.

For a week, the white Indian slipped in and out of consciousness. At times fever had him delirious. Yellow Rose never left his side for more than a few minutes at a time. Her brothers supplied them with fresh meat, and even fruit and vegetables from a Mexican village. Nine months after the leg had been amputated, Peterson made himself a wooden leg, which he held in place with leather straps. In two weeks he was able to walk with barely a limp. In another week he could run, though not as fast as the younger men.

Times were changing. There was a lot of talk about the U.S. government herding the Indians onto reservations. They were considered wards of the government, and they were assured they would be fed and housed. Not Arnold Peterson.

With Yellow Rose at his side, he rode into the settlement named Cimarron and asked for a job. Go see Mr. Maxwell, he was advised. Him? The land grabber who says he owns half the world? Yeah, him, Peterson was told, but he's not a bad feller. He's never given anyone a hard time. He's never told anyone they had to get off his land. Mr. Maxwell has fed hungry Indians, and has paid good wages to people who work for him. He's built himself one hell of a fine ranch, the finest there is. Go see him. He might have a job for you.

Arnold Peterson went to work for Lucien B. Maxwell, and lived with Yellow Rose in a two-room rock house on the home place. His knowledge of Indians, hunting and fishing, and the country surrounding them fascinated Maxwell. The two men became good friends. At the death of Yellow Rose, Maxwell tried to ease Peterson's grief by giving him some land. Twenty sections. What was twenty sections to a man who owned two million acres? Peterson could pick the spot. He knew the spot he wanted, near the confluence of the Vermejo and Otero Creek, one of the best pieces of grazing land on the whole Maxwell grant. The two men rode there and laid out twenty sections as best they could. Lucien Maxwell wrote down all the boundaries in ink on heavy wrapping paper. He gave Peterson fifty cows and eight bulls to start a herd. Peterson built a house and corrals.

Then Maxwell sold his holdings. Through ways believed by most folks to be strange and devious, the grant fell into the hands of American, Dutch, and British investors. They called their company the Maxwell Land Grant & Railway Company, and later, after a series of reincorporations, it was named the Maxwell Land Grant Company.

Then Lucien Maxwell moved to eastern New Mexico Territory. Then Lucien Maxwell died.

Now, the ownership of one million seven hundred thousand acres of land was being resolved through foreclosures, tax sales, evictions, and expensive litigation after litigation.

And gunfire.

Pegleg Peterson knew he'd have to go to court again. He wanted to do everything the legal way, so there would be no doubt he owned the land he claimed. This time he would hire a lawyer to represent him. He had some cash left from the last time he'd trailed beeves to the new railroad town of Springer, and he decided it would be wise to hire professional representation.

For five nights now he'd been sleeping on the ground outside his house, fearing another night attack. He kept the little iron box containing his deed buried under a boulder across Otero Creek. But it worried him. If he was killed, the box would never be found, and his land would no doubt go to the grant company.

So when he happened to meet his neighbor, Bill Watson, gathering cattle that had strayed too far, he told of his plan. Wild Bill decided to go with him to Springer, just out of curiosity.

Springer had sprung up with the coming of the Sante Fe railroad, and was soon named the county seat of Colfax County. A stone courthouse sat on the main street, housing county offices, a district courtroom, a sheriff's office, and a jail. It was only a few months earlier that three good men, all anti-grant men, were shot down in the street with a volley from a deputy sheriff and other members of the militia. The deputy was eventually arrested, but never tried. Instead a member of the anti-grant crowd, a prominent citizen, was arrested and jailed for three weeks. Springer was known as a nest of grant vipers, and the anti-grants didn't expect to get a fair shuffle of the cards.

The two men rode down the street of Springer, trying to ignore the stares. They had squatter and cattlemen written all over them, and anyone could tell at a glance they were anti-grant. They both carried six-guns in holsters on their right hips, and lever-action rifles in saddle boots.

"There's trouble looking for a place to happen," commented a bystander.

"I got a hunch," said another, "if anybody locks horns with them two, they better have the whole damn militia ready to shoot."

But the two weren't looking for a fight. They corraled their horses at a livery near the railroad stockyards and walked down the street, looking for a lawyer. A sign hanging over the plankwalk attracted their attention, and they climbed wooden stairs at the side of a two-story brick building to an office door. The sign on the door read Thos. A. Atwell Attorney at Law.

"What're we s'posed to do," Pegleg asked Bill, "knock on the door or holler or go on in?"

"I don't know, but just to be polite, let's knock."

Pegleg rapped on the solid wooden door with work-hardened knuckles. A man's voice came through the door, "Come in, come in." The one-legged man led the way inside, cautiously. Wild Bill was right behind him. "Are you a lawyer?" Pegleg asked the young man sitting behind a desk. "Yessir, that I am. Thomas

Atwell at your service." The young man wore a smile, a stiff white collar, a short square necktie, a thin mustache, and thick brown hair parted in the middle. His office was furnished with a desk, two chairs, and a wooden cabinet. One wall was lined with law books. A window overlooked the street below.

"Uh," Pegleg hesitated, putting his weight on his good leg, not knowing what to say. He looked at Bill. Bill only shrugged.

"What can I do for you?" the young man asked.

"Well, I, uh, let me ask you somethin'," Pegleg said. "Are you for the militia or the squatters?"

"Why, I, uh, as an officer of the court, I am neutral." Thomas Atwell put his hands on his desk, palms down.

"Nobody's neutral," Pegleg said. "You're one or the other. I need a lawyer that'll do my talkin' for me in court."

"You have a legal problem?"

"Yessir, I do. I own twenty sections of land around the fork of the Vermejo and the Otero. I got a paper to prove it. But I don't know how to talk to a judge."

"I see. Umm. I take it, then, that you are in opposition to the land-grant company?"

"Ever' inch of me."

"Umm." The young lawyer leaned back in his chair, then, as a afterthought, stood and came around his desk. He stuck out his right hand. "You know my name; would you mind telling me yours?"

Both men shook with him and introduced themselves. Pegleg reached inside a shirt pocket and pulled out two folded sheets of paper. He handed them to the lawyer.

"Umm." Thomas Atwell took his seat again, leaned back, and read the papers carefully. Looking up at Peterson, he said, "I only recently qualified to practice law in this territory. Of course, I have heard and read extensively about the legal dispute over ownership of the Maxwell land grant. Thus far, I have not been involved with either side, and have kept an open mind. Whatever the courts decide is the law, and I will abide by the court's decision." He paused, thinking, and this gave Pegleg an opportunity to put in:

"Then you know the grant folks have got more money than the rest of us, and c'n pay lawyers more."

"Yes, I, uh, I have come to that conclusion."

"I c'n pay you a fair price and no more. If that's not good enough, then give me my papers back."

"Mr. Peterson, it appears to me you have a valid deed here. The boundaries are somewhat vague, however. Yes, I will be happy to represent you in court for a fair fee, but I am certain the court will order the disputed land surveyed, and you will have to pay the surveyor."

"I c'n pay a fair price."

"Very well, the first thing we have to do is file a motion for adjudication of rights to the property, and get a hearing date set."

"Speaking of which," Pegleg said, "I b'lieve today is June twelve, and I'm s'posed to be in court at three o'clock."

"Oh?" The lawyer's eyebrows went up. "You were served a summons?"

"Yessir." Pegleg handed over the court order served by Sheriff Bowman. "I don't always keep track of the day of the month and all. I hope this is the right day."

The lawyer was silent as he read the summons, then said, "This is the day." He pulled a watch out of a vest pocket, opened the lid. "We have one hour." Looking up at Peterson, he added, "That is, if you want me to represent you."

"How much?"

"How much do you think your land is worth?"

"A hell of a lot more than I'm gonna pay a lawyer."

A tight smile appeared for a second on the lawyer's face. "Very well, my fee will be fifteen dollars for the first court appearance, and we'll just have to see what happens. There is something else I should mention. The judge does not allow firearms in the courtroom."

Wild Bill had said nothing except to introduce himself. Now, he took his court summons out of a shirt pocket, unfolded it, and handed it to the lawyer. "I got an order, too, but I ain't got no deed. There's not much use me goin' to court."

"Umm. Well, if you have no valid claim to any land on the grant, you would probably be wasting your time. However, if you want to argue the law, I will be happy to represent you, too."

"Naw. What's the use?"

"If you do not appear, you will forfeit your right to further court proceedings."

"I expected that."

Chapter Ten

In the Cimarron Cafe, the two men had dinner of red beans and fried potatoes. There wasn't much else on the menu. "I could of had this at home," Pegleg grumbled. "I see they've got some doughnuts on their list," Wild Bill said. "Reckon I'll try some."

The doughnuts weren't bad. "At least it's different," Bill allowed.

Their next stop was the livery barn, where they left their six-guns, gunbelts and all, with their saddles. Walking back on the plankwalk, Bill suddenly stopped and stared, mouth open. "What're you . . . ?" Pegleg started to ask, then said, "Oh yeah. It's Tomás Cruz and his sister. Good people. Know 'em?"

The brother and sister were riding in a buggy pulled by a team of bay horses. The buggy was freshly painted, black with red wheel spokes, and the horses were well-groomed. The harness was oiled and polished until the leather shone. Nickel silver decorated the harness in a dozen places.

"Uh," Bill sputtered. "I, uh, I met 'em a time or two."

"She's one purty lady, ain't she? Never married, they tell me. Their folks was killed by the Jicarillas 'bout fifteen year ago. He was married, but his wife died calvin'."

"Yeah, uh, one purty lady."

"Wonder if they're in town for the same reason we are?"

Wild Bill had turned completely around on the walk, watching the brother and sister ride past. He realized suddenly that he was gawking, and he cleared his throat and turned back. "Prob'ly are. The goddamn land-grabbin' foreigners're tryin' to get ever'body's property."

"Well, we better get on over to the courthouse and see what happens."

"It oughta be fun."

A wooden leg went *thump, thump, thump* on the flagstone floor of the Colfax County courthouse as the two men looked for a courtroom. They found it on the second floor. Thomas Atwell met them outside the courtroom door, put his finger to his lips, and said, "Shhh. The court's in session." While they waited on benches, the lawyer again read the papers Pegleg had given him. And Tomás and Eileen Cruz came up the stairs.

The young Mexican wore a short jacket with wide lapels, and a necktie with a big knot at his throat. His pants were tight-fitting Mexican wool, and his boots were polished calfskin. He carried his broad-brim, round-top hat in his hands, and his dark hair was combed back and parted in the middle.

But Wild Bill barely noticed. He couldn't take his eyes off Eileen Cruz. Just the sight of her made his knees weak. Her dark hair was combed carefully straight down to her shoulders, and a red rose was pinned over her left ear. He saw an oval face, flawless skin, beautiful brown eyes, a wide mouth that needed no artificial color and a round, firm chin. Covering her shoulders was a white hand-crocheted shawl. She wore it over a light gray dress that fell to the tops of black patent-leather slippers. A cloth belt, tied in front with a big bow knot, pulled her dress in at the waist—a small waist.

The young man smiled widely when he recognized Pegleg, and he walked toward him. *"Señor Peterson. Cómo 'sta usted?"*

"Poco bueno," Pegleg answered, shaking hands with the young Mexican. The two talked in Spanish from there on. Bill understood a few words and phrases, but could only guess at what they were saying.

He stood, removed his hat and wanted to say something to Eileen Cruz, but didn't know what to say. She spoke:

"Nice to see you again, Mr. Watson." Her English had only a trace of a Spanish accent.

"Y-yes, ma'am," Bill stuttered. "I mean, miss. It's surely nice to see you, too."

"I would guess," she said, "that you were served with a court summons."

"Yes, ma'am."

"It seems a lot of us were. The sheriff has been busy carrying out orders of the court."

The courtroom door opened, and a man and woman came out, dressed in laboring-class clothes, weather-beaten. The woman was holding a handkerchief to her eyes, sniffling. The man looked to be so angry he was

83

ready to chew nails. Jaws clenched tight, he led the woman down the hall and down the stairs.

Pegleg said, "Whatever happened to them, that's what we can expect."

Eileen Cruz said, "This doesn't look at all encouraging." A worry frown pulled her features together. As she clasped her hands in front of her waist, Bill noticed that her hands didn't fit the rest of her. They were clean, the fingernails were clean, but the hands were work-worn, callused, sun-darkened.

Of course. When he thought about it, he knew why. After all, she was a farmer and stock grower. She could wear a bonnet to keep the sun off her face, and her clothes kept the sun off her arms and shoulders, but her hands had to be exposed.

The hands, compared to the perfect complexion, made her even more interesting to Bill. She had all the airs and looks of a lady, but she worked for a living, and she worked with her hands.

Again, the courtroom door opened, and a young man wearing wire-rimmed glasses stuck his head out. "Is there a Mr. Arnold Peterson present?"

"Yeah," Pegleg said. "That's me."

"Your case is next," the young man said.

Thomas Atwell whispered, "Let me do the talking unless you are asked a question."

"More'n glad to," Pegleg said.

They all trooped inside; Pegleg Peterson, Wild Bill, Tomás Cruz, and Eileen Cruz. A wrought-iron rail separated the spectators from two tables with chairs and the judge's bench. Everyone sat on wooden benches provided for the spectators. Judge Wilford Mitchell sat behind a high desk mounted on a platform. He wore half-glasses on the end of his long nose, and he looked over them at the newcomers.

"Case number four-two-zero-five," he said. "The Maxwell Land Company versus Arnold Peterson. Is Mr. Peterson present?"

"Yessir."

Thomas Atwell whispered, "Stand up." Pegleg stood.

"Are you represented by counsel, Mr. Peterson?"

Standing, Pegleg said, "Yessir." Thomas Atwell stood, too. "Your Honor, I am Thomas B. Atwell. I have been retained to represent Mr. Peterson."

"Very well. Come forward."

The lawyer led his one-legged client through a gap in the wrought-iron divider. The judge said, "Be seated over there." He nodded toward one of the tables. "This hearing is to show cause why Mr. Peterson should not be evicted from a parcel of real estate . . ." The judge read a lengthy legal description. His voice showed he was weary of hearing endless arguments about the ownership of land in the grant. Weary and discouraged over what seemed to be a hopeless mess.

A lawyer for the land company began the argument, standing, buttoning his suit coat, using legal language that the spectators could only guess the meaning of. When he finished, Judge Mitchell cast a bored look at Atwell. "Mr. Atwell?"

"A-hum. Yes sir, Your Honor." The young lawyer stood and began talking. "Allow me to introduce into evidence a deed of trust, signed by Mr. Lucien B. Maxwell, and witnessed by Mr. Charles F. Bordon and Mr. Jesus B. Garcia."

"Any objection?"

"Your Honor, we would like to examine the document."

Atwell continued, "You will notice that the deed is recorded in Book 2, Records of Colfax County, pages 116 and 117 on March 14, 1870. It also has affixed a federal revenue stamp of one dollar and fifty cents in compliance with the law of the United States."

After everyone had examined the paper, the judge asked, "Do you have a legal description of the parcel in question?"

"Your Honor," Atwell said, "please notice the date on this document. It was signed and recorded before the land in question was properly surveyed. However, we do have a description of the kind that is being recognized as legal."

A small groan escaped the judge. He appeared to shrink inside his black robe. He'd seen that kind of description before. "Very well," he said in a tired voice. "Do you want to introduce that as evidence?"

"We do, Your Honor."

"Will you please read the description."

Thomas Atwell read: "To all the land beginning at a dam at the head of a ditch leading out of the Vermejo River to the right hand of a point of rocks piled a foot high as a marker, from thence running on the north side of said river to another pile of rocks on a small knoll with some willow bushes nearby, thence running near southward across said river to a piñon tree with the letter P carved on the trunk, thence running up to Otero Creek, continuing south to another rock marker thence back to place of beginning, containing twenty sections of land more or less."

"Ohhh," the judge groaned, holding his chin in both

86

hands. A lawyer for the land company smirked. "Very well." Judge Mitchell raised his head and looked everyone in the eye. "The validity of the deed can easily be determined. What remains to be resolved is the location and size of the parcel in question. That will have to be determined by a proper survey. The court will appoint a surveyor, the costs to be borne by the defendant."

Bang, went the judge's gavel. Judge Mitchell wanted to call a recess so he could visit the water closet, but he decided to hear one more case. He hoped it would be a simple one.

It was not.

Next defendants called were Tomás and Eileen Cruz. They were represented by a lawyer of Spanish descent, but his English was good and his speaking was eloquent. A lawyer for the land company repeated what he'd said many times before. In the end the judge ruled in favor of the land company, but he advised the defendants they could appeal to a higher court, and no eviction order would be issued until after the appeal.

All in the courtroom stood as the judge stood and hurried out a door behind his bench.

Tomás Cruz had to have it all explained to him in Spanish. His sister understood perfectly, and she was bitter. Outside the courtroom, she exploded, first in Spanish and then in English.

"Does that judge think we have an unlimited supply of money to pay for litigation? Are the courts serving justice or the lawyers? Are we to be chased off our land, out of our homes like gypsies? Under the Treaty of Guadalupe Hidalgo of 1848, we are citizens of the

United States just as you are." She nodded toward Pegleg, Wild Bill, and Thomas Atwell.

The Anglos could do nothing but shake their heads in sympathy. Tomás Cruz didn't understand what his sister was saying, but he knew she was as angry as he'd ever seen her. He tried to put an arm around her shoulders, but she turned away.

"Our ancestors settled on the land three centuries ago. We have built homes and churches, we have raised crops and livestock. Now the United States government treats us worse than animals. Even the Indians are treated better. The Indians have never turned a furrow or built a permanent home. Yet the United States government gives them food and shelter. We get nothing. Absolutely nothing."

Turning to her brother, she hid her face against his shoulder. No one spoke. There was nothing to say. When she turned back to them, she wiped tears from her eyes with callused fingertips and spoke in a calm voice: "I am sorry, gentlemen. I did not intend to take my anger out on you. I am very sorry." Then she turned and left, holding her head high. Her brother walked with quick steps to catch up with her.

Wild Bill broke the silence that followed. "I'd give her ever'thing I've got. I'd fight the whole Union Army for that girl."

"That there is one damn fine lady," said Pegleg Peterson.

"Unfortunately," the Spanish-speaking lawyer said, "fighting is not what she needs."

"What does she need?" asked Bill.

Shrugging, the lawyer said, "Corrective legislation, perhaps. It would take an act of Congress."

"In other words, better laws," Wild Bill said.

The lawyer only nodded.

Wild Bill said, "Fightin' might not be what she needs, but if anydamnbody gives that girl any trouble he's gonna have me on his ass like a bull terrier. Law or no damn law."

"Me too," said Pegleg Peterson.

Chapter Eleven

It was the Spanish-speaking lawyer who told the Anglos all about Eileen Cruz. "As she said, when the United States forced Mexico out of this territory, the government gave the Mexican settlers the option of becoming U.S. citizens or remaining citizens of Mexico. Whatever they chose to do, their property rights were to remain secure. Eileen's parents chose to become U.S. citizens. And since they were citizens of an English-speaking nation, they wanted their children to learn the English language. They named their daughter Eileen in hopes it would help her to blend with other U.S. citizens, and later, in her teens, she went to school in Albuquerque to learn English. Tomás is not as studious as Eileen, and has not learned the language. He probably never will."

On the plankwalk, wooden leg thumping, Peterson allowed he'd buy some coffee, a loaf of bread, and some canned fruit. "I should of brought a packhorse," he said. "I could use more than I can carry in saddlebags."

"I've got coffee enough," Bill said, "but I like those

canned peaches and tomatoes and stuff. Had a can of ham, once, and it was tolerable. Reckon I'll fill my saddlebags, too.''

"Let's take our horses over to that mercantile yonder. It's gonna be dark before we get home. I might get hungry on the way.''

"I'll be glad to get out of this town. Folks are starin' at us like we was wild injuns.''

"I'll feel better when I get my guns. I'm lopsided without a shootin' iron.''

Armed again, the two men rode their horses to the Outpost Mercantile and General Hardware, dismounted, and wrapped their reins once around a hitch rail. Inside, they tipped their hats to two women shoppers, were ignored, and stepped up to a counter.

"What'll it be, gents?'' He wore a long dirty white apron and rolled-up shirtsleeves. Pegleg named what he wanted, and the clerk fetched each item one at a time and sat them on the counter. "Three dollars and thirty cents.'' The one-legged man paid, then Bill ordered. With their saddlebags stuffed and hanging over their left shoulders, they started to leave. They stopped suddenly when they recognized the deputy who had accompanied Sheriff Bowman in serving court papers.

Deputy Jameson came through the door with three other toughs, all armed with six-guns at their hips. Jameson and another wore clothes that were out of place in ranch country. "Heard you two was in town,'' Jameson said. His derby hat was tilted to one side, and he had a cocky grin on his face. One of his cohorts sported a fedora hat. Their baggy wool pants, held up with suspenders, grazed high-top, lace-up shoes.

The other two looked more dangerous, with floppy,

broad-brim hats, riding boots, and six-guns hanging low. Pegleg and Bill looked at each other, silently asking each other what to do. Bill shrugged. Pegleg shrugged. They started to go on out the door. The four thugs blocked their way.

"I heard you wild-West micks was tough," Deputy Jameson said. "We thought we'd find out for ourselfs."

Pegleg looked at Bill. Bill looked at Pegleg. Then Bill looked at Jameson. "Does your mamma know you're out?"

"Huh?" For a second the deputy was flabbergasted.

Pegleg said, "Go tell your mamma she wants you."

The deputy's hand dropped to the nickel-plated .38 on his right hip. He had no more than touched it when he was slammed upside the head with a heavy Smith & Wesson .45. The blow knocked him to his knees. His three cohorts grabbed for their guns—and halted when they found themselves looking up the bore of Pegleg's Colt .44.

Reaching down, Wild Bill took the nickel-plated pistol from Deputy Jameson's holster and slid it across the floor. Pegleg said, "What you fellers oughta do is take them weepons out slow like and put 'em down. Didn't nobody ever tell you you could get hurt with them things?"

With their leader on his knees holding his head, and two guns covering them, the three toughs did as told, careful not to make a threatening move.

"Now kindly pick up your pardner and go outside," Pegleg said, "but don't go far. We'll be right behind you."

"You . . . you're . . ."

"Shut up."

The man shut up.

"What're we gonna do with 'em, Pete?" Bill asked out on the plankwalk. Pedestrians had stopped to see what was happening.

"What I oughta do is see how far up their asses I can poke this wooden leg."

Pondering that, Bill allowed, "Naw, Pete. You'd never get the shit warshed off."

"Mebbe you're right. Tell yu what, fellers, you just line up there against that winder and stay there till we get out of sight."

Without a word, they did, two of them holding up Deputy Jameson.

Bill kept them covered until Pegleg got his saddlebags tied in place and got mounted, then Pegleg held his gun on them until Bill was ready to ride. Townsmen stared, but kept their distance.

"What you fellers oughta do," Pegleg Peterson said in his drawly fashion, "is go back where you come from and pick on unarmed women and kids. Out here, folks shoot back."

With that, he touched his one spur to his horse and rode down the street at a gallop. Wild Bill was soon at his side. Other horsemen got out of their way. Town people only stared.

It was long after dark when Pegleg Peterson and Wild Bill Watson got to their homes. They split up four miles from Peterson's house, and Bill rode at a trot to his own shack. The moon was full, and when it shone, it put out enough light that Bill could see clearly. But clouds drifted under the moon at times, turning the world dark. "Might rain," Bill said to himself. "We could use some rain."

Before riding up to his corral, he stopped, sat his saddle silently, and listened. Listened and looked, eyes searching the shadows for any movement, anything out of place. After a long moment he rode into the corral, offsaddled, and threw the horse some grass hay he'd cut near the banks of Otero Creek. Again, he stood still, listened, and looked. The horse munching hay could have drowned out any other sound. Inside the shack, he flattened himself against a wall for another long moment.

Finally, convinced he was alone, he lit a lamp. He was hungry, and he couldn't fix anything to eat in the dark. But he did stay away from the window and door, opening a hermetically sealed can of ham, and eating standing against a wall beside the window. His grumbling stomach told him he needed a good hot meal, but after what had happened to his neighbor he was afraid to build a fire and cook.

In fact, knowing the phony militiamen liked to attack in the dark, he had built himself an escape route in the far wall of his shack. He'd cut a square hole just big enough that he could crawl through at the bottom of the wall. He'd put the cut-out piece back in place and disguised it, so it wouldn't be noticed from the outside.

But he'd be damned if he'd sleep outside. What he'd done was move his bunk against the near wall, between the window and door. Now, if anyone fired through the window, they'd miss him, and if they put their heads through the window or door, they'd be a target he couldn't miss.

"Just try it, you sons of bitches," he'd said to himself.

They tried it.

The first shot came through the window just as he'd swallowed the last bite of canned ham and was reaching for a loaf of bread. It shattered the window glass and thunked into the far wall. Immediately, he blew out the lamp and dropped to his belly near his escape door. Two more shots came through the window and two drilled splintery holes in the front door. They missed Bill by several yards. But it wasn't gunfire that worried him.

With his Smith & Wesson on his hip and his repeating rifle in his hands, he crawled through the escape door. That full moon was a curse. He could be seen.

Instinct told him to stay down, make as small a target of himself as he could. But his mind told him he had to get to a spot where he could watch the front door. Bending low, he ran, angling toward the front of the shack, but also away from it. His biggest fear at the moment was that he'd run right into the shooters in the dark shadows. He carried the six-gun in his right hand, believing he could shoot faster in different directions with it than he could with the rifle.

A man yelled, "Over there. See 'im?" Guns barked. Lead slugs whined around him.

Knowing he was a target in the moonlight, Wild Bill changed directions and ran for Otero Creek and the alder brush that grew on the banks. He dove into the brush headfirst like a man diving into shallow water, and rolled over and over as soon as he hit the ground.

Spitting dirt and last summer's alder leaves, he lay still. It was dark here in the shadows of the alders and the slender elms and young cottonwoods. He couldn't be seen here. But this was a good place for bushwhackers to hide, and he wondered if any of them were nearby. Holding his breath, he listened. Not a sound.

Then the searching fire began. Rifle slugs *panged* into the ground around him.

Wild Bill crawled on his belly to the edge of the brush, to where he could see the door of his shack. All he could do was hope the shots missed him. When the gunfire slacked off, he figured the shooters had another plan, and he could easily guess what it was.

His shack was built with rocks, cottonwood logs he'd cut along the creek, and tarpaper. The tarpaper would burn like old dry newspapers.

He'd guessed right. One man carrying a gallon can ran toward the door. "Can't let 'im do that," Bill said under his breath. He holstered the six-gun and took quick aim with the Remington rifle. His aim was too hasty, and he missed his target. But the shot caused the man to pause. Bill fired again, and this time his bullet knocked the man down.

Screams, terrified screams, came from the man: "I'm hit. Help me. Help me."

A few shots came Bill's way, but only a few.

The goon over there tried to get up, fell back. He rolled onto his side, knees against his chest, and screamed hysterically, "Help me. I'm hit. Help me."

Two men ran out to help him. Bill's first impulse was to shoot them. He couldn't miss. But another thought flashed through his mind: He'd have to fetch the sheriff or a deputy to view the bodies. There'd be another inquest. Too many dead men would be hard to explain. He held his fire.

While he watched, two men half-carried and half-dragged their partner away. In the moonlight, Bill could see their horses now, over there under the hill. They lifted the wounded man onto his horse, got mounted, and, holding their wounded partner in his saddle, rode away. Four of them.

Bill could guess which four.

The danger was over, and Bill stood and walked to his shack. He picked up the gallon can, unscrewed the cap, and sniffed. Coal oil.

"Wal," he said to himself, " can use some fuel for my lamps."

Chapter Twelve

A baile. That's what folks in northern Colfax County needed. A dance where neighbors could get together with music and laughter. Forget the land grant. Forget the lawyers and judges and court orders. The spring calf roundups were over; the crops were in the ground. Now was the time. Have fun. Those were the thoughts going through Ella Fitzwater's mind. But who would arrange it? Then she had another thought: Why not her?

It had been a bad night at Willow Springs Liquor and Games. Everyone was in a bad mood. Three fistfights had been started, and eventually broken up.

For a time earlier that year, the self-appointed vigilantes did more to keep the peace than officers of the law. After Governor Sheldon authorized Jim Masterson, brother of Bat Masterson of Dodge City fame, to head a special militia, the citizens of Raton had become so enraged that the governor rescinded the authorization. But the militiamen had remained. They were toughs, thugs, imported by Masterson. They had no intention of leaving. Not until some of the citizens organized the vigilantes.

One night the vigilantes rounded up Masterson and some of his gang and escorted them to the Colorado line. They made it understood that if the so-called militiamen were seen again in New Mexico, they would be in grave danger. That bunch wasn't seen, but other militiamen were. Not so many in Raton, but in Springer. Their new boss appeared to be a man named Hunter Howser, an easterner somehow connected with the land company.

Then came the three murders in the streets of Springer, in front of the courthouse. Three anti-grant men were killed by a deputy sheriff and others of the "courthouse crowd." A telegram to Raton brought the vigilantes to Springer on the next train south, but another telegram to Santa Fe brought a detachment of troops sent by Governor Sheldon.

A truce of sorts was worked out. No more shots were fired at the time. It appeared the land disputes would be settled in court. And eventually the vigilantes scattered and went about the business of earning a living.

Now there was no one to keep the grant crowd from coming into Raton and starting fights. No one even thought of calling in Deputy Duncan. He arrested only the anti-grant people. Marshal Dilsworth did the best he could, but he was only one man.

Ella herself had been the cause of the last fight that night. "Hey, Ella Firewater," a man in striped pants and a brocaded vest had yelled across the room.

She was used to being called that and she didn't mind. Except when the name came from one of the grant crowd. Still, she merely ignored him. She'd seen a half-dozen grant men come in together, and she feared another fight would break out. If she took offense at the name, that would start it.

"Hey, you with the curly hair, come pour me a drink of whiskey."

Ella poured drinks occasionally for friends, but not for grant men. She ignored him.

"Hey, you're in the business of selling likker, ain't you?"

"Haw-haw," a sidekick laughed. "Bet that ain't all she sells."

"I hear," the other added in a loud voice, "that she ain't had a man in years."

"Naw. Haw-haw. I hear somethin' else. I hear she peddles her ass."

That did it.

Ella grabbed a whiskey bottle to use for a club and started toward the loudmouth. But someone beat her there. A cowboy from one of the nearby ranches got in ahead of her, said, "That there lady is a friend of mine," and brought his right fist up from his knee. Loudmouth was knocked back against his friend.

The brawl was on.

Within seconds every man in the place was fighting, punching, kicking, butting. Ella yelled at them, "Stop it! Stop it!" She wasn't heard. Grunting, swearing, fighting bodies were everywhere. Chairs were knocked over. Tables were knocked over. Men rolled on the floor, punching, biting. Making her way to the backside of the bar, Ella took down the Hawken rifle. Hastily, she loaded it, pouring powder from a flask, pushing in the wadding, putting a percussion cap on the nipple. But without a ball. She didn't intend to shoot anyone, just make a loud noise. Maybe that would stop them.

On second thought, maybe it wouldn't.

Some of the men were armed, and a gunshot could have them grabbing for their guns. If that happened, there'd be dead and wounded all over the place by the time the smoke cleared.

Frustrated, Ella could only mutter, "Oh, damn, damn, damn."

Eventually, the brawlers wore themselves down. Several men were on their hands and knees, too badly beaten to get up. Others were bleeding from scalp wounds or cuts on the face. One man spit out a tooth. They stood, swaying drunkenly, gasping for breath, too beaten or too arm-weary to carry on.

"I want all you grant men out of here," Ella yelled. She knew who they were. She knew almost everyone in Raton and northern Colfax County. "Get out. Get out of here right now."

Using the butt of the long-barreled rifle as a battering ram, she herded them toward the door and finally outside. They were too battle-weary to resist.

Standing with her back to the door, rifle in her hands, she surveyed the damage. "Damn. Dammit all anyway." She went to one of the chairs that was still right side up and dropped into it. "Dammit."

"Don't you worry none, Miss Ella," a man said, rubbing the knuckles of his right hand, "we'll clean 'er up." He picked up an overturned table, righted it, then a chair. Other men joined in, and soon everything was in its place. Men lined up at the bar, bleeding, but grinning, asking for beer or whiskey.

The tension had been broken. Fellowship had returned.

Her hired bartender couldn't keep up with the demand, so Ella went behind the bar, racked her rifle, and began pouring drinks herself.

"Keep the firewater comin', Ella."

"Say, we fair kicked the hound dog out of 'em, didn't we."

"Their shirttails ain't hittin' their backs till they're plumb out of town."

"They come in here lookin' for a fight."

"They sure as hell got it."

Yes, Ella thought later that night, lying sleepless in her bed in a three-room house across the alley. They got it. Anyone looking for a fight could find it. Everyone was on edge, primed, ready to explode. We were lucky, she thought. It could have been worse. It could have ended in gunfire. Next time it would. Maybe running a saloon was no job for a woman. It took a big tough mean man to keep the peace.

It was all because of the land grant. The damnable land grant. Folks needed something else to think about. Fun. A baile. Some foot-stomping music. Good food. Good liquor. But not too much liquor. Something men could bring their families, too. Could she arrange it?

"Yes," she said aloud to the ceiling, "I can do it. I will do it."

It took all day for Pegleg Peterson to ride around his estimated twenty sections. He wasn't surprised at what he found. Rocks piled up for markers had been kicked over and scattered. A tree with his initial carved in it

103

had been cut down and dragged away. The only markers left were the Vermejo River and Otero Creek.

Peterson piled the rocks up again. He could do nothing about the tree. The stump might prove something, and it might not. Tired, angry, he stopped before he rode across the creek to his house. Stopped, studied the brush, the trees, the house. His horse herd was grazing north of the river, and a few of his cows with young calves were grazing over west. A half-dozen calves were lying in the grass, resting, while one longhorn cow watched over them. Their mommas grazed.

Shaking his head sadly, Peterson realized that this was what he'd always wanted—good grazing land, cattle, horses. Only thing missing was Yellow Rose. He had everything but her. But could he keep it?

Why, he asked himself, were there always men who wanted what wasn't theirs? The land-grant company, now, they'd pulled every kind of dirty trick there was. Over one and a half million acres was theirs, but they wanted more. They'd extended the boundaries by moving mountains and renaming rivers and valleys, and by distorting the meanings of Spanish words. They manipulated politicians. There'd been shootouts, murders, hangings—all over the ownership of land. They'd destroyed the boundary markers on his land in hopes of claiming it, too.

Aw, well, hell, that's the way the world is, he mused. The big animals eat the little animals. That's why there had been so much talk about law. The law was supposed to protect the little animals.

"We'll see," Peterson said to himself as his horse splashed across Otero Creek.

His stomach reminded him he hadn't eaten since

early morning, and the rapid approach of darkness made him afraid to build a fire in his cookstove and cook something. He'd sleep out in the grass again and eat out of a can.

Plans for a baile were taking shape. Ella Fitzwater was pleased at the way the merchants were willing to donate their time and money. They picked a flat piece of land south of town and bought enough lumber to build a big platform for a dance floor. When the dance was over, the lumber would be sold and the merchants would get some of their money back.

Would the Mexicans be invited? "Of course," Ella said. "They're our neighbors. They were here before we were. Most of us can speak a little Spanish and most of them can speak a little English, and we can talk."

But they had their own kind of music.

"Well, we all can waltz, can't we? They don't know how to dance the schottische, and we don't know how to dance the fandango, but we'll find something we can all do."

And what if some of those militiamen came around looking for a fight?

"We'll call in the vigilantes. We all know who they are. Some of the finest and most honest men around here are vigilantes. We trust 'em. Everybody else will leave their guns in their wagons or with their horses, and only the vigilantes will be armed. We'll get enough of 'em to stop trouble before it starts."

Food?

"Everybody brings his own. The bachelors, well, somebody'll invite 'em to set and eat."

Liquor?

"Everybody brings his own. And if anybody gets ugly drunk, the vigilantes will take 'im for a walk and talk to 'im."

There were a lot more men then women around here.

Ella smiled. "The women are gonna have to dance their feet off."

Everything's planned, eh, Ella?

"Not everything, but I'm workin' on it. Yessir, we're gonna have a gran baile, a ball."

Chapter Thirteen

He hadn't had a good meal in a long time. He needed it. He needed a woman-cooked meal. *Let's see,* Pegleg Peterson mused, *I can go to Raton, Springer, or Cimarron.*

Cimarron. He hadn't been over that way in years. He wondered if any of his old friends were still there. It sure would be good to see some old friends. He'd ride through the Cimarron Valley and stop and say *"Hola"* to some of his Mexican amigos. Anglos came and went, but the Mexicans stayed. They'd invite him to supper, and boy could he use some of those good Mexican pork ribs and some eggs, real chicken eggs. The Mexicans all had chickens. And Cimarron used to have a good eatin' house. If it wasn't still there, some other would be.

Peterson trimmed his whiskers, combed his hair, put on clean duck britches and a plaid shirt, dusted off his beat-up hat, and wiped his one boot clean. He saddled his best horse and put a crossbuck saddle, a pair of canvas panniers, and his bedroll on another horse. He'd bring back enough groceries to last a long time.

With his Winchester repeating rifle in a saddle boot and his .44 Colt on his hip, he rode west. The early morning sun felt warm and good on his back.

Bill Watson needed a good meal, too. He wasn't sleeping outside like his neighbor was, but he was afraid to cook after dark. It took hours to cook a pot of beans or a stew, and he used to do that in the evenings when it was too dark to work outside. They'd be ready to eat by the next evening. Beans and stews tasted better warmed up the next day anyway. Now he was eating cold bacon left over from breakfast, stale biscuits, and canned tomatoes.

"My stomach thinks I've been strangled," he mused.

He remembered a good restaurant in the St. James Hotel in Cimarron, and there was the Shuteye Hotel and Cafe in Raton. Springer might have been home to a good cafe, but he wasn't acquainted there, and he didn't like that town anyway. Being a young man, he needed more than just food, and Raton was probably the best place to go for that.

Wild Bill washed his clothes on a scrub board in a tub of warm water and laid them on top of some alder bushes near the creek to dry. Then he took a bath out of the same tub. He did that before dark. If the militia came calling, he didn't want to be caught naked. Next morning he shaved, noted that he needed a haircut along with everything else, put on his newest pair of cotton pants and a blue chambray shirt. A black silk bandanna was hung loosely around his throat. Before sunup he struck north, carrying both his guns, riding his good dun horse and leading a packhorse. When the sun came up, it felt warm and good, and he sang as he rode.

"Oh, I come from Alabama with my banjo on my knee. I'm goin' to Loosiana my uh true love for to see. Oh, Suzanna, oh don't you cry for me . . ."

What was the rest of it? Oh well, he could whistle the tune.

Bill Watson liked to sing. He remembered his mother in South Texas singing as she worked in her kitchen. His dad used to pick at a banjo, and he'd tried it himself. All he'd learned to do was play a few simple tunes. He'd sung to cattle herds while on night guard, and he'd sung quietly to help control his fear when he'd ridden alone through hostile Indian country. But mostly he sang because he liked to sing.

"Ring, ring the banjo, I love that grand old song. Come again my true love, oh, where've you been so long." He couldn't remember the rest of the lyrics, so he whistled.

Sleeping late had become a habit with Ella Fitzwater. She never went to bed before two A.M., and she needed a good seven hours' sleep. Her old maw and her brothers would have poked fun at her for sleeping till nine o'clock every morning. Her mother and dad were dead, and her two brothers had left the farm and headed west. Her brothers and her husband, all had been out of her life for a long time. Whether they were dead or alive she didn't know. She thought about them often, and silently prayed for them.

It was quiet in her three-room clapboard house across

the alley from her Willow Springs saloon. When she opened a window, she could hear wagon wheels creaking in the street, trace chains rattling, and dogs barking. Lazily, she started to dress, then remembered she'd been too tired the night before to take a bath. Once she got a fire going in the cookstove in her small kitchen, she put a bucket of water on to heat. Then she put the coffee on, sliced some cured ham, and mixed some flapjack batter.

Today was the day she'd go to the print shop and have some flyers printed. She'd find travelers who would post them all over northern Colfax County. And, oh yes, she had to find some musicians.

After a bath from head to toes and breakfast, she had to wait for her hair to dry. Sitting in her long cambric gown, her hair piled on top of her head and wrapped in a towel, she read the newspaper then started reading *Harper's* magazine.

Darn. Her hair would never dry this way. She needed to be outside in the sun. But until her hair dried she couldn't comb and brush it, and she looked a mess. Well, she couldn't spend the day sitting in the house. She'd leave it piled on top of her head and wear a bonnet. The bonnet would keep it hidden.

That was the way Ella went out onto the streets, in a wool serge business suit with wide lapels, covering a white shirtwaist with a high collar, all topped by a poke bonnet. She didn't realize how out-of-place the plain bonnet was until she saw her reflection in a store window.

"Oh, my gosh."

A fast about-face had her hurrying to her house to change. She had wanted to dress like a woman with business to attend to, but now she realized she should have worn a plain dress with the bonnet. Head down, not wanting to be recognized, she walked with quick steps.

" 'Lo, Ella. Mornin'. Or is it afternoon?"

Oh, my gosh. It was Bill Watson, sitting on a horse, grinning at her. "Wha . . . uh, good morning, Mr. Watson."

"Mr. Watson? How come not Bill?"

"Oh, of course. Sure. What brings you to town, Bill?"

"An unhappy stomach." Bill was smiling good-naturedly. "It can't stand any more of my cookin'. Soon's I get these horses offsaddled, I'm gonna go over to that Shuteye Cafe and wrap myself around somethin' to eat. Is your place open for business?"

"Well, no, not yet, but it will be by the time you're ready for a beer."

"It'll be a while. Got to get my ears lowered, too. Say, you look like a banker today."

Without thinking, she put her fingers to the few curls that were peeking from under the bonnet. He would notice, darn him. "I have some business to attend to."

Reading the embarrassment in her face and gestures, he touched spurs to his horse. "See you later, Ella."

Wild Bill walked with spurs ringing down the plank-walk to the Shuteye Hotel and Cafe. He signed for a room, then dragged his spurs across the hotel lobby to the connecting cafe. Damn. It was noon, and the place was full. Men filled all the chairs at the tables and lined the long counter like hogs at a trough. Dammit, he thought, there won't be anything left by the time I get my snout in that trough.

Outside, he stood with his thumbs hooked inside his gunbelt, and looked up and down the street for another cafe. There was the Acme Restaurant, down the street a block and across the street. He angled over there. Once inside, he knew he was out of place, but there was a table for two that wasn't occupied, and he headed for it. There was no counter in here. Taking off his hat, he ran his fingers through his brown hair, pulled a chair out from the table, and sat. The Acme was inhabited by merchants, bankers, livestock dealers, and ranch owners. And lawmen. Not ranch hands.

Across the room sat Sheriff Bowman and Deputy Duncan. The sheriff was avoiding his glance, but the deputy was staring at him like he was a skunk in a barn. Also in the room was that gent named Howser, Hunter Howser, a grant man. Howser was seated with a man in a gray business suit, a round face, and neatly combed hair. Both were giving Bill a looking over.

This was not the place for a laboring man, but now that he was here he'd be damned if he was going to let them run him out. "Oh, ma'am," he said to a passing waitress.

"Yes, sir?" She was young, pretty, with a clean white apron from her throat to her feet.

"I'd, uh, I'd like somethin' to eat."

She glanced nervously at the other customers before answering, "Yes, sir. I shall bring you a menu."

Shall? What kind of talk was that? Was she another easterner? Easterners were taking over the territory.

The menu was written in a neat hand. The first item on it was what Bill was looking for: beef steak, mashed

112

potatoes, gravy, and green beans. Now where was that waitress? Back in the kitchen, he reckoned. He waited. Other customers were stuffing their faces, chewing, talking, sipping coffee. When the young woman finally appeared again, she walked right past Bill and went to the table occupied by Hunter Howser. She picked up the dirty dishes, carried them to the kitchen, returned with two wedges of pie on saucers. Hunter Howser nodded in Bill's direction and said something to her. She glanced at Bill, then went to the table occupied by Sheriff Bowman and his deputy.

Deputy Duncan grinned and took the girl by the wrist. She tried to pull away. Sheriff Bowman said something to the deputy, and the girl was released. When she took a coffeepot to their table, she tried to stay out of reach of the deputy. He smirked.

"Ma'am," Bill said when she went past.

"Yes, sir?"

"Can a feller get somethin' to eat in here?"

"Sir, I, uh . . ." She turned and hurried to the kitchen.

There was nothing he could do about it. She had orders not to serve the laboring riffraff. He could bawl out the owner, but the owner probably wouldn't show himself. He could draw the Smith & Wesson and shoot holes in the walls, but that would do no good. He could walk out and maybe cut a big loud fart on his way out. Naw.

Damn, he hated to let them get by with this.

Aw, hell. Show them you're more of a gentleman than they are. Just hold your head up and leave. Slowly, Bill Watson stood, put his hat on, shifted his gunbelt, and sauntered toward the door.

"S'matter, squatter, won't they serve you?"

It was that smirk on Deputy Duncan's face that did it. Deliberately, Bill turned and faced him, hands on hips. "I wouldn't take advantage of a workin' girl like you just did. I'm a better man than you are any day."

The smirk left Deputy Duncan's face. He started to stand. Bill was standing spraddle-legged, right hand near his gun butt, ready.

"Dunc, sit down." It was Sheriff Bowman who spoke. "Leave it be."

Deputy Duncan sat down. His face was ugly. "There'll be another meeting, squatter."

Anger had Bill ready to fight now. He wanted to fight. "You'd better have an army of your so-called militia with you, 'cuz you ain't man enough to fight a pissant."

Again, the deputy started to stand, and again the sheriff spoke sharply. "Sit down, Dunc." To Bill, he said, "I can't say I blame you, Watson, but the best thing to do is just leave."

But Bill was too angry now to just leave. He had to do something to get even. Turning to the room, he said bitterly, "You all think you're too good to eat with a workin' man. Wal, the whole damn bunch of you ain't worth a pimple on a workin' man's ass."

Now, and not until now, he was ready to leave.

No one tried to stop him. No one made a move.

It took a while for Bill to force the anger down. For a long moment, he stood on the plankwalk, seething. Finally, he turned back toward the Shuteye Hotel and Cafe. By the time he got there he had himself under control. But one thing the deputy had said was true:

There would be another meeting.

114

Chapter Fourteen

Pegleg Peterson shot a young buck deer with fuzzy antlers, dressed it out on the spot, and slung it across the packhorse. Some Mexican family would be glad to have the meat. He rode northwest, over some timbered, boulder-strewn hills, past an old volcano, across a lava bed, and reined up on a ridge overlooking a green valley. It was a pretty valley with a small village of flat-roofed adobe houses, pens made of pine poles, and small patches of growing vegetables. The finest building in the village was the church, with a steeple over a vestibule.

Off the ridge now and down into the valley, he followed wagon ruts between green fields, waved at Mexicans with long-handled hoes who were trying to keep the wild grass from taking over the fields. At the Cruz house, he stopped in the yard and hollered, "Hello. *Hola.*" He figured they were working in the fields, and he rode around the house, noticed chickens in a wire pen, a nanny goat with two kids, and a cow with a heavy udder picketed on a grassy spot behind the house. Tomás and Eileen Cruz were working in a potato patch, bent over, pulling weeds up by the roots. Afraid his horses would trample the field, Pegleg dismounted, dropped his reins, and walked toward them.

She wore a straw hat with a wide brim, which shielded her face from the sun, and a long, colorful, but dirt-smudged dress. He said, *"Buenas tardes,* Eileen."

Straightening, she smiled, teeth white against her dark complexion. "Good afternoon, Mr. Peterson. What brings you over this way?"

"Need some groceries. Brought you some fresh meat." He nodded toward the packhorse and the deer carcass. "I shot it not more'n two hours ago."

By this time, Tomás Cruz had heard the voices, looked up, and recognized Peterson. He came forward, holding out his right hand, smiling. They shook hands, and the conversation from then on was in Spanish.

Supper was just what Peterson needed: pork ribs roasted in a clay oven as only the Mexicans knew how, refried beans, home-grown corn, tortillas, chokeberry preserves. Leaning back in his chair, Peterson smiled contentedly and said in Spanish, "There's no place in this whole wide world where a feller can buy a meal as good as this."

No one mentioned the land company or the possibility that sooner or later the whole village would have to be abandoned.

They'd wrapped the deer carcass in canvas and hung it in the shade of a tall ponderosa. Tomás said he'd butcher it in the morning when the air was cool. The Cruz family had built a small rock structure over a narrow creek, and the air inside was cool enough to keep meat for a week or longer. Pegleg slept in his bed on the ground near an irrigation ditch where the grass grew high. His two horses had a good feed, too, on the tall grass. In the morning, after a breakfast of cured ham and eggs, he helped Tomás butcher the deer, wrap the meat in wax paper, and stack it on a table in the spring house. The Cruz family would share the meat with neighbors. It would be eaten before it could spoil.

That done, Pegleg saddled his two horses, then mounted. "Be very careful in Cimarron," Tomás said in Spanish. "In Cimarron are many bad men."

"I've been in tough places before," Pegleg said, "and I'm sixty years old. But I'll be careful. Listen"— he leaned forward in his saddle, crossed his wrists on top of the saddle horn"—if there's ever anything I can do for you folks, I'm just over a couple of hills from here. And I'm not the only white man ready to help. You need anything, you just holler."

"That's very kind of you, Mr. Peterson," Eileen said in English.

"Besides"—Pegleg's smile returned—"I can't do enough to pay for that good supper and breakfast. I sure do thank you."

"Por nada."

The Santa Fe railroad had bypassed Cimarron, although there was talk of a spur line in the future. Long wagon trains hauled supplies to the town and hauled lumber out of town. A stage line carried passengers. Heavy freight wagons pulled by four-horse teams carried supplies to the ranches and farms, and lighter wagons pulled by two-horse teams carried goods from the warehouses to the stores. A sawmill had always supplied lumber for building in Cimarron, and nearly all the houses were of board-and-batten construction. A

117

few were two-story. Most of the stores had false fronts with roofs out over the sidewalks.

Peterson rode the length of the main street, looking for a familiar face. Leading a packhorse, his wooden peg in its stirrup cup, he attracted some attention, but not much. Folks came and went in Cimarron, and strangers were common. He remembered where the livery barn once stood, and he rode over there, near the river, and was surprised to see that the old barn had been torn down and a new one built. The livery pens were full of horses belonging to townspeople and travelers. Wagons and buggies of all kinds were parked in a row west of the barn. Finally, Peterson saw a familiar face.

"Pete, is that you?" The hostler was the same age, the same size, and had the same grizzled, callused, weatherbeaten look about him. But while Peterson had only one leg, Bundy Newcome had only one eye. He'd had his left eyelid sewn so no one would have to see the cavity, and now it had grown shut. "It's gotta be you. Nobody else's got a leg made out of a tree."

Grinning, Peterson said, "It's me, Bundy. Glad to see you're still kickin'. I figgered you'd be makin' the grass grow by now."

"I'm too mean to die. Still got that piece of land over east somewheres?"

"Me, I'm too mean to move. Shore, I still got that piece of land. I got 'bout a hunnerd and fifty cows now, and a half-dozen good hosses."

"Wal, jerk the leather off'n them animules and put 'em in that pen yonder, and let's go over to the St. James. If I rec'lect right, you owe me a drink of whiskey. You c'n walk, cain't you?"

118

"I can outrun you any day. And it's t'other way around. You owe *me* a drink of whiskey."

"I'd rather pay than rassle you for it, but tell you what, let's have two drinks."

Still grinning, Peterson said, "Hell, we might have three or four."

Someone had tried to dress up the saloon in the St. James Hotel, but soon discovered it was hopeless. A mahogany bar had been whittled on with pocketknives, the long mirror behind the bar had been shattered in two places, tables had initials carved on their tops, and pictures on the walls had been used for pistol targets. Even at midday the place was busy. Cowboys, timberjacks, and miners stood at the bar or sat at the tables. Bundy Newcome had strapped on an old long-barreled cap-and-ball pistol before leaving his one-room living quarters at the barn, and everyone in the room was armed.

Standing at the bar now, one foot on the rail, he said, "Been kinda quiet aroun' here lately. Ain't been nobody killed in two, three days."

The bartender was wide and solid, with bushy hair and a square smooth-shaved face. "You got any money, Popeye? Ain't no credit in here no more."

"Shore," said Bundy, blinking his one eye as he dug into the left-side pocket of his faded denim pants. "I got money I ain't even spent yet."

"I'll get 'er," said Pegleg.

They sipped whiskey from shot glasses, and Pegleg said, "How come you're workin' at the livery? I thought you was gonna strike 'er rich."

"I did oncet. Hit the purtiest vein you ever saw. Didn't have the spendulics to take out the ore, howe-

119

somever, and sold my claim. Hell," he chuckled, "it's the findin' that makes life interestin', not the minin'."

"I spent some time lookin' up in Colorado but I didn't find enough to pay for my beans. That was before the war."

"Wal." Bundy eyed his whiskey glass with his one eye. "I did get kinda tired of draggin' a jackass all over them hills, and cookin' lizards on a stick for my supper. I went to bed one night thinkin' how I'd been talkin' to jackasses more'n people." He finished his whiskey, smacked his lips, and aimed his one eye over Peterson's head, seemingly looking into the distance. A sad note crept into his voice. "But, I'll tell you, Pete, I shore wish I c'd do 'er again."

"Can't do 'er no more, huh?"

"Rheumatiz."

"Oh. Well, let's have another drink of whiskey, and let's go find somethin' to eat."

"I'm buyin' the next round of whiskey."

"You sure?"

" 'Course, I'm shore. I ain't abummin' nobody."

"I sold some beefs last winter, and I got enough for 'em to keep me a long time. I shoot a buckskin now and then, and it don't take much money to keep me eatin'."

Bundy said to the bartender, "Pour another'n, mister."

Another drink downed, Peterson was ready to look for a cafe, but Bundy said, "I got a room in the barn and a sheepherder's stove and a pot of beans and some bacon and bread. You're welcome to dig into that."

"I 'preciate it, partner, but I eat that stuff all the

time at home. Where can we get a good fresh beef-steak?"

"Wal." Bundy's eye looked down at his worn shoes. "Tell you the truth, Pete, I been eatin' my own cookin' so long I'm gettin' to like it."

"I'm buyin'."

"You shore? I ain't abummin' nobody."

"I ast you, didn't I?"

They found what they wanted in a cafe that had a one-word sign over the sidewalk. It said EATS. The beef had been butchered only two days ago, and the sirloin steaks were aged just right. The meal was topped with apple pie, and they were told the apples came from a Mexican orchard, not out of a can.

Pegleg paid. Bundy allowed he'd pay for the next meal they shared, then he had to excuse himself. "I got work to do at the barn. Got to earn my keep. It'll take a few hours, and about dark I'll come lookin' for you. Where you stayin?"

"Reckon I'll lug my change of clothes over to the St. James." He grinned. "Last time I stayed there, somebody downstairs shot a hole in the ceiling too damn close to the bed."

"They put a layer of two-inch lumber in that ceiling to protect the folks upstairs, but I wouldn't trust it too much."

The two men went back to the livery barn, where Pegleg started to open one of the panniers from his packhorse, then changed his mind. "What I need is some new britches and a couple flannel shirts, and some new blankets. When I crawled out of my bed this mornin', the blankets was so dirty they stuck to me."

Chuckling, Bundy said, "Time for a change, then. Your old squaw never let your blankets get that dirty."

Pegleg suddenly lost his humor. "No. She didn't."

"She was a good woman," Bundy said, shaking his head sadly.

"Well"—Pegleg forced himself to grin—"I'm gonna find me a feather bed and a gen'ral store. Tomorrow I'm gonna load up on groceries."

"I'll look for you at the St. James. I'm buyin' supper."

His room overlooked an alley instead of the street, and that was fine with Peterson. The street was too noisy. With a loud "Ahhh," he backed up to the feather bed and fell backward onto it. For a second he thought he was going to sink out of sight. "Now this's the way to live." But within a few minutes, he realized he wasn't comfortable. He tried, but no matter which way he lay, he couldn't get the kinks out of his back or his neck. When he lay on his back, his foot was higher than his head.

"Need a goddamn anvil to hold that end of the mattress down," he said to himself. "Aw, well, I ain't gonna sleep in the middle of the day anyhow."

On his way to the general store, he saw the stage come in from Raton, saw it was loaded with people. In the store he bought two pairs of the new Levi's, two flannel shirts, and three pairs of cotton socks. "Oh, yeah"—he looked around the long room to be sure no women were within hearing distance—"I, uh, need some under, uh, you know."

"Over here," the clerk said, all business. Pegleg thumped along behind him to another counter. "These

122

are all cotton, and they won't shrink more than one size. What size do you wear, sir?"

"Size? I dunno. Ain't bought any for a while."

"Well, let's see." The clerk held a pair of broadcloth shorts up to Pegleg's waist. Pegleg felt his face turning red as he glanced at two women customers on the other side of the room. "This seems to be the size you need. They'll shrink a little and then they'll fit. They're nice and cool in the summer."

Backing away, Pegleg said, "Yeah, yeah, how much do I owe you?"

In his room, he tried on the new Levi's and didn't like the fit or feel at all. The denim pants were cut full to allow for shrinkage, and they were stiff and awkward. He pulled them off and put his old duck pants back on. "Gonna have to boil the newness out of 'em before I c'n wear 'em," he said to himself.

Restless, he thumped his way downstairs to the saloon. He didn't need any whiskey now, but having nothing else to do he stood at the bar and ordered a shot and a glass of beer. Sipping the whiskey, he felt, rather than saw, a man standing on his right. Their reflection in the broken mirror behind the bar showed him who the man was.

Hunter Howser.

"Remember me?" Howser said. He was dressed in businessman's clothes, with a wool vest and a gold chain draped from one vest pocket to another. He also wore a six-gun in a new leather holster on his right side.

"Yeah," Pegleg said without turning his head.

"Shot any more men lately?"

"Shot at 'em. The ones you sent over in the dark."

123

Hunter Howser stood straight, looking hard at Pegleg. "Who says I sent 'em?"

Still looking in the mirror, Pegleg said, "I know about you. You sent 'em."

"That's a serious accusation."

"Bushwhackin' in the dark is a serious business."

"You'd better be ready to back that up."

Now Pegleg half-turned to face the man. His hand was near the Colt on his hip. "I'm always ready, mister."

Howser made no threatening move, but his eyes shifted to the left of Pegleg. Now Peterson felt the presence of another man, this one behind him. Out of the corners of his eyes, he looked in the mirror.

The man behind him wore a derby hat cocked on one side of his head. He had his hand on the butt of a nickel-plated revolver, he wore a deputy's badge on a shirt pocket, and he had a smirk on his face.

Chapter Fifteen

They had him. Pegleg knew it. He might draw his Colt and shoot fast enough to get one, but not both. Which one? Thinking fast, he figured the deputy would be the most dangerous, but he'd have to turn half-around to shoot him, then turn again to shoot Hunter Howser. He couldn't do it. A young man fast with a gun, like Wild Bill Watson, might do it. He couldn't.

Howser's face was ugly. "You owe me an apology, squatter. Nobody accuses me of a thing like that."

The first target would have to be Howser. The man behind him was a hired goon who'd shoot his own mother if the right man told him to. Howser was the right man. No use waiting for him to grab for his gun first. Make the first move and make it count. Pegleg concentrated on drawing the Colt. He'd have to have the hammer back and ready to shoot at the same instant the gun cleared leather.

Then he felt something poke him in the back, and the deputy's sneering voice said, "Apologize, mick, or I'll shoot you right here."

There was no chance at all now. Well, maybe . . .

maybe he could draw fast enough to shoot Howser before his spine was shattered by a bullet from the deputy's gun.

"I'm givin' you three seconds, and I hope you don't apologize."

Howser was smirking, too. "You'll be one less problem. Reach for your gun. Go ahead."

Glancing around, Pegleg was surprised that no one else in the room was paying any attention to them. The three of them were alone at one end of the bar, the end nearest the door. As far as anyone could tell, they were merely having a conversation.

"Two seconds."

Now, Pegleg said to himself. *Draw and shoot now.*

Another voice came from behind him, cold, deadly: "Mister, this old gun'll shoot a ball as big as your thumb. It'll make a hole you c'd throw a rock through. Put that there purty little pistol on the bar and do it right fast."

The pressure on Pegleg's back was removed. The nickel-plated revolver clattered onto the bar.

"Pete, if you wanta shoot that feller, go ahead. I know about him. He ain't fit to live."

Pegleg didn't look back. His eyes locked onto Hunter Howser's. "Whatta you say, shitface? Wanta fight or do you hire your fightin' done?"

Howser looked around, and said loudly, "These men are trying to pick a fight with us." Others noticed them then. "We came in here for a friendly drink and these two old codgers tried to pick a fight."

For a moment, other saloon patrons only looked, then one said, "You're Hunter Howser, ain't you?"

"Yessir, I am."

"You're one a them grant men."

"I work for law and order."

The speaker looked beyond Hunter Howser at Peterson. "Go ahead and shoot the son of a bitch." He turned back to his whiskey glass.

Peterson considered it. He was sure he could do it. It would be like killing a rattlesnake. Without turning his head, he said, "Bundy, is there a law in this town nowadays?"

"Yeah, there's a marshal."

"Well, I don't want no run-in with the law. Mister, you c'n go. Take your hired goon and git outta my sight."

Howser couldn't hold back a sigh of relief. He stepped around Pegleg and said to the deputy, "Let's go, Jameson." To Pegleg he said, "There will be another meeting."

Bundy didn't holster his long-barreled pistol until the two men were out the door. He picked up the nickel-plated .38, turned it over in his hand. "What does this thing shoot, anyhow?" He broke the gun down, ejecting the cartridges. "Wal, I reckon they c'd kill a man."

"That deputy's lookin' for a chance to shoot somebody with that little pistol. But I got a hunch he's better with a knife or a club."

"He looks like a city feller. Whar'd he come from?"

Shrugging, Peterson said, "I heered old Howser took over where Jim Masterson left off, an' he's hired a bunch of hardcases from Denver and Texas to do his fightin' for 'im. He got some of 'em sworn in as deputies."

"Wal, he ain't much of a fighter, but he don't hafta

127

be. He's dangerous, Pete. He meant it when he said there'll be another meetin'."

Bill Watson had been called nothing but Bill Watson until that day three years ago. He'd helped drive two thousand five hundred head of longhorn beeves to Dodge City, and instead of spending his wages in the saloons and whorehouses, he saddled his own horse, a long-legged dun he called Dunnie, tied a blanket and a bed tarp behind his saddle, stuffed some bread and beef jerky in his saddlebags, and headed back to Texas alone.

On the way up to Kansas, the crew had seen a few Indians, but there were eighteen well-armed cowboys in the crew, and the Indians kept their distance. The Indians were Comanches, and they hated white eyes. A man alone had to keep his eyes open and be ready to run for it.

Bill saw no Indians while he was alone. But that didn't mean the Comanches didn't see him. An Indian could hide behind a sagebush, a yucca, or almost anything. When Bill crossed a draw or a creek, he kept his Smith & Wesson in his hand. A Comanche brave would be a hero if he could shoot a white eyes from ambush and take his scalp, his horse, and his gun. All the wages Bill had in his pockets would do him no good if he was dead.

He spotted a cow outfit's remuda and chuck wagon about the same time he saw the Canadian River. When he caught up with them, they were getting ready to float the wagon across the river, using timbers another outfit had left after crossing the river from the other direction. Bill helped. A half-dozen cowboys were taking the remuda and wagon back to the Box X in South Texas after shipping a big herd at Dodge, and Bill was invited to ride along with them. He earned his keep by doing his share of the night horse wrangling. The wagon boss, a bandy-legged little man with a walrus mustache, tried to trade him out of his horse.

"Pick any horse out of the remuda, and I'll sign 'im over to you and give you twenty bucks to boot."

"Naw, I don't think so."

Walking around Dunnie, the boss said, "He's a big 'un. He'll go sixteen hands. Whatta you reckon he'll weigh, twelve hunnerd?"

"Maybe twelve-fifty," Bill allowed.

"Can he run?"

"He sure can stack the scenery behind 'im."

"How old is he?"

"Comin' eight."

The boss continued studying the horse. "Give you thirty to boot."

"Naw." Bill grinned. "I need a big horse to carry my bed and saddle pockets and ever'thing."

"Thirty-five?"

Bill just grinned and shook his head.

They were about sixty miles south of the Canadian and guessed they were ten or twelve miles east of a town called Adobe Flats when the Comanches attacked.

The cowboys saw them coming over a rise to the east, and knew they were in for a fight. Outnumbered by at least five to one, they knew they couldn't save the remuda. Each man tied a horse to the chuck wagon, hoping they could save that many. Dunnie was tied to a rear wheel.

"Boys," the boss said, "if we're lucky, all they want is the remuda."

"Nope," a cowboy said, "them's Comanches. They want scalps."

They ripped the canvas top off the wagon, and four men crawled inside, hoping the sideboards would stop bullets at long range, and hoping they could keep the Indians at long range. The other three men crawled under the wagon, lay on their bellies, and waited for the attack.

Everyone but Bill had a repeating rifle. He had only his Smith & Wesson six-gun. The Indians had guns ranging from Winchester lever-action rifles to the cavalry trapdoor single-shot carbines. Their horses ranged from scrawny mustangs to big fiddle-footed horses with collar marks captured in attacks on wagon trains. Their clothes ranged from Indian buckskins to white men's wool britches and felt hats.

They stopped four hundred yards away and formed a long skirmish line.

"We're in for it, boys."

"Try to knock 'em down before they get close. In a close fight we ain't got a chance."

"Wish I had one a them buff'ler guns."

"Wish I hadn't a made fun of that preacher man back in Dodge."

"Here they come."

"Take aim, boys. Take aim."

The Comanches came on a gallop, whooping, yelling, screaming. They started firing at three hundred and fifty yards, but their aim from the backs of running

130

horses wasn't good. The cowboys let them come within three hundred yards, then opened up.

The first volley from the repeating rifles was one continuous ear-splitting racket. Two Indians fell from their horses.

But the savages were coming closer, and their aim was getting better. Bullets were slamming into the ground around the wagon and splintering the wagon box. Bill waited for a good target, knowing it would be useless to shoot a six-gun at rifle range.

A painted savage on a big harness horse hung onto one side of the horse, keeping the horse between him and the wagon, and fired a pistol from under the horse's neck. A rifle cracked. The horse went down without a sound, kicked twice, and lay still. The Indian crawled behind the carcass and fired twice more. Bill squinted down the short barrel of the Smith & Wesson, squeezed the trigger.

The savage flopped onto his back, arms outflung, and stared with sightless eyes at the sky.

Two more Indians fell off their horses. A cowboy beside Bill grunted loudly in pain, and gripped his left shoulder. He gritted his teeth and fired his rifle with one hand.

Two Indian horses went down, one turning a somersault and pitching the rider over its head. A cowhorse tied to the wagon dropped to its knees, then collapsed. Bridle reins tied to the wagon held its head up.

"God damn it," a cowboy said, "that's my horse." He quickly added, "Excuse me, Lord. I didn't mean to use thy name in vain."

Indians were on all sides of the wagon now, and men

131

were scrambling on their bellies, turning to shoot back in all directions.

"Lord, help us," a cowboy muttered, "but don't send your son Jesus, 'cuz this ain't no place for kids."

Bill fired his six-gun, missed. A rifle cracked near his left ear. A cowboy yelped, dropped the rifle, and grabbed his right thigh with both hands. Face twisted in pain, he muttered, "Son of a bitch, son of a bitch, son of a bitch."

"Should I take your rifle?" Bill said. "It'll shoot farther than this six-gun."

"No, by god, I ain't through yet." The cowboy let go of his leg, picked up his rifle, aimed, and fired.

"We're whuppin' 'em, boys. They're runnin'. Pour it to 'em."

The Comanches were riding away, leaving two downed horses and five downed savages behind. They gathered out of rifle range, shook their guns at the cowboys, and yelled something.

Bill crawled from under the wagon and looked to his horse. Dunnie was wild-eyed, but not hurt. Three of the cowboys' horses were down. "Easy, son," Bill said. "Maybe we'll live to see another day."

"It ain't over, fellers. They're talkin' about it, figgerin' out how best to shoot us out of here."

"Next time they won't come chargin' in horseback. They'll come crawlin' like snakes to make littler targets of theirselfs."

"Maybe we can git horseback and ride for it."

"We ain't got enough hosses left, and what we got cain't run fast enough carryin' double."

"Look at 'em. See 'em?"

About half the Comanches were on foot now, but the others were riding to the west, still out of rifle range.

"They know the closest help is at 'Dobe Flats, and they're gettin' twixt us and there."

Bill had his Smith & Wesson reloaded, wishing he had a rifle.

"Boys," the boss said, "we're done for, we know that, don't we? There's too many of 'em, and they're gettin' smart. They're comin' on foot now so they can aim better."

"We'll damn sure make 'em pay."

"How far you reckon it is to 'Dobe Flats?"

"Ten, twelve miles."

"A man on a good hoss c'd get there and get back with some help in a couple hours."

"Think we c'n hold 'em off that long?"

"We can try like a steer."

"Bill," the boss said, "you got the fastest horse and one of the few that ain't been shot."

"I'll go," Bill said, standing, holstering his six-gun.

"That pistola only holds six ca'tridges," a cowboy said. "Take mine, too. I got this Winchester. If I live, you can give 'er back, and if I don't, it won't make no difference."

Bill shoved the six-gun inside his belt, went to the dun, and untied the reins. He stepped into the saddle. "See you fellers in a couple hours."

Chapter Sixteen

At first Bill rode at a trot, wanting to save his horse's strength and wind as long as he could. But the Comanches saw him, knew what he was trying to do. They came at him on a gallop from two directions, shooting. They had the angle.

"Sic 'em, boy," Bill hissed, and Dunnie jumped into a dead run. "Get 'em, Dunnie. Sic 'em."

Bullets were coming fast and furious, singing angry songs. Puffs of smoke were coming from the savages' rifles.

"Keep goin', Dunnie. Keep them long legs goin'." The dun horse had its ears back, running its best. Bill drew the Smith & Wesson, pointed it at a savage on his right. Fired. The Indian fell forward onto his pony's neck.

At the wagon, all shooting had stopped while men watched the race. "Ride, cowboy," a man muttered. Even the Indians on foot were standing still, watching.

"Think he'll make it?"

"If he don't, it won't be for want of tryin'."

Hooves pounding, the dun horse sensed the danger

it was in, and strained to run even faster. Indians were coming from two directions, firing, trying to head off the horse and rider. Bill stuck the reins between his teeth, and drew the borrowed pistol.

Shooting with both hands now, he rode recklessly, desperately, silently praying. At the wagon, the boss said, "That there is one wild man. Yes, sir, he just might be wild enough to save our bacon."

Comanches were still to the left and right of Bill, but they no longer had the angle. They were still shooting. Bill was shooting until both guns clicked on empty.

"Ride, wild man," the wagon boss said.

Dunnie was pulling away now, outrunning the Indian horses. They still were within rifle range, but their horses were jumping gulleys, dodging cholla cactus, making accurate shooting difficult. Looking back, Bill saw a savage stop his horse, jump down, kneel, and aim a long-barreled rifle. He saw the puff of smoke and jerked Dunnie to the right just as the lead ball whistled past.

"Atta boy, atta boy. Keep them long legs goin'." Now they were on a dim wagon road, and Bill knew the town was ahead. "Hate to do this to you, Dunnie, but men's lives are dependin' on you. Keep goin', partner."

It was a badly winded horse and a wildly yelling cowboy that galloped down the main street of Adobe Flats. "Indians," Bill yelled. "Comanches. They're attackin' a crew of drovers."

Within two minutes, the saloons were emptied of men. The stores were emptied. Men with horses tied to hitchrails were mounted, carrying rifles. A rancher stripped the harness of his buggy horse, grabbed a rifle from the buggy, and jumped on the horse bareback. Other men ran for their homes and stables. Still others ran for the livery barn.

Within fifteen minutes, ten men were riding at a dead run out of town, heading east. Bill had been offered a fresh horse, and he was in the lead. Ten minutes behind them another armed bunch was riding hard. While he rode, Bill again held the reins in his teeth, and reloaded his Smith & Wesson.

Long before they reached the battle site, the white-eyes could hear gunfire. They tried to urge more speed out of their horses, wanting to get there in time to save lives.

They were seen. A long, high yell came from a savage's throat. Firing ceased. The Indians jumped on their horses and galloped east. The first wave of white-eyes chased them a ways, shooting, hoping to kill Indians. But their horses were too winded to continue the chase.

"God damn it," a townsman said, pulling his horse down to a walk. "If I could run, I'd chase 'em on foot."

"I'd give my interest in hell to get a shot at them sons of bitches," said another.

The second wave of white-eyes came up on a gallop, horses blowing hard, and they too knew it was useless to go farther.

"Red men, hell," a man muttered. "Yellow, that's what they are. Yellowbellies. They won't fight 'less they got you outnumbered by a hell of a lot."

Looking back at the wagon, they saw a dozen or more dead Indians and about the same number of dead or wounded horses. "Well, let's go see how many good men are still alive."

Three cowboys had been killed. All the horses tied to the wagon had been killed. The wagon boss got to his feet and shook his head sadly. His jaws were clamped so tight he couldn't talk. A cowboy folded his arms on top of a wagon sideboard and hid his face in his arms. No one spoke. Another knelt beside the body of a friend. His lips moved silently.

Finally, the rancher on the bareback horse spoke. "Well, we'll round up your remuda for you. We'll hitch up the wagon and get y'all to town, and we'll patch you up as best we can."

In town, the story was told and retold. Bill's name was changed from Bill Watson to Wild Bill Watson. The dead were buried. Wild Bill Watson spent the rest of that summer, the next winter, and half the next summer working for the Box X. The story spread over most of the West. At midsummer, after most of the new calf crop had been rounded up and branded, Bill drew his pay, saddled Dunnie and a packhorse, and rode west. He wanted to see what was over the horizon.

It was late afternoon when Ella next saw Wild Bill Watson. He was walking aimlessly on the planks, looking dejected. Something else about him was different, too. When she realized what it was Ella had to chuckle.

"What happened to your head, Bill? You look like a peeled onion."

"Aw, that danged barber got started cuttin' and didn't know when to quit."

Still chuckling, Ella said, "He sure peeled your knob."

"Uh," Bill grunted. "My danged old hat won't fit no more. I got to hang onto it to keep it from goin' off without me."

"It is kind of flopping around." She laughed. "If the wind picks up, it'll spin around on your head like a top."

"Uh," Bill grunted.

They had to step aside to allow two women in long gingham dresses to pass. Ella said, "That's easy to fix, if that's all that's making you grumpy. All it takes is some folded strips of newspaper inside the sweatband."

"Uh."

"What else is eating on you?"

"Eatin', that's what's eatin' on me."

Cocking her head to one side, Ella said, "That needs explaining."

"I come to town to find a good meal, and all I got was leftover scraps, what them other hogs didn't eat."

"Oh. Well. Tell you what, Wild Bill, you come home with me. I bought two good T-bone steaks just yesterday, and I'll boil some spuds and mash 'em, and make some gravy, and we'll have a feast."

"You'd do that? You'd do that for a poor old broke-down cowpuncher?" He lifted his hat and ran a hand over the top of his head, frowning at the short hair. The back of his neck and the places over his ears that had been covered with hair were now woman-white.

Ella laughed, "You ain't old and you ain't broke down. But"—she gave him a quizzical look—"you are kind of spotted. Like a paint pony."

Wild Bill had to grin. "If you hadn't of invited me to supper, I might take offense at that."

"Let's get over to my place of business first. You

can have a cool beer while I make sure everything is running all right, then we'll go to the house.''

She looped her arm through the cowboy's left arm, and side by side they walked down the sidewalk. A half-dozen customers stood at the bar in the Willow Springs saloon, and all spoke pleasantly to Ella. She made sure Bill got a drink, then slipped out the back door, crossed the alley to her house, yanked off that damned bonnet, and combed out her hair.

Hours later, Wild Bill leaned back in his chair and patted his stomach. ''Now that was a meal! I couldn't a got as good a supper as that anywhere else in town. A woman's got a way of cookin' that us men couldn't match if we tried for a hunnerd years.''

''We're good for something besides having babies.''

That remark reminded Bill of how babies were made, and that reminded him of something else he'd come to town for. Would she? How to ask? He'd heard that she hadn't had a man for a long time. Maybe now was the time. His eyes followed her as she stood and picked up dirty dishes. A fine figure of a woman.

''Coffee, Bill?''

''Huh? Oh, yeah. I mean yes, please.''

''You're awful quiet all of a sudden. Something on your mind?''

He couldn't help grinning. Did she know? ''Well, uh, I was thinkin' maybe, uh . . .''

''Oh, that. Forget it, Bill.''

''Don't you ever, uh, you know.''

She placed a china cup full of steaming coffee in front of him, and sat across the table. ''Let's not talk about that.''

''Oh.'' He felt dejected again. Then he reminded

140

himself that he had just had a fine meal, and he had no reason to feel dejected. If Ella Fitzwater didn't want to go to bed with him, well, that was her business. There were the whorehouses across the railroad tracks. No, he wouldn't do that. He wouldn't go from her house to a whorehouse. Somehow, that just wouldn't be right. He rolled a cigarette, struck a match on the sole of his boot. "Well," he said, finally, "what would you like to talk about?"

She told him about the dance she was planning, and how the merchants had pitched in to help. "Wal"— Bill looked down at his coffee cup—"I dunno." Then she told him about getting the vigilantes organized again to keep the peace. "I've got two of the merchants that were among the vigilantes to promise to get the rest of them together. They'll do it."

"Might be a good idea. Think folks'll come?"

"That I don't know." Ella's mouth turned down in a frown. "It would be awful if we gave a dance and nobody came."

"Wal, you never know till you try."

"It's worth trying." She sat with her elbows on the table, her chin in her hands. Then she changed the subject. "Know what, Bill?"

"What?" he said, matching her mood.

"I'm thinking of selling my business. Running a saloon ain't what I want to do the rest of my life."

"It's a living."

"Yes. I'm not getting rich, but I'm more than breaking even. Still, I don't know. I like running a business. I wish I knew some other business. How about you, Bill?"

"All I know is cows and horses. I used to think I

could homestead a piece of land and get started in the cow business that way, but the good land is already taken and the free range is comin' to an end.''

They talked on. Feeling melancholy, Ella told Bill about her husband and the way he'd left her. She'd never talked about that before, and now, somehow, she felt like telling someone. She wanted Bill to know about it. ''I've spent many hours worrying about him and wondering if it was my fault.''

Still matching her mood, Bill allowed, ''All I can say is he was a fool for walkin' away from a good woman.''

Ella was silent a moment, then straightened in her chair. ''Do you have any plans for the future, Bill?''

''Naw. Right now, I'm thinkin' I'll stay where I am for a while and see what happens. I've been there nearly two years now, and I've had two good calf crops. My herd has grown on free grass. I drove three barren cows to the packin' house a month or so ago for eatin' money, and I won't starve.''

After another moment of silence, Ella stood. ''Speaking of businesses, I've got one to run. Are you staying at the Shuteye tonight?''

''Yep. On a soft bed where nobody can sneak up on me.''

''Will I see you again before you leave town?''

''You betcha.'' Bill drained his coffee cup and stood, too. ''There's beer I ain't drunk yet.''

Chapter Seventeen

They watched Pegleg Peterson ride out of town. Pegleg knew Hunter Howser and the smart-ass deputy were standing on the plankwalk watching. He was riding a good bay horse and leading a packhorse carrying a supply of groceries, some new clothes, new blankets, and his tarp-covered bed. He'd waited until that morning to buy his groceries, and he was getting a late start. But if he kept up a steady trot, he'd be home before dark.

The last thing he'd done before riding out was to toss three twenty-dollar gold pieces onto Bundy's bed. By the time Bundy found them he'd be out of town.

He rode over a low rocky ridge, across a sagebrush flat, across a lava field. He didn't stop at noon, knowing the packhorse would get no rest until it was unloaded. At midafternoon he picked up Otero Creek, and followed its brushy banks to the Vermejo. The sun was sitting on top of the Raton Mountains when he reined up and let his eyes rove over his house and corrals.

Someone had been there.

His water barrel had been tipped over, the bench was out of place, the door was wide open.

Heart in his throat, he dismounted and thumped over to his hiding place under a boulder. When he saw it, his heart dropped into his stomach. They'd found it.

The small iron box that he'd kept his deed in was there, but it had been dug up and forced open. It was empty. "Ohhh, god," he moaned.

Mounted again, he rode across the creek and got down at his front door. Inside, the place was a mess. Every sack of groceries had been torn open. Flour, sugar, coffee, baking soda, all scattered over the wooden floor. His bunk had been turned over, the stovepipe had been knocked loose, and the pockets of his clothes had been turned inside out and the clothes piled on the floor.

Pegleg swore. He cursed the men who'd done this, and he cursed himself for not hiding his paper better. But, hell, given enough time and enough men they were bound to find it. And they had all the time in the world. They'd no doubt hidden somewhere and seen him ride away, leading a packhorse, and knew he'd be gone for at least two days.

Shaking his head, muttering to himself, he unloaded the packhorse, led the horses to the corral, and offsaddled. By dark he had everything back in place and the floor swept. And while he was working, he remembered something that gave him hope:

He'd registered the deed with the county land office. It was on record. They couldn't steal that.

Believing the thieves had what they wanted now, he slept in his house, but he didn't sleep well. He'd no more than lain down when something else popped into his mind:

Maybe they could.

At sunup he was horseback again, heading east at a high trot. He rode past Wild Bill Watson's place, hollered a greeting, got no answer, and went on. Wild Bill was probably riding, keeping his cattle from wandering too far. That's what Pegleg ought to be doing, but his business at the county seat had to be taken care of. Shortly after noon he rode down the main street to the courthouse, tied up at a hitchrail, and stumped inside. Men and women on the streets stopped and stared. Let them stare.

"My name is Arnold Peterson," he said to a young man wearing a stiff collar. "I hold a deed to twenty sections at the confluence of the Vermejo River and Otero Creek. Will you look and see if it's still registered?"

"Why, uh." The young eyes took him in, dirty duck pants, wooden leg, floppy hat, whiskered face. "Sir, do you have a legal description of the tract?"

"No, no legal description was ever wrote. I can show you on a map of Colfax County."

"Well, without a, uh—"

"Goddamn it, young feller, that deed was registered back when Cimarron was the county seat, and that was before there was any such thing as a legal description. Go look for it."

"Yessir. You say it's at the confluence of the Vermejo River and Otero Creek?"

"That's what I said."

"Well, I don't know whether I should find it for you. Most people interested in learning who holds title

145

find it for themselves. Uh, pardon me for asking, sir, but can you read?''

"Dang right I can read, but I don't know where to look.''

"Well, maybe you should wait for Mr. Bruner. He's the county recorder. I only work for him.''

"Where's he?''

"He's at dinner, sir. He should be back in about an hour.''

Pegleg felt anger building, yet this young man was so well-mannered he couldn't get mad at him. Forcing calm into his voice, he said, "Listen here, I need to see that my deed is registered like it's s'posed to be. If I went back there and looked through all them books I wouldn't get 'em back in their right places and nobody could ever find anything again. Now, will you look for me?''

"Do you happen to know which book it is in?''

"Book two. I don't rec'lect the page number.''

"Very well, sir.'' The young man crossed the room to shelves holding stacks of thick, heavy, hardbound ledgers. He ran his fingers down a stack of ledgers until he came to the one he wanted, then grunted and strained to lift other books off so he could remove it.

Pegleg watched as the young man laid the book on a desk, opened it, and flipped pages. Looking up he asked, "Are you sure you don't remember which page number?''

Pushing his hat back, scratching his whiskers, Pegleg tried to remember. "I b'lieve it was two pages, hunnerd and sixteen and hunnerd and seventeen or thereabouts.''

"Those pages are missing, sir.''

146

"Huh? How's that?"

"They have been removed."

"Ain't that ag'in the law?"

"Yessir, it is."

"Any idee who took 'em?"

"No, sir, I'm afraid I don't."

"Aw . . ." This was what Pegleg had feared. His stomach had suddenly turned sour and a bitter bile was building in his throat. He had nothing now to prove he owned the land. He was no better off now than the squatters. The land company's hired goons had stolen his land.

"Aw." He wanted to cuss, let the world know how he felt. But this young man might be a church-goer and would be offended. "Aw." He turned on his peg leg and stumped out of the office, down the hall, and out the door.

Outside, he leaned against a wall and tried to think. Ignoring the people, he looked down at his one boot, shook his head, and tried to figure out what to do. How can anybody steal land? They can't pick it up and carry it away. Easy. They don't have to pick it up, just steal paper. Everything's on paper. The whole goddamn world would stop turning if it wasn't for paper. Some good folks have lived on their land for twenty years, and they ain't got a goddamn thing without paper.

Goddamn it.

Paper, lawyers, judges. And that gave Pegleg an idea. He stumped down the street, scowling, wooden leg thumping on the planks, until he came to the sign over the sidewalk. Thos. A. Atwell Attorney At Law. Pegleg climbed the wooden stairs and knocked on the

147

door. No answer. He knocked again. Goddamn it, was ever'body gone?

For several minutes he stood there, trying to decide what to do next. Maybe the lawyer was at the courthouse, arguing the law in a courtroom. Maybe he went to dinner late. Maybe if Pegleg went back to the courthouse he could find him. Then he saw Thomas Atwell coming up the stairs.

"Why, Mr. Peterson," the young lawyer said. "Are you waiting to see me?"

"Yeah. Yessir. I got to talk to you."

Pegleg declined an offer to sit in one of the two chairs in front of the attorney's desk. He was too worried to sit. Too scared. He explained what had happened. Thomas Atwell stood, opened a drawer in a tall, narrow cabinet, and took out a manila folder. He placed the folder on his desk, sat, opened it. Pegleg, reading upside down, recognized his name on the folder. The lawyer handed him a sheet of paper. Pegleg read it, and his jaw dropped open.

"Why, this's . . . ain't it?"

"It is. It's a copy of the original deed of trust filed with the county recorder. You will notice it has the recorder's raised seal. It is a perfectly legal document. I also copied the boundary description of your property."

Suddenly, a heavy load was lifted from Pegleg. But still he couldn't believe it. "How did you . . . why . . . ?"

"Mr. Peterson"—the lawyer leaned back in his chair, elbows on the chair arms, fingertips together—"the county recorder allows, in fact I believe he encourages, people to look up the ownership of real estate themselves. It saves work for him and his clerk. It occurred to me that something could happen to the deeds recorded by my clients. I had copies written and attested to."

Relief was spread all over Pegleg's face. "Now, that's smart thinkin'. You're smarter than I am, Mr. Lawyer. You done my thinkin' for me. That's how you make your livin', and I owe you."

"I do my best for my clients."

"How much do I owe you?" Pegleg started to unbutton his shirt and reach for his money belt.

"We'll discuss my fee later. Right now we have to have your land properly surveyed, and obtain an adjudication of rights."

"I'll pay you right now if you want."

"The judge should already have appointed a surveyor. I'll see him about that this afternoon. I apologize, I should have done that sooner."

"Well, alls I can say is I'm shore glad somebody's on my side that's smarter than me."

"It's not so much a matter of intelligence, Mr. Peterson, it's a matter of studying the law, and . . ." Thomas Atwell smiled, "what we call grapevining. I was warned that strange things have happened in Colfax County."

Pegleg was so relieved, he was smiling when he thumped down to the hitchrail in front of the courthouse and untied his horse. He felt so good about everything that he decided to buy himself a meal in one of the restaurants in Springer. Riding at a walk down the main street, he heard the train whistle north of town, heard it whistle again. He tied up in front of the same cafe that he and Wild Bill had patronized a few days ago, and went inside.

The menu, scribbled on a wall behind the counter, listed something interesting for a change: Ham hocks and navy beans. "We got just about enough left for one man," said the elderly waiter, wearing a smudged apron. "After you there ain't no more." Pegleg had lived on beans at times, but they were red Mexican beans. Navy beans weren't so common in the southwest. They were good.

While he ate, he noticed the paper pinned to the wall beside the menu. The message on the paper, printed in big type, read

DANCE. BAILE. EVERYONE WELCOME. JULY 4. RATON. COME ONE COME ALL. FAMILIES WELCOME. BRING YOUR OWN FOOD. SETTLERS, RANCHERS, COWBOYS, MINERS, MEXICANS, INDIANS, EVERYBODY OF ALL RACES COME TO RATON JULY 4 AND HAVE FUN. PEACE OFFICERS WILL BE PROVIDED.

Below that, the same message was printed in Spanish.

Feeling well-fed and satisfied, Pegleg unwrapped the reins from the hitchrail and started to get on his horse. "Uh-oh," he said under his breath.

Walking toward him on the planks were Hunter Howser and the smirking deputy in the derby hat.

Chapter Eighteen

When he thought about it, he knew how they'd gotten here so soon. They'd traveled by stagecoach to Raton, and from Raton to Springer by rail. Folks got around a lot faster now than they used to.

Pegleg stayed on the ground. In case of gunfire, a fidgety horse could spoil his aim. He stood in front of the hitchrail and watched the two men approach. They stopped in front of him.

"You're out of your element here, aren't you, Peterson?" Howser was wearing his six-gun in its new holster. He had his thumbs hooked inside his vest pockets. He was right. In Cimarron, the anti-grants outnumbered the grants. The town of Raton was evenly divided. But in Springer, the county seat where most of the legal arguments were taking place, the anti-grant men were badly outnumbered.

Pegleg growled, "What's that got to do with anything?"

"Oh, folks here don't take kindly to squatters, and you don't have your one-eyed friend to help you." Howser was smiling. The deputy was smirking.

"I don't need no help. If you're gonna start some-thin', fart and start."

"Oh my." Howser lifted his hands in mock sur-prise. "Why, we wouldn't think of starting a fight, would we, Jameson? We don't have to fight you, Pe-terson. The forces of law and order will chase you out of the territory."

Pegleg knew what he was thinking. He was thinking Pegleg no longer had a paper to prove he owned the land he claimed. At that, Pegleg had to grin. His mouth inside the beard spread into a wide smile. Chuckling, he turned his back on them and got on his horse.

"Is something funny, Peterson?"

Pegleg didn't answer, just continued chuckling.

The deputy sneered, "You're gonna be laughing out the other side of your mouth, mick."

Still chuckling, Pegleg turned his horse around and rode down the street and out of town. But by the time he got out of town, he realized something. He realized Howser and company would soon find out about those copies Thomas Atwell had.

Then the bushwacking, the night attacks, would start again.

Editors of the newspapers in Raton, Springer, and Cimarron were skeptical, but they thought a commu-nity dance was worth trying. They all printed half-page notices. Travelers posted notices in the stores, hotels, and restaurants. Soon everyone in northern Colfax County knew about it. Most felt the way a cowman living east of Cimarron put it:

"I'm goin', and I'm takin' my woman and my kids, and I'm takin' my shootin' iron."

"It says the vigilantes'll be there to keep ever'thing peaceful."

"Them vigilantes're all right in my books, but I ain't takin' no chances."

In Raton, Ella Fitzwater was busy, making the final arrangements. She had promises from two fiddlers, two guitar pickers, a banjo picker, and a man with a set of drums. They all said they knew some Mexican music as well as waltzes and the schottische. But Ella wanted a cornet. Mexicans liked guitars and fiddles, but they liked horns, too. Who could she get? Then she had an idea.

After all, she wanted the Mexicans to come, yet she had spoken to none of them. In the evening, just before dark, she walked in her wool serge business suit and high-collared shirtwaist to the south end of town and entered the Caza de Pluma saloon. Patrons stopped everything and stared. She forced a wide smile, and asked the bartender for the manager. He nodded and scurried to the back of the room.

The manager was a small, paunchy man in a short dark coat with wide embroidered lapels. His face wore a thin mustache and a question. "Yes? May I be of service to you, *señorita?*"

The face broke into a wide smile when Ella introduced herself. "I see one of our posters on the wall," Ella said in broken Spanish. "Please excuse my Spanish. I'm trying to learn." The Mexican's smile spread even farther. Ella continued, "I would like to personally invite all of you to come."

"*Sí, señorita.* It is kind of you to invite us."

"Do you happen to know a cornetist?"

The face was questioning again.

"I'm sorry," Ella said, "I don't know the Spanish word."

"Jorge," the manager said to a man standing next to him.

Jorge said, "What is it you wish, *señorita?*"

"I would like to have a cornetist to play at our dance."

Jorge spoke to the manager, *"Cornetín."*

The smile returned. *"Sí,* I know of such a man. I will ask him for you."

"I appreciate it very much. *Muchas gracias."*

"You are most welcome, Miss Fitzwater. You have treated my friends very well in your place of business. Please feel welcome here."

Walking back to the Anglo side of town, Ella vowed that tomorrow she'd visit some of the *tiendas* on the Mexican side and personally extend an invitation. "Heck," she said to herself, "all it takes is a little palaver, a little communicating."

A whole flock of those big black-and-white magpies, or satchel birds, had found something interesting in an arroyo about twelve miles west of Springer. The birds were carrion eaters.

"Somethin' dead," Pegleg said to himself as he rode toward his ranch. "Prob'ly a cow died of somethin'. Danged cows're always lookin' for an excuse to die." If it was a cow, whose? This was in Wild Bill Watson's grazing country. He turned his horse in that direction.

As soon as he rode to the edge of the arroyo, he knew

154

it was a dead man. Someone had covered the body with rocks, but enough of it was uncovered to attract the magpies. At first glance he feared it was his neighbor Wild Bill, then he noticed the shoes. They were laced brogans, worn but not ragged.

Talking to himself again, he mused, "This ain't somethin' I like to do, but I gotta know who he is—was." He dismounted and climbed down into the arroyo. The smell was so bad he tried to hold his breath while he picked rocks off the dead man's head. He'd smelled more than his share of dead animals and it had never bothered him much, but something about the smell of a dead decomposing human was enough to make a buzzard sick. The body was on its side. It was no one Pegleg knew. Looked like one of the city thugs that were once recruited for militiamen. Pegleg recovered the head with rocks and climbed out of the arroyo.

"Maybe I oughta go back to town and tell the sheriff about this," he said to himself. "Then, maybe I better not."

If he reported it, he would be questioned closely and he wouldn't get back to his ranch until next day. "Well, if anybody is lookin' for 'im they'll find 'im. You can spot them birds a mile away." He rode on.

Wild Bill had stayed too long in Raton, spending all but a few dollars of his money on groceries, and he was riding at a steady trot, leading a packhorse. He wanted to get home before dark and check for sign of prowlers. Hell, he might not have a home. He might find nothing but a pile of ashes. He was relieved when he rode into sight of the shack and saw it was still standing.

155

From half a mile away everything looked to be the same. His horses were grazing over west. A few cows and their calves were grazing between him and home. The cattle were wearing his brand, a J with a line across the top part. Cross J.

Bill rode on, stopped. A rider was coming down the long slope from the east and heading toward his shack. After watching the rider a moment, Bill recognized him. "Old Pegleg is either lookin' far and wide for his cattle or he's comin' from Springer," he said to himself. He rode to meet him.

"*Hola*, Bill," Pegleg hollered. "Been to the big wicked city?"

"Yup." Their horses were standing head to head now near Bill's shack. "Had to buy some chuck or quit eatin'. Eatin' is a habit I picked up when I was a kid." He held the reins between two fingers and rolled a cigarette.

Pegleg joked, "I tried to break myself from that habit once, and I damn near starved to death."

"There's some habits a feller can't get shut of."

"Say, Bill, you shot anybody lately?"

"Huh? Why?"

Pegleg told about the dead man he'd found.

"Yeah, I traded some shots one night a while back." Bill told about the night attack. "His partners picked 'im up and put 'im on his horse. Could be him."

"Somebody tried to hide a dead man, but the satchel birds found 'im."

"Then, somebody else'll find 'im."

"Well, whatta you think, think we oughta report it to the sheriff?"

156

Bill mulled it over. "You know, they're lookin' for an excuse to arrest me. You too."

"I guess we'd better keep quiet about it, then."

"Forget you saw 'im. Say, I've got some fresh side meat and plenty of flour and bakin' soda and stuff—come on in and let's cook up a feast."

Squinting at the setting sun, Pegleg said, "Thanks, but I'd better keep ridin'. If I keep this ol' pony a-trottin' I might get home before dark."

Pegleg missed his guess. He had to feed his horse in the dark, and find a can of beans and a loaf of bread in the dark. If anyone was watching his house, he didn't want to light a lamp. He slept outside, and at daylight he ran in his horses, picked a brown gelding as his mount for the day, and rode away at a high trot. Grazing land was plentiful and free—at least for the time—but he wanted to keep his cattle on his own land. He had enough grass on his twenty sections to graze his cattle and more.

The first cattle he saw wore Wild Bill's Cross J and had underslopes cut in their right ears. They had wandered onto his land, but he let them be. There were only four cows and their calves. Riding across land that was as flat as a table, across rugged foothills, and around a high sandstone-capped mesa, he saw most of his cattle by midafternoon. He rode along Otero Creek and stopped in the middle of a boggy meadow where he'd been cutting hay. "The grass'll soon be tall enough to cut again," he allowed. Looking at the sky, he wished it would rain, though, so the grass would grow faster. His brown horse had to hump to get through the boggy ground. Its hooves made sucking noises.

"Maybe I'd better get over here with a shovel and do some irrigatin', 'case it don't rain," he allowed. Cattle rustled their own feed in the winter, but he needed hay to feed his horses.

To play it safe, he dismounted and left his horse in some of the tall weeds and willow brush that grew along the Vermejo, and went on foot, carrying his carbine, to where he could see his house across the river.

Two horses were standing in front of the house. A man sat on the bench, smoking a pipe. One man. After studying the man and horses a moment, Pegleg went back to his own horse and mounted. The man wore a flat-brim hat with a high, pinched crown. His pants were the kind that flared at the hips and were tight below the knees. The legs were inside high laced boots. One of the horses was a packhorse, and a tripod was tied across the top of the pack.

The man stood when he saw Pegleg coming, and knocked the dottle out of his pipe on a bootheel. "Evenin'," Pegleg said.

"Good evening, sir. Are you Mr. Peterson?"

"That I am."

"I am Everett J. Godwin. Judge Wilford Mitchell appointed me to survey your land."

Dismounting, Pegleg held out his gnarled right hand to shake. "Glad to meet you, Mr. Godwin. It's too late in the day to start surveying, so put your horses in the corral yonder and pitch 'em some hay. I'll get supper started."

He served the surveyor some of the meat he'd brought from Cimarron, fried potatoes, and baking-

158

soda biscuits. Meal over, he didn't know how to tactfully advise him to sleep outside, but he didn't have to. The surveyor had a small tent and bedroll, and expected to sleep outside.

Wild Bill had also been doing some riding, and had spent most of another day irrigating a grassy spot along his section of Otero Creek. "Wish to hell it'd rain," he grumbled. Three hours before sundown, he was walking from the corral to his shack, thinking now would be a good time to get a stew and a pot of beans cooking, when he saw Sheriff Bowman coming. Immediately, he grabbed his rifle and waited. The sheriff was the only rider he saw, coming down the long slope from the southeast. No one spoke until the lawman was close. Bill waited, ready.

"Now, I don't want any trouble, Bill," Bowman said, sitting his horse. "As you can see I came alone."

Bill said nothing, but just waited until the lawman said what he'd come here to say.

"I wish I didn't have to do this, Bill, but I have to put you under arrest."

"Why?"

"We found a dead man back yonder on your grazing land. He'd been shot with a rifle. Somebody'd tried to hide his body in an arroyo. You're the best suspect."

Chapter Nineteen

"What makes you think I did it?" Wild Bill Watson asked.

"You've shot men before for moving your cattle. This one had a rifle bullet in his left side. A man huntin' meat found his horse and then found him."

"I'll bet he was one of them militiamen."

Shifting slightly in his saddle, Bowman said, "Yeah, he was. Everybody knows you've got no love for them."

"I'm prob'ly the one that shot 'im, all right. He tried to set fire to my shack here. See that can over there? He was packin' that. It's full of coal oil."

"When did this happen?"

"Four, five nights ago. They started shootin' in the dark. A bunch of 'em. I went out the back way, got around to where I could watch the front door here, and shot 'im when he ran up packin' that can. His partners got 'im on his horse and rode off with 'im."

"Did you recognize any of them?"

"Couldn't see 'em in the dark."

"Why didn't you report this?"

"I ain't in the habit of reportin' ever'thing to the laws."

Shaking his head sadly, the sheriff said, "Goddamn it, Bill, when a man is killed, it has to be reported to the authorities."

"I didn't know he was killed. Like I said, he was able to ride off."

With a sigh, Bowman said, "I wish I didn't have to do this, but I have to arrest you. Maybe when I learn more about what happened, I can let you go."

Bill was holding the Remington rifle with his finger on the trigger guard, but he didn't point it at the sheriff. "You mean you wanta lock me up in your jail. I ain't ever been locked up."

"I'll do some investigating. I'll learn everything I can about what happened, and if you were defending your property maybe the prosecutor won't charge you with a crime."

"Maybe is a big word. Them militiamen ain't gonna admit what they done. They done the same thing to Pegleg Peterson. In fact, they did set fire to his house, but I came along in time to help drive 'em away and put out the fire."

"Is that so? Did you see any of them?"

"They sneak around in the dark."

"I'll sure check on that. If Peterson backs up your story, that'll be a big help in your trial."

"Trial? I ain't goin' to no trial."

"I hope it won't go that far, but I have to take you in."

The two men eyed each other. Sheriff Bowman carefully kept his right hand on top of the saddle horn, away from his gun. Bill made no threatening move, made no move at all.

"Will you put your guns on the ground, Bill?"

No answer. No movement.

"I know you're fast with a gun, Bill. I know you can outshoot me. But look at it this way: if you shoot me, you'll be a fugitive from justice, and every lawman in the territory will be looking for you."

Still no answer.

"You'll be on the run. You'll lose everything you've got."

Finally, Bill spoke again. "If I'm locked up in jail I'll lose ever'thing anyway. You'll no more'n turn the key than they'll be out here stealin' ever'thing."

"I wish I could promise you they won't, but this is a mighty big county and I can't be everywhere. I will promise you that I'll ride over this way every chance I get. As a matter of fact, I'll be over this way again tomorrow to talk to Arnold Peterson."

Bill was silent again, thinking, then, "You plannin' to put them handcuffs on me?"

"No. No handcuffs. If you run, you'll have to keep on running. You don't want to do that."

"Can I send a telegraph?"

"Who to?"

"I don't know yet. I just want somebody to know where I am. 'Case I disappear."

"All right. I'll send it for you."

"Is that a promise?"

"That's a promise. Now will you put your guns down?"

* * *

163

It was a mystery to Pegleg Peterson what the surveyor was doing and how he was doing it. He followed the man, curious, showing him the landmarks listed on a copy of the deed of trust. Every few hundred yards, the surveyor unloaded his tripod from the packhorse, mounted his spyglass, squinted through it, made a note in his book, then went on. At every place where the described property line made a turn, he drove an iron stake in the ground. At the sharp turns, he put a yellow cap on the stake. "It's illegal to tamper with these markers," he said. This was going to take two days at least.

When they came to the stump of a tree that had been a landmark, Pegleg said, "See? This tree was chopped down not long ago and dragged away. Come over here." He led the surveyor to an arroyo and pointed to the tree at the bottom. The tree was still green. Dismounting, Pegleg said, "Come down here and I'll show you the initial I carved in this tree a long time ago."

The surveyor looked, made another note in his book, then set up his tripod at the tree stump.

"A telegram? For me?" Ella Fitzwater was puzzled. "I never got a telegram in my life. Are you sure it's for me?"

"Yes; ma'am. It came this mornin', and I brung it over. You are Ella Fitzwater, ain't you?" He was a wrinkled, skinny man in a gray shirt buttoned to his throat. He had a black bill cap on his head.

"Well, who's it from?" She stood in the door of her house across the alley from the Willow Springs saloon.

164

"Can you read, ma'am? I'll read it for you if you want."

"Oh no, I can read."

"I pasted the envelope shut so no one else can open it and read it without you knowin' it."

"Well." Ella tore open the envelope and took out a sheet of yellow paper. The message was handwritten in big block letters. It was addressed to Ella Fitzwater, Willow Springs saloon, Raton, N.M. It was simple: BILL WATSON ASKED ME TO TELEGRAPH YOU SO YOU WILL KNOW HE IS BEING HELD IN JAIL IN SPRINGER. The name at the bottom was SHERIFF MACKENZIE BOWMAN.

"Oh," Ella gasped. "Wild Bill's in jail at Springer. What . . . ?"

"Who, ma'am?"

"Oh, it's, uh, nobody you know. A friend of mine. When is the next train south?"

The skinny man pulled a biscuit-sized watch from a vest pocket and opened the lid. "She's due in a hour and ten minutes, ma'am, and she'll be pullin' out in about two hours."

"I must buy a ticket. I must make arrangements for my bartender to run the saloon for a day or two. I must . . . Thank you. Thank you for bringing this over."

"You're welcome, ma'am." The skinny man lifted his cap, turned, and walked away.

Hurrying, Ella packed a leather satchel with clean underclothes, a washcloth, and towel. She put on her wool serge business suit with the white pleated shirtwaist buttoned to her chin, and then her new hat. The hat was fine black English felt with two rows of twisted velvet around the crown. The ends were twisted upward in the shape of bird's wings. A gilded buckle was fastened on the crown just to the left of center.

She'd just bought it the day before at a newly opened millinery shop for a dollar and forty-five cents. It took four bobby pins to hold it at the right angle on her hair. "Maybe," she said to herself, "this won't make me look like a lady, but maybe it'll help me feel like one."

Two days was what it took to survey the land as described on Pegleg Peterson's document. At the end of the second day, the surveyor dismounted stiffly in front of Pegleg's house, tamped tobacco in his pipe, and lit it. Looking at the western horizon, he said, "I think I can find my way back to Springer in the dark."

"You can spend another night here," Pegleg said. "I'd reckon you'd rather sleep in a bed in town, but it's a four- or five-hour ride. I'll cook supper."

"Perhaps you're right. Shall I put my horses in your corral again and feed them some hay?"

"Shore."

By lamplight, after a meal of beef, potatoes, and beans, the surveyor went over his notes, and did some calculating with a lead pencil. Sitting in the house by lamplight made Pegleg nervous, and he excused himself and carried his rifle outside where he sat in the dark, watching and listening.

"Mr. Peterson, are you out here?" The surveyor stood in the lighted doorway.

"Right here," Pegleg said.

"I have something to show you if you'll come in here by the lamp."

Inside, the surveyor tamped and lit his pipe, took a few puffs, and sat at the table. "By my calculations and by the descriptions given me, you own twenty-two sections of land."

"Twenty-two? That's more than I thought. I own twenty-two sections?"

"Well, it's up to the courts to decide who owns it, but there are twenty-two sections within the boundaries described in the deed."

"Well, I'll be durned. Old Maxwell and me, we intended to mark off twenty sections."

"You did remarkably well, considering you had to pace it off."

"Old Lucien'd had some experience layin' out land. He owned about two millions acres."

"The latest calculations by government surveyors has the grant comprising a million seven hundred thousand acres."

"Whoo," Pegleg said, shaking his head, "who could want more? Why would that land company want more?"

The surveyor shrugged and said nothing.

"Mind if I blow out the lamp?" Pegleg asked.

"Not at all. I understand your fears. But once we have this properly recorded and the land patented, you'll be the undisputed owner, and you'll have nothing more to fear."

Sure, Pegleg thought, as he covered himself with a blanket and tarp near the creek, nothing more to fear. Trouble is, this feller don't know what kind of men we're dealin' with.

* * *

It was only the second time Ella had been on a train, and she marveled at how fast it traveled. The passenger coach swayed, the wheels *click-clacked* over the fish-plates, and smoke from the engine blew past the windows. Over east was Mount Capulin, which once spouted red hot lava, and there was a big round mesa also on the east. Cholla cactus and soapweeds rolled past the windows, and a few cattle grazed in the distance.

Seemed like only an hour before the engine was whistling its approach to Springer, and then it was hissing and screeching to a stop in front of the one-room clapboard depot. Ella climbed down the iron steps, carrying her satchel in one hand and an umbrella in the other. She carried the umbrella because a lady at the millinery shop told her that's what ladies carried.

The courthouse was easy to find, and she wasted no time walking there and asking for the sheriff's office. Sheriff Bowman wasn't in. Instead the deputy with the cocky derby hat was in. He sat with his brogan shoes parked on a scarred wooden desk and smirked.

"Thought I recognized you, mizzuz. I been in your saloon in Raton, and I seen you. A mick told me you owned the joint."

"I'm the owner, yes."

"Too bad I can't let you see Watson. He ain't allowed to see nobody."

"Why not?"

"That's for me to know and you to find out."

"Where's the sheriff?"

"Who knows? Who cares?"

Ella was beginning to fume. His smirk. His smart-aleck answers. "Listen, I came from Raton to see Bill Watson and I insist on seeing him."

"You insist, eh?" The smirk turned to a speculative look. His eyes took in the snug-fitting suit jacket, which revealed a trim waist and an ample bosom. "Maybe if you was to be nice to me I'd let you in for a visit. I might even look the other way for a while."

"What do you mean?" Ella was smoking now.

"Oh, you know, let me see what you got under that dress."

Whack. The umbrella came down hard on the deputy's head, knocking the cocky derby hat off. *Whack,* another blow was laid upside his face. Still another blow on the other side of the face had the deputy falling backward, tipping the chair over on top of him. Even before he hit the floor Ella was whacking him again, whacking until the umbrella broke. His hand went to the nickel-plated revolver. That was as far as it went. A hard leather shoe heel came down on the hand, twisting, grinding. The deputy yelped in pain.

Ella reached down and picked up the pistol, stepped back, and cocked the hammer. The gun felt strange to her, but she knew she could shoot it. "Stay there," she hissed through her teeth. "Stay on the floor. Make one move and I'll punch another hole in your head." The deputy rubbed his injured hand with his other hand, but made no attempt to get up.

Then a man came in the door, stopped, took in the scene, and reached for a gun on his hip. He froze when he found himself looking up the bore of the nickel-plated revolver. "What . . . ?" That's all he got out.

Ella hissed, "Get your sorry carcass over there, Mr.

Howser. Get over there beside your smart-face deputy. If you think I won't shoot, just try me."

Hunter Howser was too surprised to move. All he could do was stare with his mouth open.

Talking through her teeth, Ella said, "I just figured how to shoot this little gun. It don't have to be cocked. It'll shoot as fast as I can pull the trigger. I'm about to start pulling."

Chapter Twenty

Hunter Howser looked like an eastern dandy in his dark fingerlength coat, white shirt, and dark necktie. A bowler hat sat on his head. All that made him look western were the riding boots and the pistol in a new holster on his right side under the coat. He blinked, gulped, and haltingly shuffled over to stand beside the fallen deputy.

Ella was beginning to control her anger now. "Where'd you come from, Mr. Howser?" She accentuated the *Mr.* "Where are you getting the money to pay these goons? The land company paying you?"

"Why, uh . . ." His mouth opened, but not much came out. His eyes were fixed on the bore of the gun.

"Well, what did you expect? You came out here and took over where Jim Masterson left off, and you act surprised to find somebody aiming a gun at you. You the kind that hires somebody to do your fighting?"

"Now see here, madam, I—"

"Shut up. Shut up till you're ready to answer some questions. Who's paying you?" When she got no answer, Ella took a step closer and aimed the pistol at the end of Hunter Howser's nose. "Talk, mister."

Howser's eyes suddenly shifted to the door behind Ella, and relief flooded his face.

A man's voice thundered, "Ella, what in tarnation . . . Ella, put that gun down."

Half-turning, Ella said, "Welcome to your office, Sheriff. A couple of rattlesnakes almost took over."

"Ella, you . . ." Sheriff Bowman came on in and sat on the edge of the desk. "Will you tell me what's going on here? And will you put that gun away?"

Easing the hammer down on the pistol, Ella let it dangle by the trigger guard from one finger. "It's like this, Sheriff. I came down here from Raton to see Bill Watson, and this smart-mouth pile of manure wouldn't let me. Instead he propositioned me."

Hard pale eyes turned to the deputy. "Is that so, Jameson?"

Jameson got to his feet. His hat was on the floor and his dark curly hair stuck out in all directions. He was not smirking. "She's lyin'. I never propositioned 'er."

With a flip of her wrist, Ella had the gun solidly in her hand again and the hammer back. "You calling me a liar?"

"Now, Ella," Sheriff Bowman said, "don't do that. Let me handle this. I was elected sheriff, you know."

Sighing, Ella eased the gun hammer down again, and handed it to the lawman. "I've got nothing against you, Sheriff Bowman, but I wish you'd get rid of these snakes."

"I'm trying, Ella, but I don't make the laws."

"Yeah, yeah."

"Did you say you came here to see Bill Watson?"

172

"Yeah."

"That's easy to arrange. I'm letting him out."

"You are? How come?"

"I'll explain it to you both. Jameson, bring Watson out here, and be polite."

Picking up her broken umbrella, Ella grumbled, "This cost me honest money. I oughta take it out of his hide."

When Wild Bill Watson came through the door between the sheriff's office and the jail, he was blinking, trying to get his eyes accustomed to the daylight. He stopped, blinked, wiped his eyes with a shirtsleeve, and said, "Ella? Is that you?"

"It's me, Bill. I got your telegraph."

"I didn't mean for you to come down here. I only wanted somebody to know what happened to me, and you're the only one I could send a telegraph to."

"Well, I'm here, and you're out." Turning to the sheriff, she said, "How come you're letting him go?"

Still sitting on the edge of his desk, Bowman said, "I don't doubt Bill shot that man, but somebody else shot him, too."

"What man?"

Bill said, "I'll tell you about it later, Ella." To the sheriff, he said, "Who else?"

"That we don't know. The coroner found a rifle bullet in his side, and that's why I arrested you. Then while ago he found another bullet square in the heart. It wasn't a rifle bullet. More like a small pistol bullet. But deadly. The man died so quick he didn't even bleed. That's why the coroner only just now found it."

"I can tell you what happened," Watson said. "It's easy to figure out."

"All right, tell me."

"I shot the man for tryin' to set my shack on fire. My bullet didn't kill 'im, and his partners got 'im on his horse and rode off. They figured if they brought 'im to town, they'd have to answer some questions, so they made sure he didn't get to town."

"Uh-huh," the lawman said, nodding his head. "I was thinking in that same direction. You say you didn't get a look at his partners?"

"Naw, but I can guess. That jackass over there." Bill nodded at the deputy. "You said the dead man was shot in the heart with a little gun. He carries a fancy little gun."

Deputy Jameson said, "Aw, this mick's guessin'. He's just waggin' his tongue. I wasn't nowhere near his shack that night."

"What night?" the sheriff asked.

"Whatever night that happened. I was here in town, and I can prove it."

"How?"

"Mr. Hunter and some of our pals. We play cards almost ever' night. Sometimes at his house and sometimes in the Good Times saloon."

Sourly, Wild Bill said, "Sure, sure."

"Bill, do you know exactly when you were attacked?"

"Wal, I can figure it out. Let me think. I hafta count backwards." He looked at his boots and scowled while he counted the nights since the attack. Finally, he looked up. "Six nights ago. That would of been, uh, what day of the week was that?"

Now the sheriff had to do some backward counting. Ella said, "Last Monday."

174

"You're right. Mmm." Sheriff Bowman lifted his hat, ran his fingers through what little hair he had, reset the hat. "Trouble is, Bill, you're only guessing at what happened. It's probably a good guess, but only a guess. And there's a lot of small-caliber pistols around."

"Sure, sure."

"I'll do some investigating. Maybe I'll get lucky."

"Sure, sure."

"Anyway, you're free to go." Bowman opened a desk drawer and took out Bill's Smith & Wesson, holster, and cartridge belt. Bill buckled it on. "You know, Bill, that eventually you're gonna have to move."

"Someday. But they"—Bill nodded toward Howser and Jameson—"are just gonna have to wait. If they try again to shoot me out or burn me out, some more of 'em are gonna get killed."

Bowman said, "The wheels of justice are moving faster now. It won't be long."

"You know what?" Ella said. "I've been wondering and asking, and come to think of it, it's easy to understand why they want to shoot the settlers out."

Both Bill and the sheriff looked at Ella, questions on their faces.

" 'Cuz it costs too much to go to court and get 'em out that way. It's cheaper to shoot 'em or scare 'em off."

"Uh-huh," Bowman said. "That occurred to me, too. Well, why don't you two go on about your business. I apologize, Bill, for incarcerating you."

"For what?"

"Locking you up."

"Oh. Let's go, Ella. I'll buy you a meal."

"Just a minute." Hunter Howser moved over between the door and Ella. "I want to register a complaint against this woman. She assaulted your deputy and threatened me with a gun."

"Well, now." The sheriff lifted his hat again, reset it. "You know, Mr. Howser, you're going to look funny when the word gets out. How a woman got the best of you both." Bowman tried, but he couldn't suppress a small grin.

Bill looked quizzically at Ella. "What happened?"

"I'll tell you about it later, Bill, just like you told me later about the shootout at your shack."

"Well, uh . . ."

"Come on, Bill, you owe me a meal."

Seated at a table in a restaurant next door, sipping coffee, waiting for roast beef sandwiches, Ella told Bill about her fracas with Deputy Jameson. When she described it, Bill got to laughing so hard, other restaurant patrons stopped eating and tried to listen to the conversation.

When his laughter subsided to a chuckle, Bill nodded at the top of Ella's head and said, "Why didn't you sic that bird on 'im?"

"What?" Her hand went to the millinery-store hat. "Oh, that. I almost forgot about that."

"Are them little flat pieces s'posed to be wings?"

"Don't you make fun of my hat, Bill Watson."

"It's a good thing you've got it pinned down, otherwise it might fly away."

"Bill, one of these days you and me are gonna tangle."

With a chuckle, Bill said, "When that happens, I hope you ain't packin' that umbrella."

* * *

Everett J. Godwin pocketed a twenty-dollar gold coin and said goodbye to Pegleg Peterson. "I'll add my report to your deed, and I'll make a copy for your lawyer. I appreciate your hospitality. Sometimes in my line of work, I have to camp out by myself."

"I appreciate what you've done. I'm mighty glad to have this land officially surveyed. I've been wonderin', though, what happens if the land company sends its own surveyor and the two of you don't agree?"

Stepping into his saddle, taking a good hold on the packhorse's lead rope, Godwin said, "When that happens, we usually reach a compromise. But don't worry, I'm a hard bargainer."

Pegleg watched him ride away, then went to the corral to saddle a horse. "Maybe now I can get on with the business of raisin' beef," he said to himself. "Got some ridin' to do. Got some hay to cut."

The Fourth of July was drawing closer. Ella Fitzwater was both excited and apprehensive. "Will they come? Will it be peaceful? Will everybody have a good time? Will it rain?"

Walking out to the eastern edge of Raton where the dance floor had been completed, she looked at the sky. A few white puffs of clouds drifted overhead, but they didn't look like the kind that held moisture. The stockmen are crying for rain, Ella thought, and I hope they get what they want. But not on the Fourth of July.

The dance floor was splintery, and some of the green lumber had shrunk, leaving narrow gaps between the

177

boards. Oh, well, Ella thought, nobody's going to be barefoot. A small raised platform had been built at one end for the musicians. There was plenty of space out here for parking buckboards and buggies, and hitch-rails had been erected to tie horses to. Not much was left to be done.

Silently, she prayed. Maybe I'm asking too much in a territory where folks are ready to start shooting over one wrong word. But we need this. If it works, it will help folks feel better about one another. Thank you, Lord, for the vigilantes. Keep the blessings coming.

The vigilantes, however, had another job to do before July.

Chapter Twenty-one

Pegleg Peterson was the first to get wise to what was happening. When he heard cattle bawling, he knew from experience it was the sound of cattle being moved in a herd. He struck a trot, rode over a long, low ridge, and saw them. Fourteen cows and their calves. A dozen men were moving the small herd toward Springer. Almost as many cowboys as cattle. Some squatter was getting out of the cow business. Pegleg wondered who and why, and why there were so many men.

Riding closer, he recognized Tomás Cruz in his Mexican saddle on a black horse far behind the herd. Pegleg touched his one spur to his horse and rode at a lope to his friend, reined up beside him.

"Hola, Tomás. Qué pasa?"

The Mexican's face was pinched, angry. In rapid Spanish he told Pegleg about it. They had come at dawn, the sheriff and eleven deputies. The sheriff had read to Tomás and Eileen Cruz from a court order. Eileen had taken the paper and read it for herself, then in a broken, tearful voice explained it to her brother.

A judge in Santa Fe had issued a permanent injunction, barring the Cruzes from tilling the soil or grazing livestock. They were given thirty days to vacate the "herein described" property. The judge had also issued a judgment against the Cruzes, ordering them to repay the costs of litigation. The cattle were being driven to Springer, where they would be sold at auction to partially satisfy the judgment. The sheep and goats would be driven to Springer in a few days.

Pegleg listened silently. Anger was boiling in his guts. By the time Tomás had explained it, he was so angry he could barely talk. Even his beard bristled. Through clenched jaws, he said, "Now I know why it takes twelve sons of bitches to move fourteen cows. They didn't give you a chance, did they?"

The more he thought about it, the madder he got. Suddenly, he spun his horse around and spurred toward the herd and the twelve lawmen, ready to fight the whole damned bunch of them.

Sheriff Bowman saw him coming, and rode to meet him away from the rest of the crew. Pegleg pulled his horse to a sliding stop, facing the sheriff. He was too angry to speak, and the sheriff spoke first:

"Now listen, Peterson. I'm acting under a judge's orders. I have to carry out the orders of the court."

Finally, words exploded out of Pegleg: "What kind of man are you? What kind of man does it take to steal livestock from two harmless Mexicans? What kind of mean, sneaky, sons of bitches are you, anyway?"

The words were insults, fighting words, and Sheriff Bowman's face turned red. But he kept his voice calm. "Listen, Peterson, hear me out. Everybody wants law and order. To have law, we have to have law enforcement and we have to have courts, and somebody has to enforce the law and carry out the courts' orders. The only other way is gun law. Ain't you people tired of that?''

The deputies had left the herd and were gathering around the sheriff and Pegleg, hands on gun butts. At first, Pegleg ignored them. He hissed, ''If this is the way the law works, then you know what you can do with the law.'' He glanced around at the deputies. ''You and the whole damned yellowbelly bunch of you can take the law and stick it up your *culos.*''

Six-guns cleared leather. Gun hammers were cocked. But the sheriff barked, ''Put them guns away. Put 'em away, or by god I'll arrest the first man that shoots.'' To Peterson, he said, ''All right, you've said what you had to say. I intend to do my duty. You're surrounded, Peterson, but I don't want any blood spilled. I wish you'd just go on about your business.''

He was right; Pegleg was surrounded. He had no chance in a fight. But before he left, he gave each man a hard look, one at a time, vowing to himself that he'd recognize them when he saw them again.

Then, without another word, he turned his horse around and rode away at a lope.

His next stop was Wild Bill's place, but Bill wasn't there. He went to his own ranch, caught a fresh horse, and rode to Cimarron, getting there late at night. The news had spread before he arrived. He went to the livery barn and awakened his friend Bundy.

''By god, Pete, if you wanta fight 'em, I'll go with you. I can borry a horse, and I can still shoot. I never liked the goddamn laws anyhow.''

''I got this feelin','' Pegleg said, ''the way men are talkin', we ain't gonna have to fight 'em alone.''

The news spread to Raton, and Ella was outraged. "Why, those sons of pups. We can't allow this to happen. Them Cruzes never bothered nobody. They're good, honest, hard-working folks."

A merchant, standing at the bar, allowed, "It's time for the vigilantes."

Ella stomped behind the bar and took down the Hawken rifle. "By gosh, I'm goin' with you."

"We'll prob'ly go horseback, Ella. We've never had a woman ride with us."

"I rode horses since I was big enough to climb on one, and you all know I can shoot."

The merchant gulped down the rest of his beer. "I'll spread the word. We'll meet at the livery barn tonight."

Newspapers in three towns printed the ads. Editors who were grant sympathizers didn't mention where the cattle came from, only that they were to be auctioned at the railroad pens in Springer. Anti-grant editors printed the ad about the auction, but also printed stories about a dozen lawmen converging on a Mexican man and woman and taking their cattle.

News spread faster by word of mouth than by newspaper, and within a few days every rancher and farmer in Colfax County knew about it. What happened to the Cruz family could happen to them.

The auction was scheduled for June twentieth. Meanwhile, the county was paying for feed for the cattle. As one townsman put it, "When the county pays, that means us taxpayers pay." And another put in, "Who'll pocket the proceeds from the auction? The goddamn land company, that's who."

Vigilantes in Raton were ready to ride. They tried

to talk Ella out of going with them, but she couldn't be persuaded. "I'm going if I have to go alone."

They started before daylight. All mounted on good horses and all carrying a rifle and six-gun. Ella rode astraddle her horse, wearing a long skirt that covered her legs and most of the saddle. The auction was to begin at twelve noon. There were only eleven men. "There're more of them militiamen than there are of us," a rancher said.

"It's gonna be bloody."

Pegleg Peterson was riding before daylight. He veered off to the south a ways to see if Wild Bill was ready. Bill had a horse saddled. "Think we'll have to take 'em on by ourselfs, Pete?"

"I dunno. Maybe we will. But I'm mad enough to fight the whole damn Union Army."

"Way I heard it, they've got an army."

"An army of yellowbellies that couldn't whip the shit off their shirttails."

Cattle buyers had gathered in Springer, coming from southern New Mexico Territory, from Santa Fe, from Colorado, and even as far away as Texas. These few cows were the first to be auctioned off, and there would be more. The lawmen would be evicting settlers all over the territory. A buyer and seller of livestock could make a profit here.

Sheriff MacKenzie Bowman was nervous. He'd been told that the vigilantes of Raton had reorganized, and he could sense the sentiment of stockmen in Colfax County. He had a hard decision to make. With fourteen well-armed deputized men, all highly visible, he could stave off trouble—maybe. But there were men in the territory who'd fight whether they could win or not.

Those deputies could make them angrier. The deputies, full of authority, could start a fight. He'd wired the governor, and an aide had wired back that troops would be sent, but they couldn't get there until eight o'clock. That would be too late. Men would die.

What to do?

He walked the length of the main street, continually looking beyond the town limits, afraid he'd see armed men coming. The train from the north wouldn't arrive until after noon, so they'd come by horseback. Checking his pocket watch, he noted the time was eleven-thirty. A half-hour to go. Maybe nothing would happen.

Then he groaned. Arnold Peterson and Wild Bill Watson were riding in from the west, carrying rifles and six-guns. "Oh, lord." Surely, they wouldn't try to shoot it out with fourteen deputies. Surely not.

But Wild Bill Watson didn't get his nickname by running from a fight. And Peterson, that tough old boot, he was a veteran of every kind of gun battle there ever was.

MacKenzie Bowman stepped out into the street to greet them. They reined up. "I hope you gentlemen are here on peaceful business," he said.

"We ain't," Peterson said.

"Listen, I've got more than a dozen deputies here. Don't get yourselves killed."

"They're gonna pay a hell of a price."

Was there anything the sheriff could do? Anything he could say? What he ought to do was disarm these two right now before trouble started. Could he? No. They wouldn't give up their weapons. If he tried that, the shooting would start before the auction began.

Looking back down the street, Bowman saw a crowd

184

gathering at the stockyards. Four of his deputies spotted him standing in front of two armed cowboys, and they headed his way. The two riders saw them coming, and they were ready.

Thinking fast, Sheriff Bowman spun on his heels and went to meet the deputies. "Come on," he said, "the auction is about to start."

"What about them two?"

"Never mind. Come on."

At the stockyards, the auctioneer, a short fat man with a narrow-brim straw hat, sat on a wooden crate, holding a megaphone across his lap. He was waiting for the time to climb onto the crate and start his chant. Cattle buyers were sitting on the rail fence. Town people had gathered out of curiosity. Bowman looked at his watch again. He crawled through the fence and went to the auctioneer.

"We'll sell the whole herd at once. Let's get this over with."

The auctioneer climbed on top of the crate and put the megaphone to his mouth. He bellowed, "All right now. The sheriff said to sell the whole herd to one buyer. What am I bid? Who'll start the bidding?"

But no one was watching him. No one was listening. Everyone was looking to the north and to the southwest. Sheriff Bowman let out a long groan.

Eleven mounted men were coming from the north, men of all descriptions, merchants in coats and ties, ranchers, railroaders. And a woman. Ella Fitzwater, sitting straight up in the saddle like a man, carrying that long-barreled muzzle-loading rifle of hers. From the southwest came about twenty armed men, mostly ranchers and cowboys, a few farmers in baggy bib overalls.

185

No one spoke as they rode up and surrounded the cattle pen. They sat their horses with rifles in their hands, grim-faced.

Bowman looked around for his deputies, afraid they would start shooting. The ones he saw were standing stock-still, faces white, afraid to move.

Then a rancher with a walrus mustache and a high-crown hat rode forward a few steps. He cocked the hammer back on his rifle. The other riders did the same.

"This sale is over," he said. "The first one that bids gets shot."

Chapter Twenty-two

The auctioneer climbed down from his packing crate, but no one else moved. A cowboy rode his horse over to the corral gate, reached down, and unlatched it. He swung it open, then rode inside and, whooping and whistling, herded the cattle outside. The motley longhorns, not used to so much activity, were more than happy to take off running down the main street, heading for open country.

"You men know," Sheriff Bowman said, "that you're interfering with the law."

The only reply he got was a tight-lipped, "Yeah."

Then some thirty men and a woman turned their horses around and rode out of town at a lope, following the cattle. Behind them, MacKenzie Bowman let out a long sigh. "At least, nobody was killed."

"You gonna let 'em get away with that, Sheriff?" The questioner was a cattle buyer from Santa Fe.

"Yep. It's that or we'll spend the rest of the day picking up bodies."

"Your duty is to uphold the law."

With another sigh, the sheriff said, "I've got a lot of

duties, and one of 'em is to keep the peace.'' Looking down at the ground, he slowly walked back to the courthouse.

Out on the prairie west of Springer, a cowboy asked, ''What're we gonna do with 'em?''

Pegleg answered, ''We'll take 'em to my rancho. I got a deed to my land, and I don't like trespassers.''

''We'll have to nighthawk 'em,'' a rancher said. ''We oughta stick together tonight anyhow, 'case some of them hardcase deputies come lookin' to take 'em back.''

''I'm kinda disappointed. I wanted to have it out with them sons of bitches.''

''We'll never have a better chance than we had to-day.''

''Them lawdogs don't fight 'less they got the odds on their side.''

''Trouble is, gents, we cain't stick together forever. They'll be madder'n hell now, and they'll pick us off one at a time.''

''Yup, that's what they'll do.''

''Wonder why the sheriff didn't send down to Santa Fe for the soldier boys. He must of knowed we was comin'.''

''Takes time to get them soldiers together. They'll prob'ly get to Springer on the next northbound train. They'll be afoot, though, and they won't come after us.''

''I've got a brother-in-law in the regulars, and he said once if he was ordered to shoot at his own people he wouldn't do it.''

''A lot of 'em feel that way. We don't have to worry about Governor Sheldon's army.''

They spent the night camped beside a narrow stream called Chacuaco Creek because of the alder brush that grew along it. Everyone had a blanket, and some biscuits and jerky in their saddlebags. Ella Fitzwater had two blankets, and two cold steaks. Three mounted men at a time stood guard over their grazing horses and cattle. They all slept with their guns handy.

By noon next day they had the cattle within sight of Arnold Peterson's cabin. They held them there in a loose bunch until cows and their calves found one another, then left them and split up, heading for their homes.

Ella dismounted in front of the house and helped herself to a drink from the water barrel. "Pete, as long as I've known you, this is the first time I've seen where you live."

"Go on in the house, Ella, and make yourself to home."

The men waited while she went in, looked around, and exclaimed, "Why, you're a good housekeeper, Pete. I expected to find a boar's nest in here."

"My squaw, rest her soul, kept a clean house, and it sorta got to be a habit."

Turning to Wild Bill, Ella said, "One of these days I'm gonna get a look in your house, Bill."

"Ella," Bill said, grinning, "there's some things too horrible for human eyes to see."

Sheriff MacKenzie Bowman was feeling down. He'd been soundly criticized by the mayor and the prosecuting attorney for allowing armed civilians to take over the town and drive away confiscated livestock. He knew in his heart he'd done the right thing, but their harsh words were cutting and painful. He felt lower than he'd ever felt in his life. Maybe he shouldn't be sheriff. It was a thankless job and sometimes dangerous. He was nothing more than hands and feet for the judges and the county honchos. He had to make snap decisions, and if he made the wrong decisions he'd catch hell from all directions. The right decisions didn't even earn a thank you.

Now he'd made the right decision and was catching hell anyway.

And that wasn't all. Here was that long, tall drink-of-water prosecuting attorney standing in his office telling him to go out and arrest a man who didn't deserve to be arrested.

"I just don't believe Arnold Peterson had anything to do with it," he argued.

"He had every reason in the world. He was the last one to see Everett Godwin alive." Prosecutor Zachary Phipps towered over the sheriff. In fact, at six four he towered over almost everyone. But his eyes hadn't squinted at the sun enough to cause a wrinkle, and his face and hands were as smooth as a baby's ass. He wore wire-rimmed glasses that he was always polishing with a silk handkerchief which he carried in the breast pocket of his dark blue suit coat.

Bowman was seated at his desk, looking up at the prosecutor. If he stood, he'd still have to look up. "The last man to see that surveyor alive," he said, "is the man who killed him. Peterson is no backshooter."

"How do you know? Perhaps he didn't like the surveyor's findings and didn't want his findings known.

Perhaps we wanted to take back the money he paid for the survey. Oh, he had a motive, all right."

"Maybe somebody else didn't want the surveyor's findings known."

Phipps's thin feminine eyebrows went up. "For instance?"

"For instance, the land company. Peterson's got some of the best grazing land in the territory, and it can be irrigated for crops. The land company would like to have it."

"Are you saying someone hired by the land company murdered the surveyor?"

"Somebody is trying to shoot out and burn out the settlers in this territory—you know that. Did you ever wonder who?"

"You find out who is committing these crimes, and I'll get warrants for their arrest, and I'll prosecute them to the fullest extent of the law."

Bowman felt like saying something sarcastic, but he swallowed and kept his mouth shut.

"Now, I want you to arrest this Peterson. You can swear in as many deputies as you need."

"The last thing I need is the kind of deputies the county board hired. They're tough, all right, when they've got everything goin' their way, but most of 'em don't know which end of a horse kicks. And every time I tell 'em to do something, they have to check with Hunter Howser."

Sheriff Bowman paused to see if the prosecuting attorney had anything to say to that, then went on, "Besides, I just don't believe Peterson did it. If he was going to shoot the surveyor, he wouldn't have followed him to within a few miles of town to do it."

191

"He wouldn't commit murder on his own land. There's enough circumstantial evidence to warrant an arrest on suspicion."

"Got a warrant?"

"I'll get a warrant."

Pegleg saw the rider coming. He grabbed his carbine, watched, and waited. Sunlight glinted off the silver-plated star on the rider's vest. He was alone. Carbine ready, but pointed at the ground, he waited silently.

"How do, Pete," Sheriff Bowman said when he was within talking distance.

"How do." Pegleg was wary.

"Mind if I help myself to a drink of water?"

With another long look around to be sure the sheriff was alone, Pegleg said, "Nope." Bowman dismounted, dropped his reins. He lifted the lid from the water barrel, filled the gourd dipper, and drank deeply. "Aahh."

The silence that followed was awkward. The lawman couldn't raise his eyes to meet Pegleg's. Finally, Pegleg said, "You on your way somewheres or is this as far as you're goin'?"

"This is my destination, Pete." He raise his eyes then. "Pete, I don't for one second believe you did it, but the prosecutor got a warrant for your arrest."

"Did what?"

"Kill the surveyor, Everett Godwin."

"Huh? Somebody killed 'im?"

"Yep. He was found late yesterday just a few miles west of Springer. He'd been shot in the back, and his

192

pockets had been turned inside out, and his packhorse unloaded and all his stuff scattered."

Peterson swore, "Damn. God damn it."

"Tell me, Pete, did you like what he found when he did his surveying?"

"Like it? I shore did. I've got more land than I thought I did."

"Is that right? Well, tell me this, did he leave some markers?"

"He drove iron stakes in the ground at ever' turn.".

"Are the stakes still there?"

"Well, hell, I can't see all of twenty-two sections from where we're standin', but I ain't seen nobody prowlin' around."

"Then maybe his murder didn't gain anybody anything. Unless it was out-and-out robbery? Did he have any money or anything valuable when he left here?"

"Only money that I know of was the double eagle I paid 'im. He coulda had more, but if he did, I didn't see it."

Thinking out loud, Sheriff Bowman said, "Hmm. Could have been robbery, but . . ."

"It was the land company and their hired goons that done it."

Silently, Bowman agreed, but he didn't express his opinion. "Well, anyway, the prosecutor went to the judge and got a warrant for your arrest on suspicion of murder."

"Well, now." Pegleg stood squarely in front of the sheriff, stood on one good foot and one wooden peg. His carbine was pointed down but could have been snapped up in a half-second.

"The evidence against you is circumstantial and

damned weak. Before I left town I went to the lawyer you've been talking to—Thomas Atwell—and told him about it. He promised he'd meet you in my office, then try to get the judge to set bond. He promised he'd get a bond hearing arranged as soon as possible.''

"Meantime, I'm s'posed to be locked up like Bill Watson was.''

With a sigh, the sheriff said, ''I'm afraid that's so.''

Another awkward silence followed before Bowman added, ''You've got too much to lose, Pete, to be a fugitive.''

This time, Pegleg sighed, ''I reckon you're right. I ain't done nothin' wrong, and I ain't runnin' from nodamnbody.''

Chapter Twenty-three

It was a newspaper from Denver that brought the news to Ella Fitzwater this time. She liked to read, and read every newspaper she could get her hands on. Sipping her morning coffee, she went through the news and the ads on the first four pages, then scanned page five. A name jumped off the page at her:

Joseph J. Fitzwater.

Her mouth formed an O as she read on. It was in the obituary columns. "Joseph J. Fitzwater died at his home Wednesday afternoon. The cause of death is unknown, but Coroner Marvin Buckholtz said he died from natural causes.

"Mr. Fitzwater was a laborer in the Great Western Groceries warehouse. He is survived by his wife, Mrs. Margaret Fitzwater. The couple had no children. Mrs. Fitzwater said her husband came to Denver from the goldfields in New Mexico Territory, and was reared on a farm in Texas.

"Funeral arrangements are being handled by the Riverside Mortuary."

"Ohh. Ohh, my." That was all Ella could say. "Ohh." She put the paper down.

"Oh, my." Then she thought, "It ain't him. It can't be him. It's another Joseph Fitzwater. But she knew it was her husband. There could be a thousand Joseph Fitzwaters in the world, but only one Joseph J. Fitzwater who'd been in the goldfields of New Mexico and was raised on a farm in Texas.

But this one had a wife. Make that two wives. Could it be?

"Ohh." For a while she sat at the table in her kitchen, too numb to move. Then she jumped up. "I've got to go to Denver. I've got to know."

Hastily, she started packing a leather satchel, then stopped. Her face crumpled. "Oh, Joe." She remembered the last time she'd seen him, remembered it as if it were yesterday. Walking away, head down, moving his feet like a man going to his own execution. A broken man. "Joe, oh, Joe."

Tears rolled down her cheeks. She sniffed her nose. Then she wiped her eyes with the palms of her hands and finished packing.

Two thirty-ton locomotives puffed, spun their twelve big driver wheels, and strained to get a string of rail cars over the Raton Pass. From the top of the pass it was easy going. Too easy. The train rolled so fast downhill that the passengers were afraid it would jump off the tracks. Brakes screeched, the whistle hooted, and passengers hung onto their seats with both hands, fear on their faces. Finally, the train rolled out of the mountains and down to the town of Trinidad in the new state of Colorado. Both engines' wheels were sliding on the rails before the train halted with the passen-

196

ger coach a hundred yards ahead of the depot. At Trinidad, one engine was uncoupled and shunted to a side track where it waited to help the next train going back over the pass. At Pueblo, Ella had to switch trains. The Sante Fe went east from there, and she had a long wait on a hard bench for the next Denver and Rio Grande.

Rather than just sit and wait, Ella walked through the business district of Pueblo. This was a bigger town than Raton and the stores had big glass windows with displays inside the windows. There were women's clothes, the likes of which she'd seen only in the Montgomery Ward catalog. There was a silver-mounted saddle, and shotgun chaps with strings of silver conchas down the legs. And there was a bookstore. Ella went in and browsed, and bought a copy of Cervantes's *Don Quixote*.

Finally on her way again, she sat next to a window and watched the prairie roll past. This was very much like northern New Mexico Territory, with the mountains on the west and the prairie on the east. It was only two hours from Pueblo to Colorado Springs, but the rest of the trip to Denver seemed to take forever.

The streets of Denver were all shadows at night, dark and threatening, in spite of the lamps on every corner. Ella had heard about the streets of Denver, where thugs with blackjacks and daggers waited for someone to come along. They knew passengers got off the trains at the Union Station, and they knew travelers had money in their pockets. They were there, hiding in the black shadows. Other women passengers had men waiting for them, men and carriages. The men travelers walked out of the depot in threes and fours.

Ella stayed in the huge well-lighted station until daylight. At times, she dozed on the hard bench, but mostly she fidgeted, trying to get comfortable. When daylight finally came, she went to the women's water closet, washed her face with cold water, combed her hair and straightened her clothes the best she could, then went looking for a respectable restaurant.

A cab carriage took her to the Riverside Mortuary, a stone building that looked like a church. Her breakfast of eggs and toast sat heavily in her stomach. It wasn't the food, it was the apprehension. After all these years she was going to see Joe again. Joe's body. Her stomach was churning.

The room inside had a pulpit, just like a church, with rows of benches. No one else was there. Her hard leather shoe heels clicked loudly on the wooden floor.

"Hello." Her voice was uncertain and weak. She tried again. "Hello. Anybody here?" Heels clicking, she went to a door at the other end of the room, behind the pulpit, and rapped lightly with her knuckles. "Hello. Anybody here?"

The door opened, and a small plump man stood there. His head was nearly bald, with only a few black hairs combed across the top. He wore a dark suit and a white shirt with a stiff collar. His voice sounded like it came from a tomb. "Ye-es?"

"Uh . . ." Ella didn't know what to say. "I, uh, came to see, uh, Joseph Fitzwater. I read in the newspapers that he died and his body is here."

"Ye-es. He's lying in state. His funeral is scheduled for this morning. Are you a relative?"

"Yes, uh, no, uh, he's somebody I used to know."

198

A puzzled look came over the wizened face, but he said, "Come with me, please."

She followed him past three caskets, all closed, lying on black-painted sawhorses, to another that was on a muslin-draped gurney, ready to be wheeled out to the pulpit. The casket was oak. The plump man opened one end.

It was Joe.

He was dressed in a dark suit coat with a blue cotton shirt and a string tie. His hair had been combed straight back. He was white, waxen, like a wax dummy.

Ella closed her eyes and swayed slightly. "Are you ill?" the plump man asked. "No," she said, opening her eyes and looking again at the face of her husband. "No, I'm, uh, I'm all right." Then she turned and walked away.

She wanted to leave, then, just leave, but as she walked through the door to the outer room, three women came in. The plump man said, "Good morning, Mrs. Fitzwater. The service will begin in an hour." Ella had to have a look at the woman, wondering at first which was Joe's wife—other wife. She didn't have to wonder long.

To Ella, the plump man asked, "Are you acquainted with the widow?"

"No," Ella mumbled, "I, we've never met."

"Then allow me the pleasure of introducing you."

She was pretty in a plain kind of way, with light brown hair combed across her forehead, and a black pillbox hat on her head. Her long dress was black, and she wore a black shawl over her shoulders. "How do you do," she said in a voice that had a slight nasal sound.

"Pleased to meet you," Ella said without volunteering her name.

"Were you a friend of my husband?"

"Uh . . ." Ella had to lie. "Yes, I was acquainted with him years ago in New Mexico. I, uh, was in town and read about his death, and had to pay my respects."

"Are you staying for the service?"

"No, I, uh, have to leave. Uh, tell me, what did he die of?"

"It was the all-overs. We don't know what made him sick, but he was sick all over. These are my sisters, here—" and she introduced the other two women.

"Well, I'm surely sorry about J— Mr. Fitzwater's death. He was a fine man. I wish I could stay, but I have to go."

Outside, she paused, turned to the door that had closed behind her, and whispered, "Goodbye, Joe."

Denver was an interesting city, but Ella didn't stay. She had the feeling that if she stayed, someone, somehow, would find out that she was Joe's other wife, that Joe'd had two wives. She didn't want the other widow to know that. The woman had enough grief. Too, Ella didn't feel like a widow. Joe's death was no loss to her. She'd spent countless hours worrying and wondering about Joe, hoping his luck had changed for the better. She had often asked herself if she would take him back if he came back. It was a tough question to answer, and she hadn't found the answer.

Now all that was past.

Weary to the point of collapse, Ella walked from the Santa Fe depot in Raton to her Willow Springs Liquor and Games. For the past two days and nights she'd slept on hard benches and on swaying, shaking, rattling rail coaches. All she wanted to do now was to fall into bed and sleep for a week. And that was what she intended to do—as soon as she checked her place of business to be sure everything was going all right.

Everything wasn't all right. The saloon was doing fine, but the news was bad. First, she was told that Pegleg Peterson was in jail in Springer, accused of murder. Then she was told that two settlers on Rayado Creek had been burned out, and one man was seriously wounded when he traded shots with the arsonists. The man had a wife and four kids. His neighbors had taken him to Taos, where he was being cared for by a doctor, but the doctor didn't give him much of a chance.

One by one the settlers were leaving. The grant people were winning.

Without unpacking her satchel, Ella hurried back to the depot. The helper engine had been shunted to a side track, and the first engine had been filled with water. The coal tender had also been refilled. The train was ready to go again. Ella bought her ticket and got on board a few minutes before it started moving.

On the way to Springer, she wondered what she could do for Pete. She couldn't believe he'd killed the surveyor. She knew darned well he didn't. Pete would fight the Mexican army if he thought he had to, but it just wasn't in him to commit cold-blooded murder. What she could do for him, she didn't know, but she had to go see him, try to do something.

Stepping out of the coach at the depot, she looked across the tracks at the stockyards where only a few days ago she'd been part of a citizens' army that had taken the law into their own hands—and won. But as she walked toward the courthouse, she knew they hadn't really won. The battles were being fought in the courtrooms here in the county seat, in the territorial capitol of Santa Fe, and even in the U.S. government courts in Colorado.

Gunfire made a difference in the short run, but in the long run the lawyers and judges would have the final say.

Ella's spirits went up a few notches when she recognized Wild Bill Watson coming out of the courthouse. They met on the plankwalk in front of the courthouse and grinned at each other.

"They tell me," Bill said, "that you're a well-traveled woman. Why, the way I heard it, you even traveled all the way up to Denver."

"Who told you a tale like that?"

"One of your saloon customers. He comes and goes 'tween here and Raton, and he knows what's goin' on in both towns."

"Yeah, well, I did go up to Denver. In fact, I just got back to Raton in time to buy a ticket to Springer. You remember me telling you about Joe, my husband? Well, he died in Denver."

"Oh." The grin faded from Bill's face. "I'm sorry to hear that. I guess."

"I read about it in a Denver newspaper, and I had to go up there to be sure it was him and pay my respects. It was Joe. He'd married again."

"I, uh, don't know what to say, Ella."

"That's over. Right now I'm worried about Pete. Have you been in to see him?"

"Yeah. He's . . . not very happy. But that lawyer

202

feller was there, too, and he thinks he can get 'im out of there *mañana*."

"Thomas Atwell? How's he gonna do that?"

"He thinks the judge will set bail. Pete's got enough money to pay bail."

"Oh, I hope so. Poor old Pete. He must feel like an animal in a cage."

"Yeah. I promised I'd spend the night at his place. I hear the militiamen's been burning down settler's houses. If they burn down my shack I won't've lost much, but Pete's got a lot more work and money in his house."

"Yes, it would be a darned shame if he lost it."

"I gotta get goin', Ella. It's gonna be dark before I get there. You stayin' in Springer tonight?"

"I guess so. In one of these hotels. There won't be a train back to Raton before tomorrow. I don't know what I can do for Pete, but I had to come down here and let him know I'll do everything I can."

"He'll be glad to see you. Sheriff Bowman is in his office, and he'll let you visit with Pete. You'll give his spirits a boost. Well, so long, Ella. See you at the baile."

Yes, she thought as she watched Bill untie a horse from the hitchrail, mount, and ride off. At the baile. It won't be long now. And the way things have been going . . . with night marauders burning houses, the settlers will be afraid to leave home. They won't show.

Things just weren't going right.

Chapter Twenty-four

Judge Wilford Mitchell was determined to carefully consider all sides of any legal dispute and to be impartial. More important, he was determined to thoroughly study the law, the Supreme Court's rulings, and the findings of other land-court judges. But too many things had happened. Settlers attacked at night, their homes burned. A surveyor murdered, shot in the back. And he'd just learned that the settler who'd been shot and taken to Taos had died, leaving a widow and four children. The settlers were stubborn and they were quite possibly claiming land that didn't belong to them, but they were not arsonists or backshooters.

Now here was this elderly settler standing before him, standing on one good leg and one homemade prosthesis, accused of murdering the surveyor. His attorney had argued that the defendant was innocent, that he had nothing to gain by the surveyor's death, that the survey had been in his favor. The prosecutor had argued that no one knew what the surveyor had discovered, and that this settler had killed him to keep his discoveries from being known. Judge Mitchell had

had doubts when he was talked into signing a warrant for this man's arrest, but he hadn't wanted to be accused of standing in the way of a murder investigation.

Well, this wasn't a trial, only a hearing to determine whether bond should be allowed and how much.

Bang, went the judge's gavel. "It appears to me, Mr. Prosecutor, that Mr. Peterson had no obvious motive for the murder of Mr. Godwin. Further, he is a property owner, and as such is a good risk for bond. I hereby order the defendant released on his own recognizance." *Bang,* went the gavel again.

"But, Your Honor, it hasn't been determined that the defendant is a property owner."

Bang. Judge Mitchell looked down from his bench, scowling. Even the six-foot-four Zachary Phipps had to look up to him. "Are you sure, Mr. Prosecutor, that you want to argue with me?"

"No, no, Your Honor. I will accept the court's decision."

Bill Watson had spent the night in Pete's bed hidden in the alders near Pete's house. It had been a dark night, but a quiet one. Sometime before midnight the half-moon had gone behind a cloud, and by morning the sky was overcast. This was good. The country needed rain. He fried some bacon and ate some of Pete's bread, then saddled his horse and started back to his own place. With a wry grin, he wondered whether his shack was still standing.

His horse splashed across Otero Creek, and Bill pushed willow branches out of his face, then reined up suddenly. Four riders were over there, not more than five hundred yards away. Immediately, he dismounted, keeping his horse back in the brush, and watched. They rode on past, casting glances toward the creek and the house, headed somewhere northwest. Where? Bill wondered. If they were headed for Cimarron, they would have been going straight west. He watched them as they stopped, and two riders dismounted. One pulled a sheet of paper from his shirt pocket and unfolded it. The two studied it a moment, then mounted again. The four talked among themselves, then turned north. Now their horses splashed across Otero Creek.

Bill stepped into his saddle and rode to where they'd crossed the creek. Carefully, he followed their tracks, staying in the alders and willow brush. At the edge of the brush, he saw them ahead, still going north. Two of the men appeared to be uncomfortable on horseback, riding their stirrups too short for a long ride, and sitting hunched over in their saddles. The other two had spent plenty of time horseback. Bill watched them until they rode over a low rise, then followed. Before he topped the rise, he got down, dropped the reins, and walked, bending low to the top. There he lay on his belly and watched them. They were headed for the Vermejo.

Too far away to see exactly what they were doing, Bill was puzzled. They rode alongside the river, looking at the ground. Looking for what? Whatever it was, they must have found it, because they all got down and stood over it. Then two of them took hold of something on the ground and pulled up. They pulled something out of the ground, something that looked like a stake, and one carried it to the edge of the Vermejo and threw it out into the water.

Then they studied that sheet of paper again, got horseback, and turned south.

It was a surveyor that Pete was accused of killing. Pete had said the man had surveyed his land and had staked it out. Were these gents pulling up survey stakes?

Yep. Sure as shootin', that's what they were doing. They were undoing the work that Pete had paid for. That goddamn land company was still trying to prove that Pete didn't own any land or that he owned less land then he claimed.

Damn, Bill thought, I'd sure like to get a closer look at 'em so I could recognize 'em later.

Thunder rolled over the land. Lightning flashed on top of the Raton Mountains. Bill knew he couldn't follow these goons farther without being seen. If they looked behind themselves at all, they'd see him. But he was mounted on Dunnie, and the gelding's speed had carried him out of danger before.

"Well, partner," he said, "let's just see how close we can get to 'em before they start shootin'."

Fresh air never smelled so good. Arnold Peterson stood on the plankwalk in front of the courthouse and inhaled deeply. The sky was overcast, threatening rain. Good, Pegleg thought, the country needs rain. Now that he had the Cruz family's cattle grazing on his land, rain was needed more than ever to make the grass grow. Even if I get wet, even if I half-drown, he thought, let it rain.

He had to pay for his horse's keep at the livery pens, and he thought that was unfair, but he was so glad to be out of jail that he paid without a word. He couldn't get out of town fast enough. It was late afternoon, and it would be dark before he got home, and he'd holler loud and clear before he rode across the creek. Otherwise Wild Bill might shoot first and then find out who he'd shot. But he didn't get more than a mile out of town before he saw Wild Bill coming.

Bill was coming at a high trot, riding his good-looking dun horse. Pegleg went to meet him. *"Hola,* Bill, what're you doin' back in town?"

Without answering, Bill grinned and asked, "What kind of birds don't fly?"

Pegleg grinned, too, inside his beard. "You wouldn't be referrin' to me as a jailbird, would you?"

"Naw, your hide's too tough to grow feathers. What am I doin'? Wal, I'll tell you what I'm doin'. I just watched four gents pull up a couple of surveyors' stakes on your land. They saw me and shot at me and they're right behind me somewhere."

Pegleg's grin vanished. "The hell you say. Did you get a good look at 'em?"

"They spotted me before I could get a look at their faces, but I know what color their horses are and what kind of hats they're wearin'. Thought I'd get to town ahead of 'em and see if they ride in. I'll know 'em if I see 'em horseback."

"Well, goddamn." Peterson studied the western horizon. "Maybe what we oughta do is get back in town, tie up these horses, and see who comes ridin' in from the west."

"Exactly what I had in mind. I'm sure glad you're

out of jail. From what I could see, I'd guess two of those gents're hardcases.''

"Let's do that.'' Pegleg turned his horse around, and the two of them rode back to a saloon near the western edge of town, tied their horses to a hitchrail, stood on the walk, and waited. They didn't have to wait long.

Four riders came in on the main east-west street. Their horses were sweating despite the cool air, and they traveled at a shuffling trot. Peterson said, "They look like they been chasin' somebody. That dun horse of yours must of run plumb away from 'em.''

"That's them.''

As the riders went past, one of them squinted at Bill and at the dun horse tied to a hitchrail, then spoke quietly to his partners. All four heads swiveled toward Bill.

"They recognize me, too,'' Bill said. "Whatta you think we oughta do?''

"Let's foller 'em. See where they go.''

Where they went was to the livery pens. Standing half a city block away, Bill asked again, "Whatta you think we oughta do?''

"Well, we could brace 'em right there. Like you said, two of 'em look like hardcases, but the other two look more like city toughs. We c'n take 'em on.''

"Whatever you say.'' Bill adjusted his gunbelt and holster.

"But,'' Pegleg added, "if we was to shoot 'em, we'd get arrested for murder, and I seen enough of that jail. Sheriff Bowman was in his office a little while ago. Let's get him to brace 'em. If he needs help, then we can shoot the shit out of 'em.''

210

"Whatever you say."

"If you'll go fetch the sheriff I'll watch 'em, 'case they leave before you get back."

"Wal, I never was much good at runnin', but I'll get back as fast as I can." Bill left, half-walking and half-running.

Pegleg watched, waited. The four men offsaddled their horses, led them to a feedlot, and turned them loose. The livery hostler made no offer to help. When they were ready to leave, they cast wary eyes at Pegleg, talked among themselves. One walked away, going to Pegleg's left, walking fast. The others stood their ground.

If they all split up, he'd lose them, Pegleg knew. He could only follow one at a time. Come on, Bill.

Then Bill and Sheriff Bowman came up behind him, breathing hard from hurrying. "One's gone, but the other three are still over there," Pegleg said.

"All right," the sheriff said, "I'll go over and question 'em. From what you told me, I ain't got enough to arrest 'em, but I'll question 'em anyhow."

"Want some help?"

"No. This is my job."

"Two of 'em look like trouble," Pegleg said. "If they start shootin', we start shootin'."

"Mind if we get a little closer?" Bill asked.

"Stay back. Just stay back and let me do this." The sheriff pulled his hat down tighter, like a man about to get on a bronc, and walked with determined steps to the livery barn.

Pegleg and Bill followed a ways, but stayed back. They were ready if needed.

From where they stood they could hear the men's

voices, but couldn't understand what was said. The three goons were gesticulating, but making no moves toward their guns. The sheriff was talking quietly. Then all heads turned as two more men appeared. One was the goon who'd left, and the other was . . .

"Aw, hell," Pegleg said, "I might of knowed he was mixed up in this."

"I'm not surprised," Bill said. "Hunter Howser's their boss."

Talk at the barn continued for a few more minutes, then Sheriff Bowman turned and came back to Bill and Pete. "I ain't got enough evidence to arrest 'em," Bowman said.

"What's their story?"

"They said they were looking at some surveyed land that Mr. Howser is interesting in buying, and they were looking for survey markers."

"Ain't so," Pegleg said. "My land ain't for sale, and ol' Howser knows it."

"He said he thinks it might be for sale eventually, and he wants to know something about it. They denied pulling up survey stakes."

"They're lyin' in their teeth. I seen 'em."

"I believe you. I'll take all this information to the prosecutor and try to get him to get a warrant for their arrest. I have to admit, however, that I doubt he'll do anything."

"I'll bet he won't."

"Well, anyway, I got a look at their faces, and I warned 'em that if they ever get in the middle of anything else suspicious, I'll lock 'em up."

"Shore."

"Now, don't you boys go over there and start a fight. I wish you'd go back to your homes. Will you do that?"

Pegleg and Wild Bill looked at each other. "Whatta you say, Pete?"

The mouth inside the beard twisted in disgust. "Piss on 'em. Let's go home."

The rain started as they rode out of town. It was a cold high-country rain. But both men had other things on their minds.

"I think I've got 'im figured out, now," Bill said. "Ol' Howser. It was somethin' he told the sheriff."

"I'll bet I know what you're thinkin'. And I'll bet you're right. Yessir, ol' Howser is a schemer. A schemer and a killer."

Chapter Twenty-five

Everyone in the Willow Creek saloon was talking about the weather. The rain was a lifesaver. Now the grass and crops would grow, the rivers and creeks would fill up again, the country would green up, livestock would get fat.

But the dark gloomy weather had Ella Fitzwater gloomy. The drizzle that had been coming down for the past two days was the kind of rain that soaked in and made things grow, sure. But it would ruin—just flat ruin—an outdoor dance.

With a new umbrella, she walked out to the dance floor, walked in the mud, getting her shoes muddy, getting the bottom of her skirt wet. "Hell and damnation," she said under her breath. The wooden floor was soaked, and the new lumber was shrinking even more. The boards bent under her feet.

Looking at the sky, getting rain in her face, she silently pleaded, *Stop it, will you? Just for two days. Then you can rain again.* The sky was solid gray, obscuring the horizons, covering the Raton Mountains. There wasn't a break in the clouds anywhere.

Well, there was nothing she could do about it. Not one damned thing. She turned to go back to the main street. Hell and damnation.

Wild Bill was singing. While he drove a small bunch of cattle back toward Otero Creek, water dripping from his hat brim, his worn rain slicker leaking water around his knees, he sang, "Oh, it ain't gonna rain no more, no more. It ain't gonna rain no more. How in heck can I warsh my neck if it ain't gonna rain no more."

"Boy, oh, boy," he said, "this's just what the doctor ordered. Just watch the grass grow now." To the cattle, he said, "Get fat, you brutes." He knew, however, that longhorn cattle never got fat and filled out, they only got big bellies.

Otero Creek had picked up volume, and his horse waded water up to its knees. "Could irrigate some of this wheat grass along here if I had the ambition," he said. "Could cut some hay for next winter. But, hell, I prob'ly won't be here next winter."

Inside his one-room shack, he shook water off his hat and slicker, got a fire going in the barrel-shaped sheepherder's stove, and put a pot of beans on to boil. He resumed singing: "Beans, beans . . . oh, never mind. I gotta make myself act and look civilized. I gotta cut my whiskers off, I gotta warsh myself and a shirt and pants, and . . . I've got a baile to go to."

While he was doing all that, he thought, If the Almighty up there did everything just right, it would stop raining this afternoon, and the sun would come out and dry things up, and it would start raining again a week from now. Can't let this rain ruin Ella's baile.

The rain did slow to an intermittent drizzle, but the sky was still a dirty gray, and no clearing weather was in sight. Ella got some men to put up four posts and stretch a piece of canvas over them to make a shelter for the musicians. They carried some chairs from her saloon for the musicians to sit on.

It was noon on the Fourth of July, and she'd seen no one from out of town. The settlers wouldn't come, but maybe the town folks would show up. As the day wore on, Ella's morale sunk lower and lower. Then Wild Bill Watson came riding down the street, and she had to smile.

"Bill," she yelled, standing on the boardwalk, holding an umbrella over her head. "Bill Watson. Yoo-hoo."

Reining over, Bill sat his saddle and grinned. "Told you, Ella, you oughta go to church once in a while. The Good Lord's got it in for you now."

Ella went along with the joke. "Is that why it's raining today? Durn. I oughta kick myself."

"You been sinnin' lately? The Lord hates a sinner, you know."

"Well, if drinking coffee and sleeping late is a sin, then I'm the one to blame."

"Yup, yup, you're the one, all right."

"Oh, go take care of your horse, Bill Watson."

Then she saw a buckboard wagon pulled by two horses coming with a man and woman on the spring seat. "Say, lady," the man yelled, "where's this big baile goin' on?" The man and woman wore broad-brim hats with the brims turned down and canvas coats.

"Over there." Ella pointed. "You'll see the dance

217

floor, and there's plenty of space for you and grass for your horses. I'm sorry to say there's no shelter.''

"We brung our own." Two towheaded kids peeked from under a tarp in the back of the wagon.

"Where do you hail from?"

"Down by the Cimarron. It's a long day's ride."

Oh, my, Ella thought as the wagon went on down the street, I hope it's worth it.

Another buckboard came from the east, and four cowboys came riding in from the north. They offsaddled and hobbled their horses beyond the dance floor and came stomping up the plankwalk to the Willow Springs saloon. Long yellow raincoats flopped around their boots.

By dark only four wagons were parked near the dance floor. The train from Springer brought a dozen more people, and the folks of Raton began strolling over. Bill and two of the cowboys helped Ella light the lamps that hung from high poles. The lamps had tin shades over the tops to keep the rain out. Bill struck a match and reached up to light a lamp, then froze and stared at something. The match burned down to his fingers, forcing him to drop it immediately, but still he stared. Ella followed his gaze.

It was Eileen Cruz, her brother, Tomás, and another man, a Mexican dressed in a business suit with a necktie. Eileen Cruz would cause any man to stop and stare. Beautiful. Her hair was combed straight down, pulled behind her neck and held there with a silver comb. Her dress was dark, form-fitting from the knees up with a lot of colorful embroidery. A dark lace shawl covered her shoulders, and a red rose was pinned to the right side of her hair. The well-dressed man held an umbrella over her head.

Ella wasn't acquainted with the Cruzes, but she had seen them in town and had heard about them. After seeing Eileen Cruz, she looked down at herself, at what the haberdasher called a "Ladies Rainy Day Skirt" of durable plain cloth, and realized what a plain woman she was. Plain as mud.

Well, she was glad Eileen Cruz had come. The beautiful Mexican lady added class to the small group. But she felt like bopping Bill for staring at her.

"If you don't shut your mouth, you're gonna strangle on rainwater," she whispered.

"Huh? Oh."

Over by the wagons, the men had built a bonfire, fed mostly with broken wooden boxes and crates. A handful of people with pieces of canvas draped over their heads gathered around the fire, talking. Well-armed vigilantes took positions around the dance floor, about twenty of them. There were merchants, ranchers, railroaders, sawmill workers, and a few ranch foremen. Only the vigilantes were armed. Others left their guns at their wagons, in their hotel rooms or homes, or with their saddles at the livery barn. The Cruzes and a few women stood under the tarp roof that had been put up for the musicians. They chatted and seemed happy. Ella went over and introduced herself to Eileen Cruz. She was surprised at how well the Mexican spoke English and at how friendly and charming she was. She seemed to fit in very well with the Anglo women.

"We appreciate your efforts in arranging this get-together," Eileen Cruz said. "And we'll never forget how you and other Anglos saved our cattle."

"Are you going back home tomorrow?"

"Yes. We're staying with friends tonight."

Ella had to admit to herself that she couldn't blame Bill Watson for staring at Eileen Cruz.

Then the musicians began to arrive. First, a man with a fiddle, then a Mexican with a guitar, then the Mexican cornetist. Then another fiddler.

They tuned their instruments with a lot of fiddle-string screeching and guitar twanging. "Whatta you say, let's get started," a fiddler said. "How about we start with a waltz. Ever'body knows how to waltz."

"Excuse me, *señors*, but I'm not sure I can . . ."

"That's all right. You'll get your turn."

One of the fiddlers started with a slow waltz, and the Mexican guitarist picked up the tune and played accompanying chords. The second fiddler joined in. Not good, Ella thought, but it has a rhythm.

The well-dressed Mexican man led Eileen Cruz onto the floor, and they were the first couple to dance. Bill recognized the man as the lawyer who'd represented the Cruzes in court. Another couple in work-worn clothes followed. Then another. Soon four couples were waltzing on the wooden planks.

Not exactly a crowd, Ella thought, but they seemed to enjoy themselves.

After a few minutes, the waltz petered out. The musicians looked at each other. "Excuse me, *señors*, may I play my horn?"

"Shore."

The Mexican played a Spanish ballad, a song about

a broken-hearted *ranchero*. The guitarist played the chords, and soon one of the fiddlers picked up the tune.

Eileen Cruz and her partner danced well together, and other couples were able to move with the music. But no one was laughing, only shuffling their feet. "Say, fellers, let's play a schottische. That'll get the ball started."

The fiddler was right. The music from two fiddles and a guitar brought everyone to the dance floor. Now eight couples were dancing lively, stomping their feet and laughing. Men without women stood at the edges of the floor, tapped their feet and smiled. Eileen Cruz and her partner tried, but couldn't figure out the steps. They too stood aside, clapped to the rhythm of the music, and laughed.

The new, wet floorboard creaked and bent, but didn't break.

When the schottische ended, the dancers began to drift back toward the bonfire, but one of the fiddlers yelled, "Hey, you ladies, you can't quit now. There's men here that ain't got nobody to dance with." His fiddle screeched, and then went into a hoedown. Some-one sang along:

"Get outta the way for old Dan Tucker, he's too late to have his supper."

"Ella, if you don't mind havin' your toes stomped on, I'd sure admire to dance with you. Try to."

"Sure, Bill. Just move your feet and holler."

With her right hand in his left, and his right hand on her waist, he moved his feet, looking down, careful not to step on her. "Come on, Bill, I won't break."

Soon he was stomping his feet in rhythm to the mu-sic and yelling, "Whoo. Hoo, hoo." A cowboy, dancing with his boss's wife, threw his head back and yelled, "Heeyou. Hooeee."

All the women were dancing. Most men could only stand aside and watch, stomp their feet, and laugh at the antics of their neighbors.

Two more Mexican couples showed up. These women wore skirts that were wide and colorful. They had duck-cloth shawls over their heads and shoulders.

"Get outta the way for old Dan Tucker. The table's cleared, the dishes're washed, and there's nothin' left but a rotten squash."

By the time that dance ended, the dancers were winded, but happy. Their hair was plastered to their heads, and water dripped off their chins, but no one seemed to care.

Before the other musicians could decide what to play next, the Mexican guitarist fastened a capo over the fifth fret on his instrument and began drumming four fingers across the strings to make a continuous rolling sound.

That was a signal for the Mexicans. Eileen Cruz and her partner started, and soon all the Mexican couples were stamping their feet and snapping their fingers in a flamenco. The guitarist speeded up the rhythm, rolling his fingers across the strings. The dancers picked up speed, too, stamping their feet unbelievingly fast and whirling to the music. Anglos could only watch in admiration. They applauded when the music stopped.

But before the dancers could move off the floor, the musicians started another waltz. Wild Bill ran his fingers over his hair, wiped water off his face, summoned his courage, and approached Eileen Cruz.

"Pardon me, *señorita, señor,* may I . . . ?"

"Of course, Mr. Watson."

It was the first time he'd ever touched her. His heart beat so fast he thought it would jump out of his chest. His pulse raced. His knees went weak. She smiled, and her face was only inches from his face. He stumbled, mumbled a "Pardon me."

"Quite all right, Mr. Watson, you're dancing very well."

She was so light on her feet she seemed to float. Her breath was as sweet as a mountain morning. Wild Bill wanted to hold her forever.

"Mr. Watson." She spoke softly, sweetly, smiling. "The music has stopped."

"Huh? Oh. Excuse me, I, uh . . ." Damn. Did he make a fool of himself?

"Thank you very much, Mr. Watson."

"Oh, uh, thank you, ma'am." He led her back to the musicians' shelter.

Ella had been dancing with a railroader in bib overalls, and when she looked around, she was pleased. Everyone was smiling and chatting happily. Everyone was having a good time. Ella was smiling. Then her smile faded.

A ruckus had started.

Chapter Twenty-six

There was no smiling on the east side of the dance floor. Men's voices were raised in anger. One was louder than the others: "I'm an officer of the law and I, by god, ain't gonna give up my weapon."

"Nobody, and we mean nodamnbody, gets close to that floor with a gun."

"Who the hell do you think you are? I'm the law around here."

"Tonight, Mr. Deputy, we're the law."

Ella hurried over. Bill was right behind her. It was Deputy Duncan, his plump face red in the lamplight. Two vigilantes stood between him and the dance floor, and when he tried to walk around them, they moved and continued to block his way.

Bill grumbled, "Might of knowed it was him."

Trying to placate everyone, Ella said, "He is a deputy sheriff, sworn to keep the peace, among other things. Maybe we should let him keep his gun."

"We agreed, Ella, that only members of the vigilance committee carried guns."

"We didn't plan on a deputy sheriff." To Deputy

Duncan, she said, "We so seldom see you anywhere, we didn't expect to see you tonight."

"You don't see me 'cuz I'm workin'. Now, do I get up there or do I arrest the whole damned bunch of you for interferin' with an officer of the law?"

Knowing that if the deputy didn't have his way, he'd make so much trouble the dance would be over, Ella said, "Maybe we oughta let him through."

"Gentlemen," a vigilante said, "what should we do?"

"Aw, let 'im in. He's gonna throw a kiddie tantrum if we don't."

"All right, Mr. Deputy." Vigilantes stepped back and let the deputy through.

Another schottische soon had the fracas forgotten. Every woman in sight was dancing. "Like I told everybody," Ella said to Bill, "the women are gonna have to dance their feet off."

"They're havin' fun. Rain or no rain, it's workin' fine, Ella. 'Scuse me, I didn't mean to step on your toes."

"I'll have sore feet tomorrow, but meantime keep dancin', Bill."

The next tune was a foxtrot, and Ella told Bill, "Just pretend you're walking in a square, one foot at a time. You'll get it." Bill was watching his feet when a cowboy touched him on the shoulder. "Mind if I cut in?"

"Why, no." Bill did mind, but he knew there weren't enough women to go around. He stepped back. That was when another ruckus started.

This one was minor, but it brought an angry bile to Bill's throat. Deputy Duncan was trying to force himself between Eileen Cruz and her partner.

226

In three long steps, Wild Bill was there. Without a word, he grabbed the deputy by the back of his shirt collar and dragged him backward. The deputy was off balance, being dragged backward, and Bill kept him off balance until they were in the mud away from the dancers. Two vigilantes came over, but made no move to intervene.

Duncan's hand went to his six-gun. Bill beat him to it, and got hold of the gun before it cleared leather. With his right elbow, Bill punched the deputy in the face. Hit him twice more with his elbow, a forward blow and a backward blow. Then he twisted the gun out of the deputy's hand and dropped it in the mud.

Men stepped back as Bill grabbed the deputy by the hair with one hand and the shirt collar with the other. Dragged him back out of the lamplight, out beyond the circle of people. A few men followed, but Bill growled, "Keep out of this. We've got somethin' to settle."

The music played on, but fewer people were dancing.

Out in the semidarkness, Bill gave Deputy Duncan a shove, and growled, "You said once there'd be another meetin'. This is it."

"I'm an officer of the law, and—"

Bill slapped him open-handed. "You just picked on a friend of mine, you yellowbelly son of a bitch."

Moving surprisingly fast, Duncan ducked his head and came in swinging. Swinging wildly. A hard fist caught Bill on the side of his head and another connected squarely with his mouth. Staggering, Bill wiped a shirtsleeve across his mouth, then ducked as another onslaught of fists came his way. His feet slipped in the mud and he went down. A size-ten boot just missed his head. The deputy kicked again. Bill rolled away and got up just in time to dodge another kick.

His clothes, his face, were covered with mud. No time to even think about that.

Boring in again, Duncan grabbed Bill in a bearhug and butted him in the face with his head. Pain shot through Bill, blinding pain. He staggered back, trying to clear his vision. The deputy bored in, swinging hard fists at Bill's face.

Seeing an opening, Bill ducked low and threw his right fist into the deputy's stomach. A loud "Oh-o-o" came from the deputy's mouth, and he doubled over. Bill threw an uppercut that caught the deputy squarely in the face and straightened him up. A roundhouse left connected with the deputy's right eye, and another right-hand blow knocked him down.

"Get up," Bill hissed. "Get up, you son of a bitch."

For a long moment, Bill waited, fists doubled. Finally, moving slowly, the deputy started to rise. Bill stepped back to give him room.

Then suddenly, the deputy lunged forward, grabbed Bill around the waist. Both men went down in the mud. They rolled, punching with fists and elbows. Bill took a punch in the jaw that made his teeth rattle. He hit back, again and again, felt his blows connect.

Gradually, Duncan's struggles weakened. Bill found himself sitting astraddle of him. He smacked him twice more, once on the nose and once in the right eye. The deputy's struggles ceased.

Standing, slowly, painfully, Bill's chest heaved as he tried to get his wind. He was beginning to think he would never breathe normally again. Two vigilantes came up, looked down at the deputy, looked closely at Bill's muddy, bleeding face.

"Which one are you?"

"I'm . . ." Panting, Bill managed, "I'm . . . not him."

"No, I reckon you ain't him. Is he the deputy?"

"That's . . . him."

A crowd had gathered, but stayed back. A vigilante said, "It's all right, folks. It's all over. Nobody was hurt. Go on with your dancin'." They turned back to the dance floor. All but Ella and a few vigilantes.

"Bill?" She looked closely at Bill's face. "Are you hurt?"

"Naw." Grinning, tasting mud, he added, "You don't happen to have a bucket of water around, do you? If you do, just pour it on me."

Two men helped Deputy Duncan to his feet. He wiped mud from his eyes, and said, "You . . . you're under arrest."

"You gotta be joshin'," a vigilante said. "Do you actually wanta charge this man with a crime? You'd have to admit you started a fight and got whipped fair and square? There's plenty of witnesses, you know."

"If I was you," another said, "I'd keep my mouth shut."

"Keep your mouth shut and do your job and you might live this down. Make a fuss and you'll get run out of the territory."

The music started again, a lively hoedown. All the women and half the men were dancing. Someone sang, "Oh, I was drivin' down a new cut road with a tired team and a heavy load. I cracked the whip and the leader sprung, and I said goodbye to the wagon tongue.''

Deputy Duncan started to say something more, then turned and walked away.

"He had it coming," Ella said.

"Maybe," a vigilante put in, "he'll be a better man now. If he ain't, we're gonna have to load him and his wife in a wagon and send 'em down the road."

"His wife's all right," Ella said. "Don't take it out on her."

"Wouldn't think of it."

"Well, Bill." Ella took Bill by the arm. "Let's go find you a rain barrel to stick your head in." She started to lead Bill away. But Bill held back.

"No, Ella. I apologize all to pieces for gettin' in a fight at your baile. You go on back and have yourself a good time."

"Where will you sleep tonight?"

"Wal, now"—Bill grinned through the mud on his face—"you wouldn't . . . ?"

"No."

"I reckon I'll sleep in the livery barn."

"Go soak your head, Bill Watson."

The rain was still an intermittent drizzle, not heavy, but enough to get everyone wet. Men who weren't dancing found more wood to put on the bonfire. Planks on the dance floor bent under the weight of twenty feet, and the gaps between them widened. A woman's heel went between two planks, and she tripped.

Her partner thought she'd been shoved by the man behind her, and he grabbed the man by the shoulder, turned him around, and shook a big hard fist at him. "Don't you, by god, do that again, or I'll—"

Before he could finish what he'd started to say, two vigilantes had him by the arms and another was in front of him. "None of that. Behave yourselves, now."

"He didn't push me," the woman said. "I tripped."

"Oh. Wal, then, in that case I apologize, mister."

With a shrug, the man turned back to his partner and resumed dancing.

A cowboy politely asked one of the Mexican women to dance. He held her loosely, carefully keeping his distance between them. Ella wanted to dance with one of the Mexican men, just to help race relations, but didn't know how to approach him. Eileen Cruz introduced Ella to her escort, and the Mexican lawyer was put into a position where he had to ask Ella to dance.

Everyone was wet, but laughing and joking. All were enjoying themselves. Ella was pleased.

Then everything fell apart.

Chapter Twenty-seven

Gunfire came from the darkness over south. Six, seven, eight shots. Everyone scattered; the dance floor was deserted. Men ran for their guns at the wagons and at the livery barns. The vigilantes ran south, trying to see where the shots came from. Men yelled, "Over here. I think they're over here."

"Where? I don't see anybody."

"It's too damn dark to see anybody. Be careful you don't shoot at the wrong man."

"Anybody shot?"

"Don't know. Wish I could see who done it."

"I can guess."

Hoofbeats came from the dark night, going south. It sounded like a herd of horses.

"Whoever they are, they're leavin'."

"No use tryin' to catch 'em in the dark."

"The sons of bitches'll be halfway to Springer before we can get horseback."

"That's where they come from, all right."

A vigilante yelled, "Hey, anybody shot? Anybody hurt?"

No answer.

"Well, I guess nobody was hurt."

"Who was they?"

"They went south, and they no doubt came from the south. Guess who."

"Them damn militiamen. They didn't shoot at anybody, they only wanted to break up the baile."

"That's what they done."

Ella didn't chase after the shooters. She had no weapon, and she couldn't run in her long skirt. When a man yelled that the shooters were gone, the women gathered at the bonfire. Someone added wood to the fire, and the flames reached higher. Bill Watson came running, carrying his six-gun.

"What happened?" he asked Ella. "Who was shootin'?"

"Whoever did the shooting, Bill, left in a hurry going south. Nobody was hurt."

Holstering his gun, Bill said with disgust, "Them."

"Yeah, them."

"Wal, anyhow, while they was firing their guns around here, they wasn't tryin' to burn out Pete or some other settler."

"There's that." But Ella was bitter. "They sure put a stop to the dance."

A woman said, "It's awfully late, anyhow, Miz Fitzwater. It's time we all dried ourselfs off and crawled under some blankets."

"It was fun, Miz Fitzwater. I'm glad we came."

Eileen Cruz stepped up to Ella. "We had a very good time, Miss Fitzwater. This is one of the good things that has happened lately, and we owe you our gratitude."

234

"Yeah, that's right."

But Ella wasn't mollified. "It just makes me so durned mad that they'd do this. They did this just out of pure meanness."

Men came back to the fire, threw more wood on it, and tried to warm up and dry out. Looking back at the dance floor, Ella said, "Well, the musicians have put away their instruments. I guess we all might as well go to bed. But durn their hides."

Gradually, everyone drifted away from the fire. Some went home, some went to the hotels, some crawled under tarps in the bed of their wagons, and some covered themselves with blankets and tarps under their wagons.

Wild Bill looked at Ella, standing in the dying firelight, hair wet and hanging straight down, clothes wet, looking forlorn. He had a strong urge to put his arms around her and talk to her. He didn't know whether she would appreciate that. "It was a good baile, Ella. Ever'body had fun."

Ella looked at Bill. The mud had been washed off his face, and he had a split lip and a cut on his right cheek. "It didn't end right. It just didn't end right at all."

"Can I walk you home?"

"No, Bill. If you did, you'd want to spend the night."

"Wal, uh . . ."

"Good-night, Bill."

As he watched her walk away, he realized she was right. He'd like to not only spend this night with her, but a lot of nights. Days, too. Sure, Eileen Cruz was

235

beautiful, but Ella Fitzwater was a damned good looking woman. His kind of woman.

The next surveyor to show up at Pegleg Peterson's house was armed with a bolt-action rifle. He was dressed in green corduroys, the same as Everett J. Godwin, and wore the same kind of flat-brim hat. "Ev Godwin was a friend of mine," he said after he'd dismounted. "I've been surveying for the U.S. government for more than five years now, and I've never heard of a surveyor being shot before."

'Most folks've got nothin' ag'in' surveyors," Pegleg said. "Fact is, most folks're glad to see you come. They figger that when the U.S. government land is surveyed, it'll be opened to homesteadin'."

The surveyor, who introduced himself as Waddell Holland, shook his head sadly. "Trouble with surveying on this damned grant is the settlers know I'm bad news. They believe that when the surveying is done, they won't be able to claim any land."

"They're prob'ly right."

"But no one has ever pointed a gun at me."

Pegleg cooked supper for the two of them, and slept outside while Waddell Holland slept inside. They were riding at sunup next morning, the surveyor leading a packhorse.

"Ev Godwin was a good accurate surveyor. If you can show me where he drove his markers, I'll put my markers in the same spots."

"I c'n show you exactly."

By dark they'd finished. Waddell Holland had unloaded his tripod and transit five times, driven stakes, and made notes in his book. By lamplight, he wrote in his book, did some calculations on a sheet of paper, and allowed, "I make it twenty-one sections and four hundred acres, but if Ev said it's twenty-two sections, that's good enough for me.'

"That's what he said, but I wouldn't argue over the difference."

"Then, that's what I'll put in my report."

Pegleg rode to Springer with Waddell Holland, and when they saw Wild Bill Watson off in the distance, driving a bull ahead of him, he stood in his stirrups, hollered, and waved his hat. Wild Bill let the bull go and loped over on a sorrel horse.

"I'm not takin' any chances on losin' this surveyor," Pegleg said. "There's men that don't want his report to get to town."

"Wal, if you don't mind my company, I'll ride along with you."

"I'd appreciate it. Them goons won't tangle with three of us."

On the way to Springer they saw four riders off in the distance, but the four came no closer. At the courthouse, Wild Bill stayed with the surveyor while he filed his papers with the county recorder. Pegleg went to get the lawyer, Thomas Atwell. The lawyer painstakingly wrote a copy of the surveyor's report, got Waddell Holland to sign it, and got the county recorder to put his seal on it.

"That oughta take care of that," Pegleg said. "It's all done right and legal."

"It's mostly a matter of paperwork now," Atwell said.

"We oughta celebrate with a drink of whiskey," Wild Bill said.

"Come and have one with us, Mr. Atwell."

"Ahem, I'd certainly like to, but I've got a wife, you know, and I've got to get these papers locked up in my safe, and . . . ahem."

"Some other day, then."

"Certainly, some other day I'll be happy to have a drink with you. Good evening, gentlemen." The lawyer walked toward his office with short quick steps.

"Stuffy jasper," Pegleg commented, "but he's smart. Smart and honest and careful."

Standing at a long mahogany bar in the Capulin Palace, Pegleg bought Bill and himself a shot of whiskey, then Bill fished enough coins out of his pocket to buy another round. "I didn't bring my little stash of cash with me," he said, "so this is the last one for me today."

"I don't know about you, but I'm gettin' tired of my own cookin'. I'll buy us some supper."

"Excuse me, gentlemen, if you don't mind, I'd like to buy you a shot of whiskey." The man was standing at Pegleg's right. He was a cattleman, in his high-heeled riding boots, curl-brim hat, big silk bandanna tied loosely around his throat, six-gun on his right hip.

"Well, uh . . .." Pegleg didn't know what to say.

"I recognize you two as bein' among the bunch that put a stop to a cattle auction a few days ago."

"We was there," Peterson said.

"I was there, too. I came down here to buy some cattle, and I'm still lookin'. My name is Howells. Harvey Howells."

Bill said, "You here to buy cattle taken by the laws from the settlers?"

"No," the cattlemen said quickly. "I'm buyin' cattle to stock a ranch up north, just across the Colorado border, and it's true I thought I might buy those cattle, but I didn't know where they came from."

"Would it have made any difference?"

"I can't honestly say. I was ready to bid on 'em. If it hadn't been for you fellers, somebody would've bought 'em. But after hearin' about how them cow brutes come to be here, I'm glad you fellers done what you done. How about a drink of whiskey?"

Pegleg looked at Bill. Bill said, "Long's I don't have to buy you one. I'm busted."

Another round was ordered. Pegleg asked, "Where you stayin'?"

"At the Holiday House. I'm goin' up to Raton tomorrow, see if I can find some good stock up there."

"I take it," Bill said, "you're not lookin' for beef."

"No. Mother cows, mostly. Maybe some young stuff that'll be ready for market in a year or so."

"How many?"

"I can pay for a hundred head if the price is right. Know anybody that's got some for sale?"

Bill's brow furrowed in thought, then he said, "No. Not offhand. But I'll keep my ears open."

A buyer from Colorado introduced himself to Ella Fitzwater on the same day. She was in the small room she used as an office in the back of her Willow Springs saloon when he knocked on the door. Standing, walking around her desk, she opened the door. He wore

239

workingman's clothes, but his clothes were clean and he was freshly shaved. He didn't look like a workingman.

"Excuse me, ma'am, are you Mrs. Ella Firewater?"

"The name's Fitzwater."

"Oh, excuse me again. I was misinformed. My name is Nowlan, Bruno Nowlan. I've been told this establishment is for sale."

"Yes, it is. For a fair price."

"Perhaps we could talk about it. If I may, I'd like to look around a bit, and examine your sales records."

"Are you interested in buying?"

"Yes, ma'am. I own a drinking establishment in Pueblo in Colorado, and I'm interested in moving down here."

"In that case," Ella said, smiling, "be my guest."

She had news for Wild Bill Watkins when he strolled in late the next day, spurs dragging on the floor. "Know what, Bill?"

"I know a few things, but I don't know what."

"In a week I'm gonna be footloose and fancy free."

"You're sellin' out?"

"Yep."

"Wal, now. Soon's I wet my pipes with a cool beer, I'll try to figger out the meanin' of what you just said."

"Have one on me."

He picked up a mug of beer from the bar, drank deeply, and said, "Ahh. Now, let me see if I got the rights of it. You're sellin' this place, and you'll be a woman of leisure."

"That wasn't so hard to figure out, now, was it?"

"Wal, I might purty soon be a man of leisure."

"That ain't so easy to figure out. What in the blue-eyed world are you saying?"

He finished his beer, said, "Ahh," again. "There's a gent here in town that's looking for cattle to buy. Name of Harvey Howells."

"You're gonna sell your cattle?"

"Like I said before, I'm gonna have to move sooner or later, and now is as good a time as any."

"Well, what are you gonna do then?"

"Danged if I know. What're you gonna do?"

She exaggerated his drawl: "Da-anged if Ah know."

Chapter Twenty-eight

Pegleg Peterson was riding, trying to keep watch on the surveyor's stakes, keeping his cattle within his own boundaries, watching for strangers. Once he saw riders off in the distance, but they kept their distance. The rain had changed the land. Red cactus flowers were blooming, little yellow flowers were growing out of the ground, the sagebrush smelled like lilac water, and the grass looked to be two inches higher than it was before the rain.

Then shortly after noon one day Pegleg saw riders coming toward him, coming at a lope.

He spurred his own horse into a lope, and rode down into an arroyo. There, he dismounted, carrying his lever-action carbine. He fired a shot in the air to let the riders know he was armed and not friendly. There were four of them. They stopped about two hundred yards away.

For a while they sat their saddles as if trying to decide what to do. The four of them could get on all sides of Pegleg and shoot him out of his arroyo, but he'd get at least one and probably two of them. He hoped they wouldn't want to pay the price.

While he watched, one rider separated himself from the others and rode forward at a walk, cautiously. When he was closer he stopped and yelled, ". . . just want to talk."

Pegleg recognized him then. Hunter Howser, now wearing a cattleman's hat.

"I'm not armed," Howser yelled. "Just want to talk with you."

"What about?" Pegleg yelled back.

"Can I come closer?"

Staying down, only his head and shoulders above the top of the arroyo, Pegleg yelled, "By yourself. Keep your hands in sight."

The rider came closer. Pegleg yelled again, "If any of those other jaspers move, I'll shoot you and then I'll shoot them."

"Agreed."

The rider came on until he was within talking distance. Pegleg climbed halfway out of the arroyo, but kept the rider between him and his three cohorts.

"I want to talk business."

"Talk."

"I'm ready to make you an offer for your ranch."

"It's not for sale."

Hunter Howser lifted his hat, a new pearl-gray Stetson, wiped sweat from his forehead, reset the hat. "Hot, isn't it?" When Pegleg said nothing, he continued, "Everything's for sale if the price is right."

Still, Pegleg said nothing.

"Let's be sensible about this, Mr. Peterson. I know you've got a deed and the land has been surveyed, and the surveyor's report is properly filed. But you haven't received a patent yet." He paused, then went on. "We

244

can contest the deed in court. We can tie it up in court for a long time. We can file motion after motion. We can appeal to the Supreme Court. The legal fees would be high, and we might win. Think about that, will you?"

Pegleg thought about it, but said nothing.

"I'll pay you a fair price for the land, and I'll buy your cattle, too. You can retire, take it easy, and forget about court battles, the Maxwell land grant, and everything but your own pleasure. How does that sound?"

"I don't trust you, Mr. Howser."

"You trust cash money, don't you? If we can strike a deal, I'll pay you in cash."

"Nope."

"Look at it this way: As long as the dead is being contested, you can't sell the ranch to anyone else. You're no youngster. You have no heirs. If anything was to happen to you, the ranch would be turned over to a court-appointed administrator. I could buy from him. Cheap. Now, what do you say to that?"

"That sounds like a threat."

"You give it some thought, Mr. Peterson. I'll ask you again in a few days, but only once more. Think about it." Hunter Howser turned his horse around and rode back to his cohorts.

Think about it. Pegleg could think of nothing else. Here he was afraid to sleep in his own house, eating whatever could be fried in a hurry over an open fire, living like a coyote, and looking like a coyote. And this Hunter Howser. For a long time the anti-grant people had thought he was working for the land company.

Now, Pegleg, Wild Bill, and probably a few others believed he was working for himself.

Oh, he was probably getting money from the land company. Somebody in the company was bankrolling him. One man couldn't afford to pay those ex-militiamen. It was like Ella Fitzwater had said: the company would get the land through litigation, but that took too much time and money. Whereever settlers were burned out, shot out, or scared out, the company took over without paying legal costs.

Maybe Hunter Howser was an investor in the company, but he was representing himself now, ready to take advantage of the dispute and buy land for himself cheap. He could have made a deal. Run the settlers off, save the company time and money, and in return the company would sell him the abandoned property.

Now here was Arnold Peterson with a deed to a big chunk of one of the best pieces of land on the whole grant. That had to rankle old Howser. That had to be a thorn in his hide. He couldn't let a one-legged old bat like Arnold Peterson stand in his way. He'd do anything.

Pegleg was horseback early next morning, heading for the county seat and the attorney Thomas Atwell. When he rode out of Springer late on the same day, he felt better; a worry had been lifted from his mind. Let the sons of bitches come.

Over two years, what had started with twenty-three cows and four bulls had grown to a herd of fifty-two. The herd was a mixture of cows with this year's calves, yearling steers, and heifers, two yearling bulls and four old ones. That was after Wild Bill had culled the barren cows and sold them and four yearlings to raise some cash. It had been a profitable two years—he'd lived fairly well and more than doubled his money—and Bill didn't feel too bad about having to leave the Maxwell land. He'd had two years of free grazing.

Still, he wished he could buy the land and build a better house, a barn, and more corrals. But, aw hell, a man had to have a lot of money to start a ranch. Men had tried to start with a one-hundred-sixty-acre homestead, but they couldn't graze more than a few cows on a hundred and sixty acres. Only a sodbuster could survive on that, and damned few of them survived. Cowboys had tried to start small and grow on free range with a big loop and a running iron, but most of them ended up hanging from tree limbs. And soon there would be no more free range. A feller either had to buy the land or lease it. It took a lot of money.

Well, he'd collect over a thousand dollars from Harvey Howells and find something else to do. What, he didn't know, but he liked working for himself, and wanted to continue being his own boss. He didn't intend to lie around town and spend his money. He'd look. He'd find something.

Howells had ridden over Wild Bill's grazing territory and bought the cattle on sight. He'd be ready to gather them in a few days and start the drive over the Raton Mountains. First, he wanted to buy a few more head if he could find them. Four days after he'd bought Bill's cattle, he showed up with a cowboy he'd just hired in Raton.

"Ready to move them cows?" he asked Bill.

"You figger it'll take three men to move 'em?"

"I bought another twenty cows from a sodbuster, and, yeah, it'll take three of us to drive 'em over them mountains."

"Wal, they're your cattle soon's we get 'em gathered, but I'll help you trail 'em up to your ranch for wages."

"I didn't expect you to work for nothin'."

"I've got four good horses, but that won't be enough."

"I bought four in Raton, and I'll buy yours. That'll be eight for three men."

"I'd like to get paid before we go very far."

"We'll camp for a day east of Raton, and when we get that far, I'll gather my other twenty head and pay you there."

"Good enough."

It took three men five days to drive seventy-two head of cattle over the Trinchera Pass to the Picketwire River in Colorado. The hired cowboy stayed, and Bill rode back over the pass on Dunnie. He had a horse and saddle and one thousand three hundred dollars.

In Raton, he put Dunnie in a livery pen and went looking for Ella Fitzwater. The Willow Creek saloon wasn't the same. Bill stopped suddenly when he walked through the door. First, the door was shut. Ella never shut the door in the summer. Second, there was sawdust on the floor, and pictures on the walls. The Hawken rifle was no longer hanging behind the bar. The bartender wore a black wool vest, a striped shirt with a high collar, and a handlebar mustache.

"Where's Ella?" Bill asked.

"Ella Firewater?"

"Fitzwater."

"She don't own the place no more, and I ain't seen 'er since Mr. Nowlan put me to work. Mr. Nowlan is in the office back there."

Bill went back outside, walked around the building to the house across the alley. Ella answered his knock, stood in the door, put her hands on her hips, and smiled. "Bill, I ain't seen you since you talked to that Howells fella, and I was getting worried. Where've you been? Did you sell your stock? Come in here and I'll put some coffee on."

Inside, sitting at the table he'd sat at before, Bill sighed, "I'm out of business. I'm like you said, foot-loose and fancy free."

"Me too, and I don't much like it."

"Got any plans?"

"I'm looking for a business to buy, but I haven't heard of anything, except for the Raton Livery and Freight."

"That's no business for a woman."

"No. I've got a good head for business and I've learned how to keep books and records, but freighting is a man's work." She smiled a weak smile. "Freighting and running a saloon."

"How come he wants to sell?"

"He's old. About sixty-five, I'd guess, and he's worried about the railroad putting him out of business. He hauls freight from the railroad warehouse to Cimarron and some of the other towns in the territory."

"I hear the Santa Fe's gonna build a branch line to Cimarron."

"They will, but there's other towns and there's stores in those towns that depend on horse and mule power to keep 'em supplied."

249

"Wonder what he expects to get for his business."

"Don't know."

"Maybe I'll go ask 'im."

"It won't hurt to ask. When was the last time you saw Pete?"

"Oh, 'bout a week ago. Think I'll ride down there *mañana* and see how he's doin'."

"Maybe I'll go with you."

"You wanta go with me? It's a long ride down there and back in a day. I was plannin' on stayin' the night."

"I'll take some blankets. I've slept on the ground before. And I'll take my rifle."

"That old Hawken?"

"It'll shoot, and I can shoot straighter than any man in the territory, and I hear the militiamen down at Springer are getting meaner all the time. Two more families came through here with their furniture and all their belongings piled on their wagons. They said they were going up to Colorado where there's still land open for homesteading. I asked one woman why they were leaving, and she said the grant people shot some of their cattle and warned them to move out or get shot. You might be glad I took that rifle."

"You could be right. I'm kinda worried about ol' Pete."

Chapter Twenty-nine

Arnold Peterson was worried about his neighbor, Wild Bill. When he crawled from under his blankets and tarp and strapped on his wooden leg, he saw smoke over east. It was either a grass fire or Wild Bill's shack burning. And the grass had so much dew on it that morning that it wouldn't burn. It was Wild Bill's shack.

What was more worrisome was that he'd heard no gunshots. Wild Bill's place was a good four miles away, but sound carried far at that altitude. Did they sneak up on him? He should have heard something.

Without breakfast, he quickly saddled his night horse and rode at a high trot to his neighbor's. The closer he got, the more convinced he was that the shack was burning. The smoke was black, the kind of smoke burning tarpaper makes, and when the breeze shifted his way he got a whiff of it. When he saw it, his heart dropped into his stomach.

Only a few sticks were left standing. The corral was empty and there was no sign of life anywhere.

Jaws clamped tight, afraid of what he might find, Pegleg dismounted, dropped his reins, and walked as close as the heat allowed. Red-hot ashes covered the spot. Two of the vertical posts that once held the roof were charred but standing. The stove was tilted, but right side up. Everything else was ashes or covered with ashes.

His eyes went over everything carefully, hoping against hope that he wouldn't find a body. The ashes were too hot to poke around in. All he could do was look. The bunk. He made out what was left of it. There was nothing that looked like a man's body near it. If Bill was burned to death, he'd be near the door, trying to get out. If he was shot, his body could be anywhere.

The flat rock that Bill had used for a doorstep was covered with ashes, but Pegleg managed to pry it out with a piece of a pole he'd found. The doorframe had collapsed and burned. All that was left was this piece of a pole that had been burned on one end. A stout pole, cut from a young cottonwood. What did Bill use it for?

When a possible answer came to him, Pegleg groaned, "Oh-h, no-o." The only door had opened outward, he remembered, and the pole could have been used to hold it shut.

Yep. After studying the ground in front of the cabin, he saw where one end of the pole had been held on the ground. The other end had been propped against the door to keep Bill from opening the door. One man holding the end against the ground could have kept Bill trapped inside.

They could have thrown some coal oil through the window, struck a match to it, and held the door shut. Bill couldn't have climbed through the window or shot through it because the window was burning. They'd

252

held the door shut until the screams from inside and the pounding on the door had stopped, then jumped back out of the way before the fire got too hot.

Only there were no screams. Wild Bill wasn't the kind to scream. He'd try with his last breath to get out of there. His body was in there under those ashes. It was murder. A cruel kind of murder—burning a man alive.

Or was it? Hope suddenly rose in Pegleg's chest. Didn't Wild Bill say something once about a little trapdoor he'd cut in the other side of the room? Yeah, come to think of it, he said he wasn't about to sleep outside, and that if they tried to burn him out, he'd crawl out through that trapdoor. Matter of fact, he did that once. He'd crawled out and shot the hell out of 'em.

Maybe he got out. But where was he?

More hope surged through Pegleg. Come to think of it, Wild Bill said he might go up to Raton and hunt up that Harvey Howells and see if he'd pay a fair price for his cattle. Said he knew he was going to have to move, and maybe it'd be better to sell now and move before the governor sent the army to move him.

"Huh," Pegleg snorted with a grin. Old Bill wasn't here when they burned his shack down. And he was planning to move out anyway.

Just to be sure, Pegleg got on his horse and rode through the creek brush and around all sides of the ashes and the corral. Nope, no body. By now the ashes were beginning to cool, and he used the piece of a pole to probe through them. He found a few cooking utensils, broken sections of stovepipe, and that was all.

Grinning to himself, believing now that his neighbor

253

was alive, Peterson got on his horse again. His stomach reminded him he hadn't eaten that day, and the sun was almost straight up. Old Bill will be some unhappy when he gets back, but he'll know he's lucky to be breathing. He won't complain.

Turning his horse west and north, Pegleg started for home, then reined up. Two riders were coming from the north. At first they were too far away to recognize, but when they came closer he recognized Wild Bill. Who was the other? Looked like a woman. If it was a woman, it had to be Ella Fitzwater. Yep. That's who it was.

He waited for them. They rode up, looking from Pegleg to the smoldering ashes. Ella said, "H'lo, Pete. I see things got hot around here while Bill was gone." She wore a floppy hat and a long broadcloth dress that covered her down to her ankles as she sat astraddle her horse.

Bill said nothing until he'd rolled a cigarette and lit it. Then he grinned. "Did it take that big a fire to cook your breakfast, Pete?"

Grinning with him, Pegleg said, "Well, you know, when I got started cookin', I couldn't quit till I cooked ever'thing in sight."

Ella said, "Whatever grub was in there is surely well-done."

No one asked what had happened. But Bill did ask, serious now, "Did they get over to your place again?"

"Not yet. I saw the smoke when I got out of the sack this mornin'. For a while I was scared you was burned up, too."

"Wal, with me gone, they had an easy time of it. I didn't lose much. Sold my cattle and horses."

254

"They tried to kill you, Bill. C'mere and let me show you somethin'." He showed them the burned piece of pole, and told them what he guessed had happened. "They thought they had you trapped in there."

Grim-faced now, Bill said, "Yeah, and they would've blamed the fire on a lamp that got too close to the tarpaper, or somethin'."

"We were worried about you, Pete," Ella said. "That's why I came along. Bill's shack is gone. Now we have to defend yours."

They sat their horses near the ashes, wrinkling their noses at the sharp bite of smoke. Peterson said, "Sometimes I think we oughta do like we done once in the war, 'steada waitin' for the enemy to attack, we taken the war to the enemy."

"Trouble is," Ella said, "if we went to Springer and started a fight, we'd be on the wrong side of the law. If we killed somebody, we'd be hung."

"Too bad we can't sneak around in the dark like they do," Bill said. "I'm tired of waitin' for them to attack."

"Come on over to my wickiup and let's eat," Pegleg said. "I've got plenty of grub."

Bill chuckled, "I hope we don't have to burn the house down to cook it."

They put their horses in Pegleg's corral, tossed them some hay, and went into the house. Again, Ella commented on the neatness, "You're a better housekeeper than some women I know. I wouldn't have expected it of you."

"It's a habit. Hope you folks don't mind flapjacks and boar belly. I ain't had breakfast yet."

They ate pancakes covered with sorghum. Ella in-

255

sisted on washing the dishes. Then they went outside and talked. Ella and Bill sat on the bench near the door, and Pegleg sat on the ground, good leg crossed over the wooden one.

"I know what he's up to, that Howser feller." Pegleg said.

"Let me see if I can guess," Bill said. "The land company's payin' 'im to run off the settlers, but he wants some country of his own, and he kept some of the ex-militiamen around to do his dirty work."

"That's right." Pegleg told about his meeting with Howser and three of his cohorts. "Yestidy I went to Springer and made some medicine talk with that lawyer feller, Thomas Atwell. Like I said, he's one smart gent, and he's been askin' some questions hisself. We had old Howser figured out—almost. Here's what the lawyer told me." Peterson recrossed his legs, leaned back on his hands, and continued:

"Old Howser has money invested in the land company, but like you said, he wants some land of his own. He come from Chicago and he likes it here and he wants to own a ranch. Bein' an investor in the land company, he c'n buy land cheaper than a outsider, but first he has to run off the settlers."

Ella said, "Let me take it from there. I've been doing some thinking and asking some questions, too."

The two men waited for her to go on.

"He wants to be a rancher. He wants to own a big enough ranch that he can hire the work done instead of doing it himself. He wants your ranch, Pete. This is one of the best spots on the whole grant. He was disappointed when he found out you've got a deed, and he tried to steal your deed or burn it, and next he tried

256

to keep you from getting your land surveyed and the results of the survey recorded. The first surveyor was killed, and Hunter Howser had a hand in that. You said you have no heirs. If you were dead, he could deal with the court-appointed administrator of your estate. And he could resort to bribery or something else underhanded.''

Wild Bill added, ''Yeah, he knows by now he'll have to buy the land, but like you said, Pete, bein's he's already got an interest in it, he can buy it cheap.''

''You hit 'er just right, Ella. That lawyer said the same thing. If I was dead he could buy my propity from somebody that might be as crooked as he is. If he can get my twenty-two sections, he can buy more country around it and have a big cow outfit.''

''And,'' Ella said, ''he can be what the magazines call a country gentleman.''

They were silent a moment while Bill rolled another cigarette, struck a match on the sole of his boot, and lit it. Then Ella said:

''We know what this means. Hunter Howser can't scare you off, and it wouldn't suit his purpose now to burn your house down. Pete, he wants you dead.''

Chapter Thirty

"It does give a feller the willies," Arnold Peterson said, standing, stumping his way to the water barrel. "Knowin' somebody's gonna try to kill me and not knowin' when or where or how."

"If he's smart," Ella said, "he'll try to make it look like an accident."

Wild Bill stood too and said, "There's been too many cabins and barns burned down to make anybody b'lieve you accidentally set your house on fire and burned up in it."

In the late afternoon, horses watered and fed, they decided to have supper early so they wouldn't be targets in the lamplight. Inside, they continued their conversation, and while they talked, Ella peeled potatoes, quartered them, and dropped them into a pot of boiling water. Pegleg put a big iron skillet on the two-hole stove, salted and peppered three steaks he'd cut from a quarter of venison. Bill stood in the open doorway, watching for riders. Flies came through the door and buzzed around inside the house. Everyone was used to flies and mostly ignored them.

Finished with the potatoes, Ella wiped her hands on an empty flour sack that had been washed and was used for a towel. "I'm trying to think of how they'd do it, but I just don't know."

"I think," Bill said from the doorway, "they'll try to shoot you out, Pete. Old Howser'll send his hired guns to do it while he stays in Springer and makes sure plenty of people see 'im there. That way the laws can't say he done it."

The skillet was hot enough by now, and Pegleg dropped the steaks into it. "Now listen here, you two, don't worry none about me. I've been in some mighty boogerish spots, and I've lived a long, long time."

"A body can get in just so many dangerous spots, and the odds are gonna catch up."

Pegleg tried to joke. "I'm so tough, ever'time the devil got his jaws on me he broke a tooth."

Realizing then that her friend didn't want to talk about it anymore, Ella changed the subject. "Bill's looking for a business to get into. So am I. Any ideas?"

"Nothin' comes to mind right now. 'Course I don't get around much to hear what's goin' on."

"Turley Woods, who runs the livery barn and the stage and freight lines in Raton, wants to sell out."

Bill said, "He's askin' a lot more money than I've got."

"The freightin' business might be good," Pegleg said, "but somehow I can't see Wild Bill sweet-talkin' a bunch of stage passengers."

When the steaks were burned on the outside but pink in the middle, Pegleg forked them out of the skillet, dumped a big spoonful of flour in with the cooking grease, stirred it until it was brown, then added water.

Their meal was venison steak, boiled potatoes, and water gravy. Ella, knowing Pete had nothing for dessert, cleaned her plate, and said, "Delicious. I can't eat another bite. I think I'll skip dessert, Pete, thanks just the same."

Ella slept inside the house that night while Pegleg and Wild Bill unrolled their beds outside. The moon was bright, and Bill, lying awake, saw a skunk wander close to the sleeping Peterson's bed, then go on. Two coyotes cried and yap-yapped at each other somewhere off in the distance. Nothing else happened.

In the morning, Pegleg talked them into leaving. "It's not that I don't like your company, but there's no tellin' when they'll come if they come. I'll keep my eyes and ears open. Don't worry about me."

No use arguing with him. He just didn't want to be bodyguarded. Ella and Wild Bill rolled up their blankets, saddled their horses.

"I'll be back in a couple or three days, Pete," Bill said.

"We'll worry about you," Ella said.

They rode away, Ella's long dress covering her and most of her saddle. Pegleg watched them go, then saddled a horse.

Turley Woods was easy to dicker with. Yep, Wild Bill could buy part of the business, any part of it he wanted, and he could move into the room in a corner of the barn. The room had a bed with springs, a coal-burning stove, a clothes tree, a lopsided chest of drawers, a wooden floor, and a stout door with a padlock. Somebody would come along and buy the rest of the business. It could be divided any way a buyer or buyers wanted to divide it.

When Bill knocked on Ella's door he had news. "I'm gonna take over in a few days," he said. "I bought two four-horse teams and harness and two big freight wagons. Oh, uh, I brought some papers Turley gave me. They're the papers he keeps his business records on, you know, what he buys and how much he pays and what he gets for it."

"You want me to look at them?"

"Wal, you been in business before and you know more about this stuff than I do."

Ella sat on the padded upholstered sofa and read the papers while Bill sat in an overstuffed armchair and watched her face for any sign of pleasure or displeasure. "It looks like," Ella said, "you're planning to haul freight to Capulin and Morrison."

"Yep. Ol' Turley's been haulin' over there for a long time and the mercantiles've been countin' on 'im. He gave me a list of the stuff he usually buys at the railroad warehouse, and he said them merchants take all of it. They give him lists of things they want that he might not have on his list."

"Capulin is east and Morrison is southeast. Can you deliver to both towns yourself?"

"Yep. Turley said it's two days round trip to Capulin, and two long days to Morrison and back. I've got two teams and two wagons. One can rest while the other works. What with loadin' and unloadin' and ever'thing, it'll take six, seven days a week, but I'm used to that."

"What if somebody else comes along and buys the barn?"

262

"Old Turley said he'd guarantee me use of a pen for my horses and the room in the barn for me."

"Well, it looks like, from these figures, you oughta make a profit."

"I'll be tickled just to make a livin'. And if it don't work, I can get my money back by sellin' the horses and wagons to some rancher."

Ella got up and sat on the padded arm of Bill's chair. She put a hand on his shoulder. "You're a businessman now, Bill. How does it feel?"

"Wal, a little worrisome. I feel like I don't know what the heck I'm doin', but, wal, I'm gonna give 'er a try." Her closeness made him aware for the hundredth time that she was a very desirable woman, which made him squirm. "*Mañana* I'm goin' down to see how Pete's doin'."

"Do you mind if I go along?"

"Wal, no, if you want to."

"I'm tired of doing nothing, and I like to sit on a horse and see the country."

"Pete seems to like your company."

"Do you mind if I sit on your lap, Bill?"

"Huh? Wal, uh, no. Not a-tall. No, ma'am, not one little bit." He shifted uneasily in the chair.

Sitting on his lap, her arms around his neck, she pressed her lips to his. Then she took his face in both hands and kissed him again. He didn't know what to say, so he said nothing. Instead, he put his arms around her waist and pulled her tighter.

The lamp on a small table had burned its fuel and the wick was smoking. No one noticed. Finally, Bill managed to say, "It's, uh, gettin' close to bedtime. Reckon we could, uh . . . ?"

"No, Bill." She stood and looked down at him.

"No? But after this and all, I thought . . ."

"Not tonight, Bill." She smiled sweetly. "But don't quit trying."

When Pegleg finished breakfast, washed the dishes, and went out to saddle his mount for the day, they were waiting for him. They'd circled and come from the north so their tracks wouldn't be noticed. Deputy Jameson with the cocky derby hat was waiting around the corner of the loafing shed where Pegleg kept his saddle. He pointed his nickel-plated revolver at Pegleg's face.

"Reach, you goddamn mick son of a bitch."

Pegleg had no choice. Jaws clamped tight, he raised his hands. Footsteps sounded behind him and another voice said, "Take his gun. I got 'im covered. One move, you one-legged bastard, and I'll blow your backbone in two."

Jameson lifted the Colt out of its holster. More footsteps meant more men. Pegleg swiveled his head and saw four of them, all pointing guns at him.

"It worked the way I said it would, didn't it? I said, if we rode most of the night, we could catch 'im unawares at daylight."

Hunter Howser said, "Sure, Jameson, you were right for a change. Tie his hands, saddle his horse, get him on his horse, and let's get this over with."

Chapter Thirty-one

They weren't surprised to find Peterson gone when they rode up to his house about noon. A cattleman had to be horseback, not sitting in the house. They dismounted and took a drink from the water barrel, then Wild Bill walked over to the corral and loafing shed. Habitually, his eyes took in the creek brush, the country around him, and habitually, he studied the ground. Stopped suddenly. Then he walked with quick steps back to the house and the bench where Ella was waiting.

"They was here. At least three of 'em and maybe four."

"Oh no." Ella stood, fear showing in her face. "How do you know?"

"Tracks. Them tracks wasn't here before. Men's tracks and horse tracks."

"Does that mean . . . ?" Her voice was close to cracking, and she was close to tears.

Grim-faced, Bill said, "I don't know for sure what it means, but it don't look good. Let's get horseback and see what we can see."

Wild Bill had tracked cattle over much of the south‐
west, and the tracks of five horses were easy to follow.
They led toward a rocky ridge southwest of the house.
Four miles from the house he saw Pegleg's horse. It
was the blue roan, standing with its head down. The
saddle was turned so it hung on the horse's left side.

Next they saw the body.

Pegleg was lying on his back, eyes wide open. His
head and his one foot were bare, and his clothes were
torn so badly he was half-naked. Bloody cuts covered
his face and body.

Bill rode to him on a gallop and dismounted on the
run. He stood over the body, rage building within him.
Ella was slower getting off her horse, and she too stood
silently over her dead friend. Tears began rolling down
her cheeks.

In a wavering voice, she asked, "What . . . what
happened, Bill?"

"He was dragged," Bill said through clenched teeth.
"Over them rocks. Them rocks beat 'im to pieces."

"By that horse over there?" She wiped her eyes with
the palms of her hands.

"I don't think so."

"Why? Why don't you think so?"

Without answering, he walked toward the horse,
stopped when he saw the boot on the ground. Squat‐
ting, he studied the boot a moment, but didn't touch
it. He looked at the horse, knew the animal was un‐
comfortable with a saddle hanging on its side, but de‐
cided to do nothing about it. Turning on his heels, he
went back to the body and Ella.

Her eyes were red-rimmed, but she had stopped cry‐
ing. "What should we do, Bill?"

"I guess the right thing to do is go to Springer and fetch the sheriff—if the sheriff is there." He paused a moment, then added angrily, "Ain't no use bringin' one of them goddamn deputies. They ain't worth a good goddamn for anything. Sheriff Bowman is the only lawdog in this whole goddamn county that's worth a good goddamn. He'd better, by god, be there when we need 'im." After a moment, in a softer tone, he said, " 'Scuse me, Ella, for cussin'."

"It's all right. There's times when a man has to cuss."

After a moment of silence, he said, "One of us has to stay here. This happened yesterday, and the coyotes and satchel birds ain't found 'im yet, but one of us has to stay here case they do."

"You're riding the fastest horse. I'll stay."

"It won't bother you none, guardin' a dead man?"

"He's not just a dead man, he's a friend. I'll stay."

"I'll get there and back as fast as Dunnie can carry me, but it'll prob'ly daylight in the mornin' before we get back. You'll have to stay here all night."

"I've got my rifle and I've got a blanket roll and some bread. I'll stay."

Bill gathered the dun horse's reins and stepped into the saddle. "I hate to leave you here like this, Ella. I'll be back as fast as I can."

"Be careful, Bill." Her eyes were red-rimmed and moist. "Don't get in any fights with the deputies or anything."

"I won't. I promise. If the sheriff ain't there, I'll come back without 'im." He touched spurs to the horse and rode away at a lope.

Ella watched him until he was out of sight, then sat

on the ground near the body, her knees drawn up
elbows on her knees, chin in her hands. She had an
urge to close Pegleg's eyes, but it occurred to her the
sheriff might not want her to touch anything.

Suddenly, looking at the dead face, she started sob-
bing. "I'm sorry, Pete. I'm so sorry."

Eventually, she wiped her eyes with the hem of her
skirt and stood. Her bay horse was cropping the grass
that grew among the sandstone and shale rocks. She
unsaddled the horse and used the saddle blanket to
cover Pegleg's face and upper body, then tied a rope
to the bridle reins and held the end while the horse
resumed grazing.

Wild Bill had said he didn't think Pete was dragged
by that horse over there. If not, what had happened?
Wild Bill had followed the tracks of more than one
horse. Did Hunter Howser and his bunch have something to do with this? Was this murder?

The sky was clear and the day was warm. Flies flit-
ted around the uncovered part of Pegleg's body. She
wished she had something else to put on it. Pulling the
tall grass gave her something to do, and if she pulled
enough she could cover the bare part of the body with
it. By late afternoon, she had it pretty well covered.
Enough that the flies were bothering her and her bay
horse more than anything else.

"Damn flies," she said aloud. And suddenly she
couldn't stay quiet anymore. She'd told Bill it was all
right to cuss, now she felt like swearing. Which she
did, loudly:

"Damned Maxwell land grant. Damned land.
Damned greedy, grubby, grabby, thieving sons of
bitches. Damn them all. Goddamn every goddamn one

of them. That dead man there was worth more than a hundred of them money-grubbing Englishmen and Dutchmen and eastern sons of bitches and all their god-damn money. God damn the lawyers and judges and all the other self-righteous bastards."

And she burst into tears again.

She hadn't eaten since before daylight, but at dusk she hadn't even thought of eating. She wrapped herself in a blanket, sat on the ground, and leaned back against a low rocky ledge. Her long-barreled Hawken rifle was across her lap. She caressed the gun, its well-oiled stock, the polished silver sideplate, the hammer. The gun was loaded with everything but a percussion cap. One didn't carry a single-trigger percussion gun with a cap under the hammer. If it was dropped, it would fire. The old flintlock rifles were safer and, some believed, just as dependable. Her powder horn, bag of lead balls, and leather box of caps were in one of the saddlebags. One cap was in a pocket of her dress. If a coyote came sniffing around, she could place the cap on the firing nipple in a matter of seconds.

The bay horse had wandered a short distance, but wouldn't go far dragging a thirty-foot rope. Pete's blue roan was still standing over there, enduring the discomfort of a saddle hanging on its left side. Poor brute, she thought. She had an urge to go over and take the saddle off and let the horse go. But again it occurred to her that she ought to leave everything the way they'd found it.

At dark she wrapped her other blanket around her shoulders. She sat against the low ledge until her backside ached, then stood and walked in circles until the ache went away.

Now she could see only a dim outline of the body. She didn't want to look at it, but she had to keep watch. Coyotes could sneak up without a sound. Late in the night she dozed.

Around midnight she awakened with a start. Did she hear something? Trying not to breathe, she listened. Nothing. The body was a dark shape. Nothing moved anywhere. Again, she dozed.

Next time she awakened, she was sure she'd heard something. Eyes wide, ears straining, she was sure. Yes. Something moved over by Pete's body. A black shape the size of a coyote. Standing, she yelled, "Git. Git away from there." She waved her arms, then grabbed the Hawken, ready to slip a cap on the firing nipple. The dark shape moved away and disappeared into the night.

"Git away from there. Don't you come back, damn you. If I see you again I'll shoot you to pieces."

She didn't dare sleep now. Walking in circles again, in the dark, carrying the Hawken, she worked the aches out of her body and waited for daylight.

The dun horse had given its best, but couldn't go much farther at this gait. Bill had let it slow to a trot, but touched its sides now and then with his spurs. He could think of nothing but Ella, sitting all night with a dead man.

"It'll be daylight soon," Sheriff MacKenzie Bowman said.

"We're almost there. Ain't far now."

Deputy Duncan kept quiet.

Bowman had explained about the deputy. "He ain't none too popular up at Raton, but he's honest if nothing else. I moved him and his wife down here, and gave him a good talking to. I think he'll be a pretty fair lawman now. He's the only deputy I've got that I can trust."

When Wild Bill and Deputy Duncan had met at the sheriff's office, they avoided each other's eyes. The deputy didn't want to incur the sheriff's wrath, and Bill didn't want any fights at the time. Bowman and Bill talked very little, and Duncan talked not at all.

Now Bill pointed ahead. "That's it. That rocky ridge up there." When they got closer, they saw Ella, standing, holding her long-barreled rifle. At the body, they dismounted, and Bill wrapped his arms around Ella.

"Was it bad?"

Forcing a small smile, she looked up at Bill's face. "It wasn't the best night of my life, but it wasn't too bad."

Sheriff Bowman squatted, uncovered the body. His eyes roved over it, then squinted at the blue roan horse. "It's easy to figure. His saddle turned on him and his boot went through the stirrup and the horse dragged him. He was dragged over enough rocks to beat him to death before his boot came off."

Bill said simply, "Nope."

"What?" the sheriff said, standing. "What makes you say that?"

"C'mere," Bill said, walking over to the boot. Everyone followed. "See the top of that boot, right above where his ankle was? See how it's pinched in? That looks like rope marks, like a rope was tied tight around his ankle. It had to be tight to keep the boot from comin' off."

Squatting again, Bowman picked up the boot, examined it. "Does look kinda peculiar. But there might be another explanation."

"Come back over here." Bill led the way back to the body. "See them marks on his wrists? Rope burns, sure as shootin'."

"Hmm."

"And that's not all."

"What else?"

"See that horse? See the high withers? Pete always had a hair pad and a double blanket under the saddle on that horse to keep the saddle gullet off of his wither bone. The hair pad is back there in the corral. Somebody else saddled that horse."

"Peculiar." Bowman walked to the horse, untied the cinches, and let the saddle fall to the ground. The horse walked away, slowly, stiffly at first. Bowman went back to the dead man, looked down at him a moment, then went on, head down. He squatted again, studied the ground, stood, and came back. "There was a roan horse and your two horses, and there were more. Don't know how many more, but there were more."

"At least three," Bill said, "and maybe four."

"Wish we'd brought the coroner with us, but there ain't no question about the cause of death."

"No question a-tall," Bill said.

Squinting at Bill, at his deputy, at Ella, at the horizon, Sheriff Bowman said, "It was murder."

272

Chapter Thirty-two

"We know who was responsible," Ella Fitzwater said.

"Who, Miz Fitzwater?"

"Pete told us about Hunter Howser trying to buy his ranch and threatening him if he didn't sell. It was Mr. Howser's hired hands and your deputies who burned down Bill's shack, and probably all the other houses that have been burned down."

"Can you prove it, Miz Fitzwater?"

"What kind of proof do you need?"

"Anything. A witness would sure help."

While Ella mulled that over, Deputy Duncan spoke for the first time. "I seen Mr. Howser and three men, includin' that Deputy Jameson, ridin' past the hotel last night."

All eyes turned to him. "Exactly what did you see, Dunc?"

"You know, my woman and me ain't found a house yet and we're stayin' at the Blue Sage Hotel. Our room overlooks the alley on the north, and I just happened to be standin' there in the dark, lookin' out of the window, tryin' to get a breath of fresh air, when I seen 'em ride by. They was comin' from the north, though."

"Are you sure you recognized Hunter Howser?"

"I'm sure. He's got that brand new Stetson, and he always wears that long coat no matter how hot it is. And that deputy with the derby hat, I'd recognize him if it was darker than a stack of black cats."

"It wasn't all that dark last night," Bowman mused.

Bill said, "They circled around and came from the north to try to fool anybody that happened to see 'em."

Head down, speaking to himself as much as to anyone else, Sheriff Bowman said, "I for sure wanta have a serious talk with that gentleman."

They buried Arnold Peterson on top of a low hill behind his house. Bill carved his name on a short piece of one-inch board, fashioned a cross, and put it at the head of the grave. Sheriff Bowman uttered a short prayer. Ella wept.

"I can't help it," she sniffed. Bill put his arms around her. "You just go ahead and cry, Ella. I wish I could. Somebody oughta cry for Pegleg Peterson."

Wild Bill and Ella said they would stay the night at Peterson's house, then leave tomorrow. Sheriff Bowman said he and his deputy would go back to Springer, make out a report on Peterson's death, and question Deputy Jameson and his boss Hunter Howser.

"I wish I had some solid proof," he said. "That prosecutor won't charge them with a crime without solid evidence."

"He charged Pete without solid evidence, and me."

Bowman wanted to say something sarcastic about the prosecuting attorney, but decided not to.

"I s'pose," Bill said glumly, "that Pete's property and ever'thing he owned will be turned over to the courts, now."

The sheriff was just as glum. "Yeah. If he has no kinfolks, that's the way it'll work."

"It's a darn shame," Ella said. "Pete worked so hard, and now it'll all go to the lawyers and the darn money-grubbing investors."

All Sheriff Bowman could do was shake his head and shrug.

Wild Bill spent the night in his blankets outside while Ella slept inside. Romance didn't enter their minds, not now, not here. In the morning, after a breakfast of bacon and flapjacks, Bill caught one of Pegleg's horses and rode all around the house and corrals to be sure all of Pete's horses were free and able to forage for themselves. Ella picked some wildflowers and decorated Peterson's grave. Their own horses munched hay in the corral.

Just before noon, they ate an early dinner, and while Ella washed the dishes, Bill went to the corral to saddle their horses. That was when he saw four riders coming.

He recognized two of them immediately, but he assumed the sheriff had questioned them, and now that Pete was dead they were no longer dangerous. A bitter bile formed in his throat, though. His upper lip curled. They had killed Pete. Bill didn't reach for his rifle, but he kept his right hand close to the Smith & Wesson as they rode up.

Ella was working over a dishpan in the house and didn't see or hear them.

The four dismounted, and Bill barked, "Nobody invited you to get down. You got no business here."

"Oh yes, we do," Hunter Howser said. He was wearing his new pearl-gray Stetson, and had a blued-steel revolver in a new leather holster. "This is my ranch now."

"Can't be. The judge'll decide who gets it."

"It will be mine. You can be sure of that."

Deputy Jameson was circling to Bill's right. The other two riders looked like hired gunslingers, with six-guns in well-worn holsters. They stood beside Howser, their hands close to their guns.

"Until it is," Bill growled, "you've got no business here."

"As much business as you do. More. I'm an investor in the Maxwell Land Company, and this is company land."

Ella heard men's voices and looked out the window. When she recognized Hunter Howser, she grabbed her Hawken rifle, put a percussion cap on the nipple. She saw Deputy Jameson circling, aiming to get behind Bill. She poked the rifle through the broken window, got him in the sights, her finger on the trigger.

Bill knew what the deputy was up to, and he growled at Howser, "Tell that gunsel to get over here with the rest of you. Tell him now, or I'll shoot him, then I'll shoot you."

"There are four of us."

"Four sons of bitches."

"Now listen here, as a part owner of the company I came here to inspect this property and I found you

276

looting the place. I have every right to shoot you on the spot.''

''You're a liar.'' Bill knew he was in a bad way, with three guns in front of him and one off to his right. Thinking fast, he decided Howser wasn't much of a threat, but the two gunslingers were. He'd have to shoot them first, then try to turn fast enough to shoot the deputy before the deputy could shoot him. If he was still alive after that, he'd shoot Howser right through that smirking face of his.

Howser's smirk only widened at the insult. ''Do you step aside or do we shoot us a looter? I hope it's the latter.''

The time for talking was over. Four against one. Wild Bill concentrated on drawing the Smith & Wesson and shooting the man next to Howser, cocking the gun, and shooting the next man. He was glad he'd replaced the mainspring on the gun so it would take only a slight pressure to pull the hammer back. He thought of Ella, and wished he could protect her. They'd have to kill her, too. His move had to be lightning fast. It would be the last move he'd ever make.

His mind screamed, *Now*.

Wild Bill's thumb was the first finger to touch the Smith & Wesson. In a split second he had the hammer thumbed back and gun clear. The first shot hit one of the gunslingers in the middle of the chest, knocking him back and down. Bill fanned the hammer with the edge of his left hand and got off another shot just as the second man's gun was coming up.

Two shots in a split second, and two men down, dead or dying. But Bill didn't have time to even look at them. He spun, started to fan the hammer back. Too late.

Deputy Jameson had the nickel-plated revolver aimed right at Bill, and his finger was already squeezing the trigger. He was too close to miss. In his mind's eye Bill could see the bullet coming, feel it smashing into his heart.

Kapow.

The shot came from behind Bill, from the house, and the tin star on the deputy's chest suddenly had a hole in it. So did the deputy's chest. He dropped like a wet rag.

Bill turned to be sure the shot had come from the house. That was a mistake. When he looked back at Howser, he was looking into the bore of another pistol, a new double-action revolver.

"Well, now." Howser had a cruel smile on his face. "That was real fine shooting. Yes, sir, I wouldn't have believed it if I hadn't seen it. Three fast shots and three men down. Yes, sir. I'll tell everyone about it. You'll be remembered as a man quick with a gun. But this gives me an even greater right to shoot you."

What the man said had Bill wondering whether he knew about Ella, where the shot that killed Jameson had come from.

Inside the house, Ella moved as fast as her hands and fingers could move. She poured a premeasured amount of black powder from her powder flask down the Hawken's barrel, yanked the ramrod from its bracket under the barrel. "Hurry, fingers, hurry," she muttered. Next she put a cotton patch on the end of the barrel, pushed it in with her thumb, then pushed a lead ball in with her thumb as far as she could. Instead of taking time to use a short ramrod first, she used the long one, rammed the ball and the patch all the way home. "Dammit," she cried, grabbing her saddlebags off a chair, groping for her leather box of percussion caps. Fingers flying, she picked a cap out of the box, pulled the hammer back to half-cock, stuck the cap onto the firing nipple.

It had taken too long. Too damn long. Why didn't she use Pete's repeating rifle? Why did she just have to use this damned old black-powder muzzle-loading Hawken?

Finally, with the rifle loaded, she poked the barrel out the window, thumbed the hammer all the way back, looked for a target. "Oh, god," she groaned. Hunter Howser had a gun pointed at Bill not two feet from his chest. Bill's gun hand hung down at his side. The gun wasn't cocked. No matter how fast Bill moved, it wouldn't be fast enough.

Ella squinted down the barrel. "Oh, no," she groaned again. Howser had stepped in front of Bill. Bill was standing squarely between her and Howser.

Bill saw the cruel glint come into Howser's eyes, saw his finger tighten on the trigger. The hammer on the self-cocking gun started moving back. It would go back just so far, then trip forward, striking a firing pin, which would strike a center-fire cartridge, which would shoot a bullet into Bill's heart. Could he throw himself to one side? Could he cock his own gun and bring it up? Could he do anything?

"Don't entertain any thoughts of outshooting me.

279

I've been practicing with this gun. One little move and you're dead."

From the window, Ella couldn't see Howser's gun, couldn't see Howser's head. She had nothing to shoot at. Whispering, she pleaded, "Move, Bill. Just two inches. Give me two inches. Please, Bill, honey, just move your head. Please."

Something—if Bill lived to be a thousand he'd never know what—but something told him to move his head. Stalling for a few seconds, he said calmly, "You've never killed a man before, have you, Mr. Howser?"

"No, but it's going to be a pleasure." The cruel glint in his eyes, the cruel grin, spelled death. Bill moved his head to the left. Didn't jerk his head, didn't move suddenly. Moved slowly. Just two inches. Howser was enjoying himself, knowing he'd won, slowly squeezing the trigger. His finger tightened a little more.

Kapow.

Bill felt the heat of the lead ball as it passed his right ear, saw the side of Howser's head disappear, saw the man spin and fall facedown.

For a long moment, Wild Bill stood there, unbelieving. He just couldn't believe it. When he looked back, finally, Ella was running to him, holding her long skirt up to keep from tripping over it. Then she was in his arms.

They couldn't talk. Not for a while. Just hugged each other. Then Bill stepped back, grinned a crooked grin.

"Look at me, Ella."

"Why, Bill, honey?"

"Is my right ear still there?"

"Yes. Why?"

"I felt that ball go by. It couldn't have missed me by more than a hair."

Smiling slowly, she said, "I never miss by as much as a hair."

"That was . . . Ella, that was the dangdest shootin' I ever did see. Nobody's gonna believe it."

"Don't tell anybody. I win shooting matches with men who can't believe a woman can outshoot them."

"I b'lieve it."

Looking around then at four dead men, Bill said, "Wal, that's the end of Hunter Howser and gang."

No longer smiling, Ella asked, "What're we gonna do with 'em?"

"Danged if I know. Go get the sheriff and let him worry about it."

Looking past him, Ella said. "We won't have to go and get the sheriff." Bill followed her gaze and saw the sheriff coming, him and Deputy Duncan. They silently watched the two riders come up and dismount.

Shaking his head sadly, Sheriff Bowman and his deputy went to each body, looked down at them. "All dead," Bowman said.

To Bill, he said, "You outshot all four of 'em?"

"Me and Ella."

"Tell me what happened."

"Him"—Bill nodded at the remains of Hunter Howser—"he said he had a right to be here because he's an investor in the land company. He accused us of stealin'—lootin', he called it—and said they had a right to kill us."

"And you were convinced they were going to kill you?"

"I didn't doubt it for a second."

"Uh-huh. I see. Hmm." Bowman looked down at his boots, looked at Bill, at Ella, at the horizon. "Well, I'd say that's a pretty good case for self-defense."

Ella asked, "How'd you happen to come back here today?"

"Dunc saw 'em ride out of town, going in this direction. He told me about it when I got back from the mayor's house, and we decided to come out here to see what they were up to." He paused, looked at the horizon. "Mr. Howser lied to me. I asked him last night where he was the night before, and he said he was playing cards with his pals. He was lying. I can prove that."

Ella asked another question. "Do you think the prosecutor will charge us with a crime?"

"I don't think so. I don't think so, because if he does I'll testify for the defense. Naw, he'd be the loser if we went to trial, and he doesn't like to lose."

Deputy Duncan spoke, "I will too. I'll testify for the defense."

Bill asked, "You will?"

"Yessir, I will."

"Besides that," Bowman said, "I've got news. Arnold Peterson had a will. The lawyer, Thomas Atwell, came to see me and told me about it. Peter had a will made out and he left everything to Tomás and Eileen Cruz."

"Why," Ella said, "that's wonderful."

"Yep," Bill said, "they're losin' their place, house and all, and now they've got another place, a damned good ranch. I'm glad ol' Pete done that."

282

"It'll have to be probated, but as far as I'm concerned they can move in any time."

Smiling broadly, Ella said, "That's just wonderful. I am really happy to know that."

"You two can go on about your business. Dunc and I'll take over here. One of us will have to go back to Springer and get a wagon, but that's our job. If the prosecutor wants to question you, you can come down to Springer on the train or he can go up to Raton. I have to ask you, though, not to leave the county for a while."

"We'll be available," Ella said.

Bill shook hands with the sheriff and with Deputy Duncan, then went to the corral to saddle their horses.

As they rode north, Ella was quiet, her face pinched. Bill said quietly, "You never shot a man before, did you?"

"No. I've fired a lot of rounds, but I've never even pointed a gun at a human before."

"I can guess how you feel, but you saved my life. Remember that."

"Yes." She forced a weak smile. "I saved the man I love."

They rode stirrup to stirrup while Bill put an arm around her.

Epilogue

Eileen Cruz married the Spanish-speaking attorney and moved to Santa Fe. Her brother got two of their cousins to help him take over Peterson's Rafter P Ranch. Wild Bill moved into Ella's house, but not until they were married. They named their business the Firewater Freight Company, and business was so good they bought another team and wagon and hired a teamster. Ella did the bookkeeping, ordered the goods, paid the bills, made out the vouchers, and was especially happy when she took orders for women's clothing. One day in the fall she met Sheriff Bowman on the main street of Raton. They stood on the plankwalk and talked.

"I think the shooting is over now," Bowman said. "All the fighting is taking place in the courtrooms."

"I guess," Ella said, "that's the way it oughta be. Has to be."

"I don't think I'll run for reelection."

Ella stepped in front of him, faced him. "Why?"

"I keep thinking about all those evictions. I'd rather not have to do it."

285

"Listen to me, Sheriff Bowman. If you don't do it, somebody else will, and there'll be more shooting. You're the only official in the whole county that's got any sense at all. You're calm and quiet and honest, and you don't go around trying to bully folks. You treat everybody with respect, and folks respect you. They like you and trust you, and they'll do what you ask them to. We need you, Sheriff Bowman."

"Well"—the sheriff of Colfax County scratched his jaw—"I'll think about it."

Wild Bill was on his way back from Capulin with an empty wagon. He was singing, but he'd learned not to start a verse with "Oh." Harness horses interpreted that as "Whoa." He sang:

"Uh, it rained all night the day I left, the weather it was dry. The sun's so hot I froze to death, Suzanna, don't you cry." His voice went up an octave:

"Uhh, Suzanna, uh, don't you cry for me. I come from Alabama with my banjo on my knee."

Mrs. Ella Watson was cooking one of Bill's favorite meals, chicken and dumplings. A peach pie was baking in the oven. She hummed a tune herself.

Bill would be home soon.